9
THE

Lives
of
Ray
"The
Cat"
Jones

Also by Stewart Home

— Novels —

She's My Witch

The Nine Lives of
Ray "The Cat" Jones

Mandy, Charlie and Mary-Jane

Blood Rites of the Bourgeoisie

Memphis Underground

Tainted Love

Down and Out
in Shoreditch and Hoxton

69 Things To Do
With a Dead Princess

Whips and Furs
My Life as a Bon Vivant, Gambler
and Love Rat "by" Jesus H. Christ

Cunt

Blow Job

Come Before Christ
and Murder Love

Slow Death

Red London

Defiant Pose

Pure Mania

— Non-Fiction —

Re-Enter The Dragon:
Genre Theory, Brucesploitation
& the Sleazy Joys of
Lowbrow Cinema

Confusion Incorporated
A Collection of Lies, Hoaxes
and Hidden Truths

The House of Nine Squares
Letters on Neoism,
Psychogeography and
Epistemological Trepidation

Cranked Up Really High
Genre Theory and Punk Rock

Neoism Plagiarism and Praxis

Neoist Manifestos

The Assault on Culture
Utopian Currents from
Lettrisme to Class War

— Short Stories —

No Pity

— Poetry —

SEND CA$H
Collected Poems

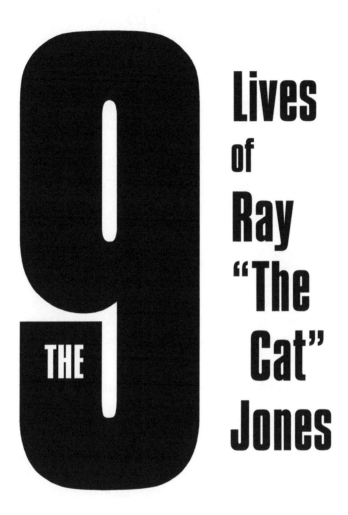

THE 9 Lives of Ray "The Cat" Jones

by STEWART HOME

CRIPPLEGATE BOOKS   MMXX

Published by
CRIPPLEGATE BOOKS
London

ISBN:
978-1-8382189-0-4 Paperback
978-1-8382189-1-1 Hardback

February 2021

First published by Test Centre,
London, 2014.

Graphic and text design by Luther Blissett

CONTENTS

PROLOGUE

I'm a face. My breakout from Pentonville in 1958 has been praised as one of the greatest prison escapes of all time by the likes of south London gangster Mad Frankie Fraser. The details differ somewhat in the various accounts but here I'll put the whole thing together, just in case you can't be bothered to track down the lurid descriptions that have found their way into a slew of book and newspaper accounts.

It was a dark and wet winter evening with the London smog obscuring everything. Johnny Rider and myself were able to get onto the roof of the prison because it was being repaired and there was scaffolding going up the courtyard wall. The screws had been distracted by a disturbance I'd arranged to take place in the library class.

Johnny and myself made our way over the tiles and across to the sheer prison wall on the other side. Scaling down this almost impossible obstacle to my freedom, I smashed my right kneecap. Pain jolted through my body like an electric shock and I lost my grip on a windowsill and fell, breaking my left ankle. Rider coming down behind me clocked my mistakes and was able to make a safe descent. We then had to scale a second wall, and this time I broke my left leg as I jumped. Johnny, who was uninjured, made it safely to the ground.

Rider picked me up and tried to carry me from the prison wall to freedom, but I told him to leave me and get away. It would be better if at least one of us made a clean escape. Johnny ran, and because I couldn't run I crawled to a house door and asked the man who opened it if he'd help me. His wife came to see who was calling, and after telling her husband I was scary, she slammed the door in my face. I then made my way to a block of flats hoping to find somewhere to hide. I took the lift as far as it would go and then made my way onto the roof. There was a skylight and, as I was trying to prise it open, I fell headlong through the glass and knocked myself out.

I was raised back to consciousness by flashlights being pointed at me. From the conversation going on around the smashed skylight above me, I could tell I'd been found by the authorities.

"Looks like he's dead." The screw's voice was emotionless.

"In that case let's go after the other one and get the body later. No point kicking in doors and getting in a row over the damage. Since he can't move, let's raise the caretaker later and get him to let us in."

I could hear movement, and when I was sure that those who'd been chasing me had left me in temporary peace, I gathered all my strength. Somehow I made my way out of the block of flats and dragged myself down the street by using my hands to pull my wrecked body along some railings. Despite being giddy with pain, I managed to get across the mainline railway tracks, then found a place to hide in a garden. When I saw a man getting into a butcher's van close by I shouted to him, and asked if he'd help me as I'd had a bad fall. He guessed I was an escaped prisoner but I was in luck because it turned out he was an ex-con who was willing to aid me, and became keen to do so when I offered him fifty nicker for his assistance. Together we struggled to get butcher's clothes and a dirty apron over my prison uniform; then I crawled into the back of his vehicle. It would probably have been better if I'd fallen asleep but I couldn't relax sufficiently. We had to get through a police roadblock and their dogs went bloody mad around the van.

"What you got in there?" the old bill asked my driver.

"I'm a butcher, I've got meat in the back."

"Can you open it up?"

"Happily, but only if you'll guarantee your dogs won't become even more crazed than they are now. If they damage my stock then you'll have to pay for it."

"The dogs must be able to smell the blood, I think we'll leave it."

I gave the butcher directions to my cousin's pub in Paddington, told him to go in and tell my relative I'd escaped and that we needed a key for a flat. My saviour came back and drove me around the corner to a room my cousin kept in case of emergencies, but when the landlord saw the state I was in he told us to piss off out of his building. So we went back to the van and I got the ex-con to drive me to my fence Benny Selby's place in Highgate. Once Benny had given the butcher fifty quid and got him out of the door, I told the fence to call my wife Ann, a nurse who worked nights at Queen Elizabeth Hospital in Hackney Road. It turned out she'd already been visited by the cops, and that was how she'd learnt I'd escaped from jail.

When Ann's shift finished she came to see me with a doctor who she knew we could trust. They patched me up, and my wife and her doctor friend saw me through my convalescence, which took months and months. I only stayed a night at Benny Selby's pad; the next day Ann found me a room in Hoxton where I could recuperate. I spent more than two years on the run, during which time I pulled off a series of daring jewel raids — including one against screen legend Sophia Loren when she was filming in England — before finally being recaptured, after a grass gave the fuzz a tip-off as to my whereabouts. Unluckily, Johnny Rider was nicked in Chingford the day after our breakout, so he wasn't over the wall for nearly as long as me.

It is tales like these that made me a legend, but what I want to do is tell you the complete and true story of my life, so you can understand me as an ordinary working-class man who acted as he did because of extraordinary circumstances. But rather than start at the beginning, I'll fast forward to where I am now, and then take you back to how it all began.

ONE

Here I am lying in a hospital bed terminally ill with cancer. It's January 2000 and I haven't got long to live. A year or so at most. I'm Ray The Cat Jones, and I've done more in a single lifetime than most people could pack into nine. That said, to the hospital staff and the other patients I just look like any other shuffling old man who is about to croak. I wasn't born in London but the doctors and nurses aren't curious about how I landed up in Hackney. Why would they be when there are people here from all over the world? I've so many stories to tell but I can hardly speak so I'll write them down. The people around me mostly look through me, and they'd never guess in a million years that I very nearly became the middleweight boxing champion of the world, or that because my dreams of sporting glory were shattered by a corrupt cop I went on to become the greatest cat burglar of all time.

You wouldn't think I'd ever been anyone if you saw me stuck here in the cancer ward. There's pain all around me but also an irrepressible humour in the face of death. I think Kevin Connor, who is in the bed opposite me, must have watched the 1959 movie *Carry On Nurse* at least one time too many when he was a young man. Only someone who is terminally ill could get away with being as fresh with the female staff as he is. About half an hour ago he got me in trouble with a buxom matron. Just before she came into the ward he threw down his newspaper so that it landed at the side of my bed. Naturally enough, when the matron got to my bay, she bent down to pick up the tabloid and handed it to me.

"That's my copy of *The Mirror*!" Kevin shouted as I took possession of it. "Ray said he'd give me a tanner if I threw it down by his bed so he'd get an eyeful of your knockers as you retrieved it! And while you were doing that I got a lovely view of your arse! You've got the perfect backside matron!"

"Really Raymond," the orderly scolded as she snatched the linen out of my hands and gave it to Kevin, "at your age I'd expect better behaviour from you!"

Kevin keeps me amused with his pranks and jokes, but that's enough about Homerton Hospital for now. Let's turn instead to my life story. I was born on 5 August 1916, right in the middle of the First World War. It was the day on which the Turkish bosses" dream of controlling the Suez Canal was finally smashed in the Battle of Romani. British Commonwealth forces had more or less won the battle the day before, but it was on the day of my birth that they finished the fight. British victory wasn't something those I grew up around celebrated. I'm a Welshman from Nantyglo in Ebbw Vale, Monmouthshire. Both my family and the working class of Ebbw Vale knew a thing or two about armed insurrection against the British ruling class.

To take my family first, my maternal grandfather Timothy Callaghan hailed from the great republican city of Cork in Eire. When he was a boy, Tim and his best friend Michael McCarthy took part in an uprising against the British imperialists. Tim was fast approaching his sixteenth birthday and his pal had already reached that milestone, so McCarthy was treated as a culpable adult by the merciless authorities. Michael was executed for his part in the uprising and Tim deported to Wales. My grandfather found himself in the south Wales valleys as the nineteenth century raced to a close and the place he landed up in was little different to the Wild West. The quest for coal and industrial goods engendered a spirit of lawlessness that might more readily be associated with the Californian gold rush.

When I was a boy, my grandfather liked to tell me stories of posses of men riding pit ponies and, armed with pickaxe handles, being employed by the mine owners to hunt down those who were sufficiently self-possessed to take some of the area's natural wealth for themselves. My grandfather was not averse to taking coal and other items for his family, and when I was small he'd tell me how he'd been chased across the valleys by those who were prepared to sell out their class for a few pieces of silver. He'd hide in caves and potholes, and he once set a trap for his pursuers by leaving a false trail that made it look like he was ensconced in a remote cavern. When the six men chasing him dismounted and went inside what they believed was his hideout, he threw brushwood he'd placed beside the cave in front of the entrance and set fire to it, trapping his pursuers inside for several hours. The cavern was deep and the men who'd been chasing him had to go a long way inside it to get away from the smoke and flames. In the meantime, my grandfather led away their ponies and sold them to a farmer for a knock-down price.

The British bourgeoisie was a vicious exploiter of the working class, and there was nothing in Nantyglo ranging from man to mineral from which it didn't attempt to turn a profit. In English the name of my hometown means "brook of coal", but in the middle of the nineteenth century it was also the most important iron-producing centre in the world. The Bailey family owned both the iron and coal works, and their fear of the thousands-strong workforce in their employ was so great that they built the last castle-styled fortifications to be thrown up in the British Isles, the Nantyglo Roundhouses. The Baileys were so intimidated by the riots that broke out from time to time that they wanted somewhere they could hole up and feel safe from those they paid a pittance to sweat themselves to death before the great capitalist god of profit. The Baileys were scum who got themselves elected as MPs, bought land at agricultural prices and then made a fortune from the coal beneath it. They ran railways too, and eventually landed an aristocratic title.

Growing up, I heard many a tale of the Baileys" greed and misdeeds. There was also a particularly ribald mythology about Lady Mary Ann Bailey, the second wife of Joseph Bailey, since she was reputed to have been a nymphomaniac. After her husband's death in 1858, Mary Ann allegedly bedded a different young buck every night until she finally shuffled off her mortal coil in 1874. Lady Bailey's table talk was something of a local legend. When I was a boy many examples of it were passed down to me in the form of a folklore that had been honed in its constant retelling. Mary Ann apparently didn't care if her guests or the servants heard what she said to her young playthings. When Lady Bailey threw a large dinner party there was always a young working man seated next to her. These horny-handed sons of toil were drawn from as far afield as Nantyglo and taken to the Glanusk Park estate, the seat in south Wales to which Mary Ann and her husband had retired shortly after their marriage. The lustful old lady's servants procured a succession of youths for her. Many a time I heard it said that Lady Bailey's standard icebreaker with these toy boys ran as follows:

"I'm told your manhood is huge."

"It's bigger than average," a particularly well-endowed coal miner of twenty replied just a few months before Lady Bailey's death.

"Excellent! I like the hard and chiseled body manual labour has given you too."

"Thank you."

"I don't want you to thank me, I want you to pleasure me. Do you know what I'd like you to do for me?"

"No your lady."

"I'd like you to push your manhood deep inside me as we ride completely naked along a beach on a white horse."

Not even Lady Godiva had days like that! While Mary Ann Bailey possessed more than enough silver to pay young men to satisfy her lusts, she could never buy their loyalty. The working class of Nantyglo and the rest of south Wales understood the value of solidarity just as well as the Baileys, and it should go without saying that the bosses opposed our attempts to unionise. The greatest nineteenth-century armed rebellion to take place on the British mainland was organised in Nantyglo. Led by the Chartists Zephaniah Williams, John Frost and William Jones, a huge column of men marched from my hometown to Newport in 1839. The Newport Uprising will live forever in the hearts of working men and women who value freedom, and its lessons were not lost on my family or my childhood friends. We always knew that the interests of the British imperialists were opposed to those of the man and woman in the street.

I know what it is to struggle as much as the next man. My family barely survived through the depression years of the twentieth century. When work was short there was less food on the table. It wasn't just my father Owen who often lacked employment, so too did many of my uncles and cousins. The first Hunger March from south Wales to London took place in November 1927 and the men of Nantyglo had their representatives among those protesting about the restriction and refusal of relief for unemployed miners, and a new government bill harassing those who found themselves out of work. Not long after this protest Wal Hannington praised these fearless marchers with the following words: "… these men are… lighting a lamp that reveals the tortuous path the toilers have had to follow, and which lights up the road of struggle for the battle with the forces of reaction and the conquest of power by the workers…"

Despite privations, I wouldn't say my childhood was grim. I was loved by my family, and like all the local kids ran ragged through the town and neighbouring countryside. We were happy enough playing with twigs and bits of string. That said, I didn't enjoy going to school, where the learning by rote system didn't suit me. I didn't like the ideas about discipline the teachers had either. I'd get hit for not paying attention, but what normal child wouldn't want to stare out of the window on a sunny day? I was one of the kids who'd turn up in the morning to get my attendance marked down on the register, before I disappeared for the rest of the day whenever I could get away with it. Out on the street, dodging the truant officer was a game I frequently played, and I was very good at it. Given how fast I could run, he didn't stand a chance against me.

Remembering my grandfather's tales of imprisoning the Baileys" enforcers in a cave, one day I set a trap for the school board inspector. I was with two friends and we allowed the truant officer to follow us to the edge of town by running at half our usual pace. After turning a corner, me and another bigger boy ran quickly and hid behind a woodshed. As we'd planned, the school board inspector was just fast enough to see the smallest of us disappear into the hut. We pulled our friend out through a small gap at the back. When the truant officer ran into the shack, I raced around to the door he had gone through and bolted it shut from the outside. Our pursuer stopped chasing us after that because he was too big to get out of the gap in the shack and was stuck inside the woodshed for several hours.

The cops proved harder to evade than the school board inspector. I received my first criminal conviction in a juvenile court at the age of twelve. I'd stolen a few lumps of coal, some milk and a pair of shoes — all things my family desperately needed and couldn't afford. I didn't take them for myself. I took them for my parents and siblings. I didn't try the shoes on: I wanted them for my brother Dai and they looked about the right size, so I just picked them up and tried to walk out of the shop with them. I was seen, and not only the shopkeeper but two of his three customers came running after me. I got away, and reaching home put the shoes beneath a bed with some milk and coal I'd stolen earlier in the day. I then got under the blankets and pretended I was sick and asleep. At least one of the customers who chased me knew who I was and before long a policeman was knocking on the door. My mother let him in and my faking sickness act didn't cut much ice with plod, especially when he found the newly stolen shoes under my bed. I didn't plead for leniency either when I was asked by the juvenile court if I had anything to say before I was sentenced.

I wanted to say the following, but at twelve years of age I didn't have the verbal skills to put it as I would now and have here: "What I did was fully justified and morally right. Why should the rich man have a full belly and a poor man one groaning with hunger? I'm following the example of those unemployed miners who marched in protest all the way from here to London. Those who need food, clothes and fuel should take what they require where they can find it. Every man, woman and child has a right to life and thus a right to the things that are necessary to sustain that life…"

I don't remember the exact words I used in the juvenile court, but what I said would have been a lot less coherent than the way I just expressed it above. Nonetheless, I got my point over well enough to really wind up the magistrate. He told me to shut up and sit down before I'd even finished. I was shown no mercy. It was reform school for me. The magistrate said he might have let me off with a warning and a fine if I hadn't made it clear I felt no remorse for what I had done, but that now it was necessary to make an example of me. I thought then and I still think now that he was lying—and even if I'd got a fine, how would my family have paid it? I'm still proud of my boyish self for standing up against my oppressors rather than accepting their punishment meekly.

Reform school was my first time away from home. The regime was strict and it was supposed to re-educate me, but it wasn't me who needed changing; the problem was an exploitative capitalist society that did nothing for working-class families like mine! At reform school it was the same thing day after day. Rise at 6am and get sent out to run a couple of miles. If you were too slow covering the distance you got no porridge. Breakfast, like every other meal, was plain and simple. Then everyone did cleaning followed by different tasks like building work and digging ditches. During the week you got some classes in English, maths, history, basic science. Sunday you went to chapel. And there were lots of gym classes, which is the one way approved school made a man out of me. They taught us boxing and I was good at it, much better than any of the other boys. When I got in the ring all I wanted to do was win. No pain, no gain. I could take the punishment from other boys" fists, and I could really dish it out too. I quickly acquired the nickname Slasher thanks to my vicious punching technique.

I guess my early life filled me with the fighting spirit. Unlike those born with a silver spoon in their mouth, I've always had to struggle for everything I've got. And the same was true for the other kids who were in the juvenile slammer with me. The sports master didn't let me fight when I was new to the approved school gym, although as soon as I saw other boys slugging it out with each other I wanted to get into the ring. But it was first things first, and that meant training: hitting the bags, sparring, shadow boxing in front of mirrors. I had to train for months before they let me have my first proper fight. I was up against a kid called Evans who'd come into the reform school a bit before me. He'd had five fights and lost them all, against my total lack of experience. Evans was taller than me, had a longer reach, but he just didn't want to win as badly as I did. My arms were like windmills, they were moving that fast. I was well ahead at the end of the first round, and in the second I just pummeled Evans. He took a load of jabs, I was raining them in on him left and right, then I hit him with a right hook smack on the side of the face and he went down. It was my first knockout.

The whole time I was at approved school I only lost a couple of matches, and they were on points. In a street fight situation I'm sure I'd have won even those. I was able to soak up punishment and my surest route to victory was a KO, because I was a brawler. We had matches every weekend and I always proved myself the dominant boxer in the ring. When I lost on points this was because my opponents were superior sportsmen to me, rather than tougher fighters.

I was only out of reform school a couple of months before I was nicked again for stealing food my family needed and couldn't afford to buy. I went into a butcher's and stuck a leg of mutton under my coat. The shopkeeper saw me and came charging at me with a cleaver. I didn't even get through the door before a copper who'd seen what was going on from outside in the street came in and grabbed me. Once he'd got a pair of bracelets over my wrists, plod told the butcher to back off.

"Let me hack him to pieces, that'll save the time and expense of a trial!" the shopkeeper screamed.

"You do your job and I'll do mine," the PC told the butcher. "If you hacked every criminal in Nantyglo to pieces I'd be out of work."

"But they deserve it."

"Try it and you'll be up before the bench on a heavier charge than this little thief."

"If I see him again, I'll cut him up."

I knew the verbals were a charade intended to frighten me. They didn't. That said, the resultant court case wasn't a joke and I was sent down again. Borstal wasn't much different to reform school, although obviously the inmates were slightly older. I used borstal as an opportunity to hone my boxing skills. I also found myself taken out of Wales for the first time in my life, to Portland in England. I was imprisoned in a fort-like building on a windswept outcrop, joined to the mainland by a causeway.

The institution was run as a parody of English public schools, and there was supposed to be sporting rivalry between the various naval-inspired divisions the borstal inmates found themselves assigned to. I ended up in Drake House. Of course the houses meant nothing to us. The Welsh defended the Welsh regardless of which house they were in, just as the Londoners stuck with each other, and the Scousers sided with those from their hometown of Liverpool, and so on. I was made to work hard, but the compensation was boxing. Once again I was either winning or every now and then losing on points.

I really hated it if I didn't come out on top in a fight. In one, after a points decision went against me, I saw red. I still had my gloves on when I went over to the master who was acting as the referee, and I hooked him hard enough to knock him down. That was the end of my borstal boxing. I was banned. More immediately I found myself strapped naked to a gym vaulting horse. My arms were tied together under its middle and my legs to the supports at one end. The first stroke of the birch on my backside really hurt; the pain actually seemed to lessen as more skin was broken and the bleeding increased. I was bloodied and blue by the time I'd taken a dozen strokes. But that wasn't the end of my suffering; the next day I was made to stand on the punishment wall for eight long hours. It was inhumane and if I fell from this narrow perch I was not only likely to hurt myself, but I'd be given another beating on the vaulting horse. The wall was about four feet high and very thin, just the width of a single brick. Still, I somehow managed to stay on it all day. Borstal could be hard but it definitely toughened me up.

When I returned home from borstal it was to go down the mines, while trying to follow my dream of becoming a world champion fighter. I joined the local Glendower Boxing Club and Michael Williams who ran it really brought me along. He sharpened up my technique and insisted I improve my footwork. Williams confirmed my belief that the fitter I became the greater my chances of winning at the fight game. So at every opportunity that presented itself to me I was running, lifting improvised weights and jumping rope. I went to the club a couple of nights a week where I'd hit the heavy bag, work on pads and spar. Some of the other boys in Nantyglo looked down on my fitness regime, and even suggested skipping was a pastime for girls. That was until they saw how vicious I was in the ring, which would always shut them up. Jumping rope is really great cardiovascular exercise and it requires good coordination too, so even if those who'd initially criticised me didn't take it up, they soon learnt better than to knock my training regime.

The Glendower Club was situated in an old hall that was falling down. There were a couple of rings at the club to spar inside, two heavy bags, some dirty mirrors for shadow boxing, and a few weights. In the back there were a couple of cold taps we could wash under once we'd finished a training session. The place stank of stale sweat and damp but I loved that boxing club. The facilities may have been primitive but the enthusiasm of Williams and his boys was palpable the moment you set foot inside the building. Both my technique and my fitness came along by leaps and bounds. It was a matter of focus; I narrowed my thoughts to one goal, to win at boxing, and excluded anything from my mind that wouldn't take me there.

My first amateur fight after I left borstal was in Pontypool. My dad and brothers came along to support me. It was good to know they were there but while I was fighting I was just focused on the task of winning. The event was crowded with the families and friends of the fighters, plus a load of guys who liked to watch kids knocking lumps out of each other. Since my previous fights had been in approved school and borstal, I didn't have an amateur record. The boy I was up against, Gareth Morgan, had won one fight and lost another. Thus according to the amateur records he looked slightly more experienced than me, but it was in fact a total mismatch. After the bell for round one sounded, I started to batter him. I got a good solid hook to his head in the first few seconds of the match and after that he just didn't know whether he was having a shit or a shampoo. Morgan was dazed and unable to block, parry or weave around my blows. I landed punch after punch to his head until he went down, and he stayed down way beyond the count. Half the crowd loved it, but not those who knew Morgan as a Pontypool boy.

I worked hard and, when I wasn't inhaling coal dust, I was fanatical about my training. My boxing was shaping up and looking better than the curves on a beauty contest winner. By adding skill to my ability to soak up punishment, my coach Michael Williams was turning me into an unbeatable fighting machine. No one ever knocked me out, although a boy called Ivor Johnson brought me to my knees in an amateur match in Newport, one of the few I lost, and again that was on points. In the third round I let my guard drop and Johnson—who was a southpaw—caught me with a vicious uppercut. I went down on my knees and got straight back up. Johnson was good and he outclassed me in that match. The humiliation, which was maximised by the fact that some of my uncles and cousins who lived locally had come along to watch me fight, gave me the motivation to train even harder so that when I next stepped into the ring there was no question about the fact that I'd leave it with a win. After that loss to Johnson all I wanted to do was get back in the ring with him and avenge the defeat. I KO'd my next six opponents, and when I finally came up against Johnson again, I KO'd him too.

Of course I had a few knockabouts in the street too. In Nantyglo my reputation travelled ahead of me, and few were prepared to challenge my martial supremacy. My grandfather's funeral took place in Newport and I wasn't well known there. After the service the men of the family went to a pub. I was the only one not drinking, and the drink led to arguments with some locals. We ended up fighting with them in the street outside the pub. Most of my family were tough, so I wasn't the only one knocking guys down, but I was faster than everyone else, so the three I beat unconscious was a KO more than anyone else. A lone copper approached as I battered the last of my opponents, and when he blew his whistle I raised a fist at him. Plod turned and moved briskly away.

Since the men we'd been fighting were either unconscious or had fled, I went back inside the pub with the other men of my family. It should have been obvious that before long the law would turn up mob-handed, but I was sad about the passing of my grandfather and wasn't really thinking straight. I had to climb out of a back window and make my way back to Nantyglo double-quick coz plod had seen me fighting. My relatives stayed on with their drinks and denied having anything to do with the altercation. They told the old bill that all those who'd been involved in the dust-up had fled.

Despite my employment down the mine, many of those around me were still without work, and they left for London in droves because that's where they stood some chance of earning money. In the end I decided to go to The Smoke too, because if I was to fight for a living then that's where I'd find a full-time boxing career and middleweight opponents who might survive more than a round or two with me.

On my first attempt to reach London I never made it out of the valleys. I left home on a bicycle without anything beyond the clothes on my back. Before long I was hungry and thirsty. I could see a large house not far from the road, so I cycled down the driveway and knocked on the open door. No one came to see who was calling and so I walked into the house. I found food in the kitchen—bread, cheese, cold cuts of meat—and I ate some of what was there. While I was feasting my curiosity was aroused by a box on the table at which I'd seated myself. I opened the container and inside there was cash and jewels. I stuffed the cash in my pockets and walked out of the farmhouse with the sparklers in the box. I pushed my bike across a field and through a hedge. I buried the jewels in their case among the roots of a tree, then manoeuvred my way around a copse and eventually made it to a road. I couldn't believe my luck and, instead of going on to The Smoke, I cycled back to Nantyglo.

Life at home was dominated by my mother Julia. She was a short woman, just over five feet tall, and when I was younger she was skinny with fair hair and blazing blue eyes. After the Second World War my mother's hair was grey and her girth grew to match her sense of determination: the piling on of pounds was triggered by the anabolic steroids she was prescribed to treat her brittle bones. My dad Owen was a quiet and reliable presence. He was a miner who suffered—like many others—long bouts of unemployment. My dad was a full seven inches taller than my mother and had dark hair and brown eyes.

My three brothers and one sister—Patrick, Kevin, Dai and Catherine—were as boisterous as me. We were very well behaved when our mum was around to rule us with her rod of iron, and riotous when freed from her stern but loving influence. It was my mother who made me who I am. She knew how to struggle, and she could handle whatever pain it took to get her wherever she needed to go. It was because of her example that I was able to take punishment in the boxing ring. No amount of agony and no obstacle would ever stop me, because I'd learnt from my mum that a winner never quits. Nonetheless, my mother's stoical attitude never stopped me from wanting to help her and make her life a little easier.

When I came back with that bundle of notes from my first abortive attempt to reach the bright lights of London, I didn't want to spend it on myself—I wanted to give it to my mother. But the rub was that after my spells in approved school and borstal she would never accept anything from me unless I could prove to her that I'd earned it through hard graft at honest work. I couldn't openly give my mum the money I'd purloined because I'd have to tell her how I got it and if she knew that she'd tell me to return it. I knew my family needed that wedge more than the wealthy landowners who'd left it lying around, but my mother didn't accept this logic, although almost anyone else in Nantyglo would have understood it.

Although my dad was nominally a Methodist, my mum was Catholic and she spent too much time listening to the local priest. My dad's parents only agreed to him marrying my mum on the condition that their kids were brought up Protestant. My father didn't care for religion, so we didn't go to church. My mother and her family viewed atheism as better than Protestantism, and since it had been agreed before we were born we'd have nothing to do with the Catholic church, my mother made no effort to get us to listen to non-Methodist sermons. My mum was deeply religious, which was why I had to slip her the cash I'd stumbled across surreptitiously. So every few days I'd put one of the notes I'd taken into my mother's purse. The plan worked well for a few weeks, then one afternoon when I was alone in the house with my mother she said to me:

"Ray, I think someone's looking out for me."

"Why's that mum?" I replied.

"Because, Ray, every time I open my purse there's more money in there than when I last closed it."

"Are you sure about that?"

"Of course I'm sure! I've been watching you and I've seen you slipping notes into it! Where did you get the money Ray?"

"I found it."

"Don't lie to me Ray, you stole it!"

"I found it in a house I went in because the door was open."

"You stole it. You come upstairs with me Ray, coz I'm going to tie you to the bed and I'm going to thrash you with a belt. I'm gonna beat the thieving that's got into you, out of you. I don't want to thrash you Ray but it's for your own good. If I don't teach you right from wrong then you'll always be a thief!"

So we went upstairs and I undressed and my mother tied me to the bed, and then she began to beat me with the buckle end of the belt digging into me and making me bleed. She thrashed me and she just kept on thrashing me; I honestly don't know where she got the strength from to beat me like that. It was agony and then after a while I didn't really feel anything at all, my mind was someplace else entirely. It was as if time itself had stopped and so I've really no idea how long this went on. Eventually my father came into the house, rushed up the stairs and found my mother giving me a hiding, and the bed sheets covered in blood.

"Stop Julie, stop! You'll end up killing the boy. Whatever he's done he's been punished more than enough."

And while my mother ruled our home and my father rarely said anything, when he spoke his words were respected. So my mum stopped beating me, and although I could still feel the pain of the thrashing for days, the agony of it gradually subsided and I healed quickly as youths do. Since my mother had spent some of the money I'd obtained, my father's view prevailed and it was decided I should not take back the rest of the cash I'd nicked. I'd been punished by my mother and that was punishment enough. My family preferred to keep me away from the courts. The remaining notes — and they added up to nearly thirty quid — were given to the Nantyglo branch of the South Wales Miners" Federation. After that, the incident was never spoken of again, and I got back to practising my boxing. My younger brothers took up boxing too, and while they weren't bad at the sport, they weren't nearly as good as me.

After winning a bunch more amateur fights, as often as not with knockouts, I decided I really did need to make the move to London before I was twenty years old if I was to do anything worthwhile with my life. If I didn't, the most exciting thing I'd ever do was work down the mines. I was convinced there was no way I could become middleweight boxing champion of the world if I stayed in Nantyglo, so in 1935 I got on my bicycle to head to The Smoke once again. This time the only thing that detained me on the way was retrieving the jewels I'd buried amongst the roots of that tree a year or so earlier. The sparklers were still lying untouched where I'd hidden them, so I knew my life in London would get off to a flying start. It was a long and dirty cycle ride and I slept under the stars on the way. Nonetheless, the exercise made me feel good and my heart was singing—as well as pumping hard as I peddled furiously—all the way.

The first thing I did when I got to London was visit my Uncle Dinny, one of my mother's brothers. He was in protection, but could fence jewels no problem. I know Dinny Callaghan didn't give me as much as he might have done for the tom, but it was enough to set me up for the start of my life in The Smoke. When he was young Dinny got in endless trouble with the filth. The south Wales fuzz got so fed up with him that one day they picked him up and took him across the border into England. They told Dinny that if he returned to Wales they'd kick seven shades of shit out of him, then get him locked up for a long long time. Dinny headed for London and settled down to enjoy richer criminal pickings than he'd encountered in Wales. I should also add that once seen, Dinny could never be forgotten! He looked as tough as nails and was missing an eye; he'd lost it in a fight over protection pitches at The Derby.

Dinny offered me the opportunity to get involved in various family ventures but I wanted to be a professional boxer, and politely declined his offer of a foot-up on the ladder of crime. The oldest of my cousins, Dennis Junior and Michael, both a few years younger than me, were already experienced burglars. In the early 1940s I was to learn the basics of housebreaking from them, before going on and taking that craft to a far higher level of perfection. But that was a future I'd never even imagined in the mid-1930s, when my only goal in life was to become the greatest middleweight boxer on earth. I stayed with Dinny and his brood in Paddington during the first few days I spent in London, but within a week I'd bagged myself a room in Lauderdale Road, Maida Vale. Back then the area was very different to what it became later; it was full of prostitutes and Eastern European immigrants wanting to escape from London's East End. I immediately felt at home among these refugees from various forms of discrimination.

I joined the Grand Union Boxing Gym, above the pub of that name at 45 Woodfield Road in Maida Vale, and got stuck in. I went out running along the canal in the daytime and at nights I skipped rope, punched bags and sparred with other young men. I got myself work as a fruit buyer, so at the crack of dawn you'd find me in Covent Garden market, and the rest of the day was free to train, and train, and train, and train. Once I'd finished work on Saturday morning, I'd often head down to the south coast and take part in fairground fights. You paid a fee and would take on whoever the boxing ring booth operator was offering as an opponent. Most of the boxers employed in this way were sluggers who could take a lot of punishment. Since I was interested in picking up purses and making a profit, as well as perfecting my craft, I'd usually wait until later in the day before taking on an opponent. That way they were tired and I could just go in for the kill without having to wear them out myself. During one of these fairground fights I even KO'd Freddie Mills.

The first fight I got in was pretty typical of most. The booth operator was offering ten nicker to anyone who could last three rounds with his fighter. The boxer must have been in his thirties and had no neck. He was all arms and chest. The promoter was waving a fistful of pound notes in the air and asking if anybody fancied their chances of winning them, as the previous challenger—who'd been knocked spark out—was dragged from the ring. I got down the front and shouted I'd take the gorilla on. The men running the booth obviously thought I was a right mug because I looked so young compared to their man, and I was a lot lighter too. But weight isn't everything, and I knew I was fast—they didn't.

I got in the ring and put on the thin gloves that were offered to me. As soon as the bell rang I got in a quick flurry of punches, mostly to the stomach. My opponent came back at me but I just danced out of his reach, and when I felt the ropes against my back, I swung a hard right hook at his head as I moved forward. He went down on one knee but before I could finish him off the bell went. We'd been fighting for less than a minute but those running the booth claimed we'd done a full three! They no doubt hoped this ruse would save their man from losing.

The booth boxer was still a bit dazed when the next round kicked off late. They only rung the bell coz the punters around the ring were getting impatient and screaming the match was a fix. I went straight at my opponent and delivered half a dozen jabs to his stomach. When this caused him to lower his guard, I finished him off with another hook, this time from the left. What followed was the longest ten count I've ever heard in my life. It gave the booth boxer the opportunity to regain a little of his wind. The crowd was jeering by this time because as objective observers they could see that I should have won already. It took my opponent more than thirty seconds to get up, but moments later he'd been decked again—brought down by my uppercut—and this time he was out cold.

I demanded my money but the promoter accused me of being a ringer, a professional boxer, and he insisted my obvious skill at the noble art invalidated my claims to a payout. I told him to hand over the cash or I'd give him a worse beating than the one I'd already given his man. A bunch of guys in the crowd hollered they'd back me up in this, and also tear up the booth to demonstrate their disapproval at the way it was being run. These threats resulted in ten pound notes being very reluctantly passed over to me. I left a happy man, since the fight was an easy way to make a tenner. Of course, I blew the money on bets, food and fair rides before I even got back to London.

Since people paid to watch fairground boxing, the promoters knew that the non-fighting spectators accounted for their profits. As a consequence, after the war it became more and more difficult to get a fight as a punter. On the whole, those who wanted to challenge the professionals at the booth were either drunk and didn't stand a chance, or else determined to prove they were a hardman and needed knocking out quickly if the defending boxer was to avoid injury. From the point of view of the crowd, either scenario resulted in a bad fight. So what happened was that there were plants in the crowd to ensure a good professional — albeit pretty much fixed — match. That's what the punters wanted, and by the late forties it had become almost impossible to walk into one of these booths off the street and get a fight. Fortunately for me, it was in the thirties that I was most interested in making money from such challenges.

I've already mentioned I took on Freddie Mills in a fairground bout. He didn't have a lot of technique but he had a lot of guts and I really admired him as a fighter. His determination was enough to make him world champion a division up from me. Like Mills, my approach to boxing was attack, attack, attack; but nonetheless practise and know all the defensive moves just in case you find yourself in trouble and need them. The best boxers have lots of courage and can soak up the punches, but add some fast footwork and other fancy moves and you're gonna be a total winner. In a fight I'd always go for a knockout where I could get it, but sometimes that just isn't possible and to win on points you gotta have endurance.

The legendary boxing promoter Jack Solomons saw me as a future world middleweight champion very early in my professional career, so by 1937 I was in training in order to conquer the world in 1938. No "peace in our time" for me; back then I thought the Nazis deserved a bashing from all those who were up for it (which unfortunately didn't include Tory toffs like Neville Chamberlain). I'd have welcomed the chance to beat scum like Hitler well beyond the point of unconsciousness, but I was even more hell bent on beating my opponents in the ring.

My first professional fight was right at the end of 1935 against Eddie Maguire at East Ham Baths. We were at the bottom of the bill that night. My focus was on the match, and I was only dimly aware of my opponent fiddling with his gloves before the bell went for the first round. I got my retaliation in first by hooking Maguire in the mouth, and he responded with a couple of blows to my midriff. As I moved backwards, Maguire followed me. When he rushed at me, I slipped past him, spun around and hammered some blows into his body as he was turning to face me. He swung at me and I danced back, then came forward and jabbed him on the nose. Maguire then got a good shot to my stomach, and despite the pain I held myself upright and went back at him. It was like that for the rest of the round, and the fight. We were trading blows evenly and the crowd was appreciative of the fact that we were both putting on a good show. Given my lack of professional experience, it perhaps isn't that surprising that the fight ended in a draw. Still, I'd put on a fine display of my pugilistic skills and from then on I had no trouble getting regular fights.

Professional boxing was a different game to the amateur scene; the greater number of rounds required more endurance and it was necessary to up your defensive game because the guys fighting really knew how to hit. I put my failure to win my first professional bout down to experience — or lack thereof — and promised myself I'd do better next time. I was able to fight virtually every week, and I needed to do this simply to earn enough money to live on, since the purses for bottom-rung professional fighters weren't huge. As the months flew by my boxing skills became sharper and sharper, and slowly but surely I made a solid reputation for myself. I was fighting so frequently that I inevitably suffered the odd defeat, but mostly I won. The public liked my aggressive style and many of my victories were achieved with spectacular knockouts.

Boxing was a huge sport in the 1930s, as popular as football is today. As a fighter I wanted to please the crowds, but I also had to use enough defensive tactics to avoid the fate of a figure like the London-based but Welsh-born Nipper Pat Daly. Nipper was just that, a kid, when he started out in professional boxing, and his impressive career was over by the time he turned eighteen in 1931. Daly had a number of problems, one of which was that as he grew his trainer tried to keep him in the lower weight categories he'd done so well in as a youngster: he should have gone up a division or two rather than starving himself so that he could fight beneath his natural weight. He was also fighting too often and taking a lot of punishment. He ended up completely battered and concussed from bouts with Johnny Cuthbert and Seaman Tommy Watson. After being KO'd by these two men, Nipper lost his fighting sparkle and retired at just seventeen years old.

The most tragic of the punch drunk boxers of the 1930s was Del Fontaine. The public loved the way this Canadian fought but his defensive tactics were weak and he ended up damaged. Having established his reputation in North America in the 1920s, he came to England in 1932 to pursue his boxing career. Battling against many of Britain's best punchers, Fontaine had a great fight record during his first eighteen months in the UK. Then, at the end of 1933, his form went to pot and he lost most of his matches.

While in England, Fontaine got into a relationship with Hilda Meeks, and when in July 1935 he discovered she was arranging dates with another man, he shot her dead at her parents" home in south London. Fontaine went on trial and his defence of diminished responsibility should have been accepted, as he was obviously punch drunk. I'm not saying Fontaine shouldn't have done some bird for killing his girl-friend, since what he did was obviously wrong, but he should not have been hanged. Despite protests and a huge petition for a reprieve, he was executed at Wandsworth Prison on 29 October 1935. That's British justice for you, and as far as I'm concerned it's not justice at all.

By slugging away as a professional boxer for a couple of years, I was able to pull myself up the professional ladder by my glove straps. Come the end of 1937, all I had to do to get a crack at the British middleweight title was win my next fight. Jack Solomons was convinced I would claim victory in both bouts and then move on to the world title. But it wasn't to be. Instead Jack had to wait until the start of the 1950s when he was able to do with Randy Turpin what he'd planned to do with me a dozen years before—create a middleweight world champion the people would truly love. The cause of my downfall was taking a Sunday constitutional with an ac-quaintance I'd made through my Uncle Dinny, the fence Ber-tie Holliday. I saw no reason to stay away from my family or their friends. They were criminals and I was a former fruit buyer and coal miner turned professional boxer. The law saw it differently, in particular the filth in the form of Metropoli-tan Police heavyweight boxing champion PC Nobby Spratt.

On the first Sunday of December 1937, Spratt clocked me walking away from Hyde Park Corner, where the speakers on their soapboxes with their crazy takes on the world had been entertaining Bertie and me. Spratt liked to watch up-and-coming boxers, so I'm sure he knew who I was. There can be no doubt the copper would have recognised Holliday too. So Spratt and a colleague legged it after us. I wasn't paying any attention coz I'd got nothing to hide, and I wasn't much interested in looking to see who the fuzz were after as I made my way towards the Edgware Road. You can imagine my disbelief when Spratt clapped his hand on my shoulder and his mate collared Bertie.

"I'm arresting you on SUS," Spratt told me after I'd been separated from Holliday.

"You're what?" I replied.

"I'm arresting you," Spratt said again.

"You're not arresting me," I told the burly pig, "I haven't done nothing."

"You're a suspected person. You may have committed a crime."

"Come off it, I ain't done a thing."

Spratt wasn't the type to waste his breath on talk. He just grabbed me by the collar, half-strangling me with his left hand, then delivered a sucker punch to my face with his right fist, before loosening his grip a moment later. I staggered backwards spitting out gouts of blood. Although I fell on my arse, I was able to spring back by using my arms to propel me up from the pavement. Spratt was used to the guys he hit going down and staying down, and just stood there open-mouthed and defenceless in the face of my counter-attack. It hadn't occurred to this bully that I was more than able to defend myself. Likewise, he'd become so obsessed with boxing that he'd forgotten it wasn't the same thing as street fighting. I put all the force I could muster into my punch and the pride of the Mets went down, and the two hard kicks I gave him to the head made sure he stayed down for the count and some more. That's the rule of the street; even if you seem to have knocked someone out you still put in at least two more blows to make sure they don't come back at you—if you think Queensberry Rules apply outside the ring then you're a mug. I didn't hang around to see if Spratt needed assistance to come back to his senses; I was on my toes.

The first thing I did was head home to my room in Maida Vale. I hurriedly packed a couple of suitcases and left. Next I went down Paddington way for a conflab with my Uncle Dinny. It was obvious to both of us my professional boxing career was over. We also agreed that it would be stupid of me to give myself up to the law. I suggested I could go to Spain to fight against fascism. It was my dedication to becoming a champion boxer that had meant volunteering to see action in Spain was inconceivable to me before this point in my life. The civil war there raged from July 1936 until April 1939, and it was the biggest political issue of the day.

Uncle Dinny rightly pointed out that the International Brigades were controlled by the Stalinists and that given my views I'd never fit in; he tried to throw my own words about this back at me but wasn't able to articulate the insight that I'd be branded as suffering from the "infantile disorder" of left-wing communism and risk a bullet in the head from those that kowtowed to "Uncle Joe's" Moscow line. I can't remember the exact words used but I knew what my uncle was trying to say as he attempted to redeploy my own argument against me.

Dinny followed this up with an even better line of attack: joining the International Brigades was illegal in the UK. Volunteers slipped out of the country by posing as tourists. I didn't even have a passport. The chances were I'd be nicked as a fugitive from so-called justice if I tried to leave British soil. In the end, me and my uncle figured that a move south of the river was my best option. I'd stick in London where the transient crowds provided cover, but a part of the city in which I wasn't known. And I'd carry on with my prize-fighting, but I'd switch to bare-knuckle boxing which wasn't licensed and therefore wouldn't make me as vulnerable to arrest as the legal rules version of the sport.

So after relocating to Lambeth, it was a new way of fighting in the ring for me. My first bare-knuckle match was in Brighton against a northerner who fought as Scheming Stephens. I'd not seen him fight but I knew his reputation; he liked to hold back, and when his opponent charged at him he'd flatten them with a haymaker that added the force of their forward motion to his punch. When our match officially kicked off I barely left my corner and pulled a few frowns in the hope of fooling Stephens into thinking I was nervous. The crowd booed us for failing to do anything more than square up against each other. Eventually Stephens charged at me, and stepping to the side I used his tactics against him. When he went down I gave him a few kicks to the head to make sure he stayed there. The crowd didn't like it because most of their money was on Stephens, who up to that point had never lost. Dinny and my cousins grabbed my winnings and we got out of Kemp Town quick, before the punters turned on us.

Later in 1938, during the Epsom Derby and after four further bare-knuckle fights, I had a rematch against Stephens and handed him his second defeat. At that encounter I reversed my tactics and charged right in at him. He wasn't expecting it and didn't have his sucker punch ready for me. Most of my unlicensed fights went the same way — they were over in a few minutes. Once I'd had a few victories the crowds around London were usually happy to see me win since their money was on me. We'd still get out quick, although there was less need for it. When I went up north to fight in Manchester and Liverpool against local men, if they'd been given half a chance the punters would have beaten me to death for defeating their boys. So we made it a rule to grab my winnings and get out fast no matter where we were.

Moving from the specific to the more general, as a rule you stay further back from your opponent in a bare-knuckle match than in Queensberry-style boxing. But I was good at both styles and was more than able to live from the unlicensed side of the sport. The fights often took place just off racing courses when horse meetings were on, and as the winner I'd often walk away with several hundred pounds (a lot of money at the time). I used the name Slasher Davies and with every big money victory I won, I bought myself a new suit, and despite this extravagance I still had plenty left to live on. The cops were to make much of those suits in 1940, but it's always been my opinion that a man should take pride in his appearance and this was one of the ways I took care of mine.

A lot of money was laid on my bare-knuckle fights and I never let down the men who backed me; all I can say of those who put quids on my opponents is that they made a foolish choice and it isn't my fault if they threw their money down the drain. As for me, I had cash to burn. When I went back home to see my family I even travelled first class on the train. It made the rich toe-rags who more usually enjoyed this luxury sick to the guts when I opened my mouth and they realised where I came from — they didn't like to see a smartly dressed working man who'd obviously pulled himself up by his bootstraps doing as well as they were on inherited wealth.

I wasn't the only Welshman at the top of the fight game at this time. I may have been forced to drop out of the legal boxing circuit but Tommy Farr was one of a number of boys from the valleys who knew how to keep his end up in the licensed ring. Like me, Farr had started his working life as a coal miner, before going professional in the fight game. The Tonypandy Terror — as Farr was known — fought his way to the Welsh light heavyweight title, then switched up a division in 1936. The following year he became British and Empire heavyweight champion. After beating Tommy Loughran, Bob Olin and Max Baer, come the summer of 1937 Farr lost on points against world heavyweight champion Joe Louis. I'm not the only person who thinks that decision was unfair; the crowd in New York booed when Louis was handed a narrow win.

After the fight even Louis admitted he'd been hurt by his opponent. Now don't get me wrong, Joe Louis was a great fighter and I admire him for his boxing skills first and foremost; but I respect him even more because he was man enough to say that despite the bookies" odds running completely in his favour, Farr matched him punch for punch in the ring. The Tonypandy Terror remained in the States for a couple of years but had little luck there, and a lot of people think this was because of his sporting refusal to cooperate with match-fixing mobsters and bookies.

When I was working the unlicensed boxing circuit, my uncle — who'd noticed I liked a bet on the ponies — took me aside on more than one occasion to try and get me to think differently about the way I gambled. He saw me as a mug punter, I saw him as too calculating. From a rational point of view his advice was sound, but I didn't bet for rational reasons, so I never heeded what my uncle had to say.

"Ray," Dinny said to me one time at Ascot. "You never do the maths right. When you place a bet, it's all about probability and averages, whereas you just try to pick the winner of a race. That's a sure-fire way to lose money."

"What do you mean?"

"You need to look for value when you bet, not the obvious winner, which is usually the favourite."

"I don't understand."

"When you're buying a suit do you pay more than you need to?"

"No."

"So you wouldn't go to the most expensive tailor you could find if you liked the work of one who was cheaper just as well?"

"No."

"So why don't you approach betting on the ponies in the same way?"

"You've lost me."

"Look," Dinny said, "you have to look at the odds the bookmakers are giving and pick those that represent the best value on a horse with a real chance of winning. Either that or lay against."

"Betting against horses isn't sporting!"

"Some people make good money from it. Not big money on any one bet, but regular income."

"Sometimes an outsider wins."

"Once in a blue moon. Average it out and you'll take the odd loss against much more money coming in over the long term. You can't lose on laying against if you do it right."

"But where's the gamesmanship?"

"It ain't about sport, it's about parting the bookies from their cash."

"You do that with protection."

"Sure, and some people do it by studying form and odds properly. Now I'm going to repeat myself because I don't seem to be getting through to you. Only mugs look for the winner. What you should be doing is looking for bets that represent good value, where the horse has a better chance of winning the race than the odds the bookies put on them. This is something that will average out in your favour. Every horse in a race has a chance of winning it because they've been entered. The favourite doesn't always win or the bookies would go broke. The outsiders rarely win, although there are odd flukes. You've got to look for the good-value bets and if you keep placing those you'll come out on top when everything is averaged out over the months and years."

"That's not my style!"

"Are you telling me, Ray, that your style is to lose money? Come on, be realistic about this! Clued up betting is a matter of applying your knowledge of the horses running to the mathematics of odds."

"There's no escape from this world in doing that!"

"Yes there is — after you've won some bets spend the money you make on yourself."

"I do that when I've won a fight."

"Same principle."

"Not to me."

"Ray, use your loaf. Look at it mathematically! Don't be a loser!"

And so it went on. There were variations on this conversation with my Uncle Dinny at race meeting after race meeting. Of course, when we went to the horse tracks Dinny and his boys wouldn't simply be looking after me during my fights; they'd also be protecting bookies. If someone felt they didn't need protection then they'd find heavies hanging around their pitch and putting the frighteners on anyone foolish enough to try and place a bet. If money was still not forthcoming from their mark, then the legitimate bookmaker would be chased off and his pitch let out to someone else at a premium rate.

My cousins would also go up and down lines of bookies with a bucket of water and sponge; anyone who didn't drop a big enough coin into the bucket had the odds wiped from their board well before it needed cleaning. Dinny also hired out chalk to bookies so they could mark up their odds. If they tried to use chalk they'd bought for a fraction of the cost of Dinny's, they found themselves in serious trouble. Sometimes my uncle and cousins simply demanded money from bookmakers. The individual hunks of dosh weren't huge, but added together they totalled more than a pretty penny. This may not have been sporting but it enabled them to make a lot more money from dogs and ponies than even professional gamblers did by betting!

Returning to my hard-won reputation as the Welsh Wonder of the bare-knuckle fight, this eventually came to be my undoing. It was not unknown for the filth to take a dim view of this sport and the bets that accompanied it. Especially as those running the contests were often the same men offering bookies protection at the racetracks; and as I've said, many of the fights took place in fields adjacent to horse racing meetings. Of course, the old bill only took the view that these illegal matches were a threat to the very fabric of our society when bent cops weren't being paid to turn a blind eye to the sport — since they often attended the fights and put money on the combatants. It was partly through detectives who were taking a drink that my reputation as an invincible fighter spread far and wide. Eventually all sorts of people in the Met got wind of this and some of them wanted to nick me.

You should have seen the spectacle when I was lifted at Sandown Park. I'd just won my fight, and the cops appeared out of nowhere completely mob-handed. The crowd melted away, which made those bookies who weren't collared very happy coz they got to keep everyone's money without paying winnings. They had a big trial of the guys running books and even brought my opponent Battling Tommy Lancaster before a beak. The lying filth told the court that Tommy's unknown opponent got away. All those on trial refused to name me; the fuzz told them in advance they'd be for the high jump if they did. It went against their nature to grass anyway.

After I was pinched, the filth in Gerald Road nick told me they weren't gonna do me for my involvement in unlicensed boxing, since I'd wounded the pride of the Metropolitan Police when I'd decked PC Spratt. They preferred to blacken my character and paint me as a thief. I'd managed two years on the run and the old bill didn't want the public to know that I'd maintained myself through hard toil at sporting endeavours. They made much of my association with men they branded criminals, but I knew these characters because they were organising bare-knuckle fights. That said, some of those connections were to keep me in good stead in the years to come when I indulged in the kind of monkey business that can bring a lagging in its wake. But back in the thirties my connections to these heavies were entirely innocent, and only to do with sport.

Another reason the fuzz were never going to let on they'd nicked me at a bare-knuckle fight was that if the general public had known this, they'd have sussed I was being fitted up; they understood well enough that unlicensed boxers participate in matches set up by entrepreneurs who are at best shady, and at worst the scum of the earth. On the other hand, it wasn't in my own best interest for me to explain the money-making line I'd been in—because strictly speaking it was illegal and therefore wouldn't sit well with a middle-class jury. And if my participation in bare-knuckle fighting was brought up at my trial, there was also the chance I'd find myself facing charges over that. So I kept mum when the old bill committed perjury in court and claimed to have nicked me at my home in Lambeth.

My chief tormentor was a truly evil copper called Detective Donald Hope. This scumbag was an expert at fitting up innocent people and planting evidence. Hope claimed in court that I'd assaulted him as well as Spratt. I don't deny that I hit Spratt, but that was in self-defence, after I'd been attacked by the bullyboy. Despite all the lies he told in court, Hope was unable to make most of his shit stick. He claimed to be one of innumerable coppers I'd beaten with my fists and left unconscious in my apparently endless bids for freedom. Hope was such an inveterate liar that he even falsely claimed at the Old Bailey that I admitted assaulting a dozen police officers to evade arrest.

The only copper I KO'd was Spratt, and that was after he attacked me! I was able to prove that I was with my family in Wales when I was supposed to have assaulted Hope. The Mets also falsely claimed that for the two years I was on the run I lived on the proceeds of housebreaking. This was another of their porky pies, and one they failed to prove to the satisfaction of the jury. Nonetheless, on 7 March 1940 I got two years for grievous bodily harm against Spratt and an "attempted" — not an actual — theft from a car. I felt the way that boxing champion Ted Kid Lewis must have done at Olympia in 1922 if you buy into the urban myth of what happened there, and I know some don't. The popular story runs that Georges Carpentier chinned Lewis with a knockout punch when The Kid turned in protest to referee Joe Palmer, while the official's hand was still on his shoulder. The blow the cops delivered against me in 1940 was far lower! After he was defeated, it is claimed Lewis said: "I felt cheated, but I didn't bear any grudge." After getting a two-year stretch for defending myself against that windbag Spratt, I'd have been a mug if I'd acted like there wasn't a chip on my shoulder.

I'd been stitched up like a kipper and the papers had a field day with my story; I soon discovered to my cost that the media loved lying every bit as much as the filth. The press reported all the false talk at the trial about my having made "numerous" assaults on coppers. I would like to stress that I was only found "guilty" of one assault, and I was innocent of even that alleged "crime". "Caught After Two Years — Labourer's Savage Attack On Policeman" screamed *The Times* after my appearance before the beak. The *Daily Mirror* of 8 March 1940 damned me with the headline: "Thief Celebrated With 21 Suits". The *Mirror* also twisted my story when it talked of the fifty quid in my pockets and blackened my name by saying that for two years my "fists kept me free". Well my fists did keep me free, not by beating coppers but by earning me the prize money that I won fair and square in bare-knuckle bouts. And those winnings accounted for the twenty-one suits the cops found at my home in King Edward Walk after they'd arrested me, and the fifty quid in notes I'd left in the pocket of one of those whistles. The fuzz had found a laundry ticket on me when I was nicked, and used that to trace my home address — there was no way I would have provided them with such information.

I was down but not out, and let me tell you what happened next dragged me so deep into the black pits of despair that it took me a long time to come back up. I knew my dreams of becoming middleweight champion of the world had been shattered, but I still had my family and they meant a lot to me. The war was going on and it wasn't easy for my nearest and dearest to come up from Wales to see me. They had to get a train to Paddington, cross London and then catch a second mainline service to Chelmsford where I was in prison. My family made a lot of sacrifices to do this and I really appreciated it. By the time my youngest brother Dai came up to visit me in early November, the Blitz was in full swing and London was being bombed night after night by the scumbag Nazis. I was overjoyed to see Dai but little did I know that I would be the last person in my family to see him alive. He died that night in a Nazi bombing raid, just hours before he was due to catch a train back to Wales. So my brother went home lying in his coffin, not smoking and playing cards with the other passengers on the Swansea train.

I was a very tough young man and I could take a lot of punishment in a fight, but when I learnt of Dai's death I lay on my bed and cried and cried and cried. Between them the cops and the Nazis had taken from me two of the things that most mattered in my life. It was hard to live with the loss of my dream of becoming middleweight boxing champion of the world, but up to that point I'd coped with it. Adding the death of my brother to the misery I already felt about being fitted up was the proverbial straw that broke the camel's back. If it wasn't for those lying bastards Spratt and Hope of the Gerald Road cop shop, I would have never been in jail, my brother might have lived a full life, and I'm sure I would have been a boxing legend to boot.

I don't know how long I cried but eventually I fell asleep, and it was then that my brother appeared to me in my dreams. He was dressed in the suit in which he'd visited me in jail, and he looked radiant and happy.

"Listen to me Ray," Dai said in my dream. "Don't let the bastards grind you down! Become a thief Ray, become a thief!"

"What do you mean Dai?" I replied.

"The rich and their lackeys the boys in blue stuck you in here on a fit-up charge didn't they?"

"Yes."

"And didn't they put an end to your boxing career?"

"Yes."

"And ultimately the same people share equal responsibility for my death with the Nazi bombers who blew me to pieces!"

"Why?"

"Because I wouldn't have been anywhere near London if you hadn't been in jail."

"You're right."

"So Ray you must avenge yourself, and me, and the entire working class by becoming what they falsely accused you of. Become a thief Ray but steal only from the rich."

So that night in November 1940 when I woke suddenly from the dream in which my dead brother spoke to me, I swore in my cell in Chelmsford that I would avenge myself against the police, the judiciary and the ruling class. I vowed I would rob only those who flaunted their wealth before the majority whose poverty they perpetrated. Like Robin Hood, I'd steal from the rich in order to settle a few of the all-too-many scores between the privileged elite and the endlessly abused working class. I would hit back at the rogues that had wrongly condemned me by becoming the greatest cat burglar and jewel thief that ever was.

I kept that vow and I never ever stole from anybody poor. I only robbed the ruling elite and most wealthy such as lords, ladies, dukes, duchesses, multi-millionaire industrialists and three of the world's richest film stars — Elizabeth Taylor, Sophia Loren and Bette Davis. I also rifled the house of the best Home Secretary of all time, R. A. Butler. In my thirty-year burglary spree I became a one-man crime wave, stealing goods worth in total more than a hundred million pounds at today's prices!

TWO

Prison was the same thing day after day. It was like reform school but with hard labour rather than sports and educational classes. Wake up at 6am and slop out. Breakfast was porridge. Then you applied yourself to some thankless task for the rest of the day, and in my case this meant sewing mailbags. The bombs were falling all around us but Chelmsford didn't take as much of a battering as London. The London jails had been decanted of us ordinary villains. British Intelligence used Wormwood Scrubs as an operational base against the Nazis. Wandsworth and Pentonville were used to house spies, as well as caging enemies and political prisoners.

Despite Chelmsford lying thirty-odd miles outside London in the county of Essex, there was great excitement in the prison when on 10 December 1940 a double execution of the German spies Jose Waldberg and Karl Meier took place at Pentonville, then a week later on 17 December 1940 another Nazi agent called Charles Albert Van Der Kieboom was hanged in the same nick. After that, wartime executions under the Treachery Act were moved to Wandsworth Prison until 1944, except for the only one to be made by firing squad, which took place at the Tower of London. Josef Jakobs was an enemy alien who'd injured his foot while being parachuted into England to act as a spy. He was the last condemned person to meet their death at the Tower of London. A lot of the lads in Chelmsford had been moved out of London jails to free up those institutions for more urgent wartime uses. Although we'd been spirited away from the scenes of these killings, news of them travelled through Chelmsford like wildfire and caused much wonderment.

I spent my free time exercising, whenever possible in the yard but mostly in my cell—mainly push-ups, sit-ups, squats, running on the spot and shadow boxing. I wanted to keep myself fit. Every day I'd bend down and place my palms flat on the ground. Then I'd swing my right leg up into the air and use it as a counterweight, before lifting up my left foot, so that I was standing on my hands. With my legs pushed straight up above me, I'd bend my elbows and lower my head to the ground, before pushing myself back up to my full upside down height with my arms fully extended beneath my shoulders. After only a few of these handstand push-ups the sweat would be pouring off me, and by the time I'd done thirty I was dripping wet.

Although I had to exert myself to stay fit, my hatred of the ruling class remained as sharp as a blade without much effort on my part—all I had to do was think of the old bill who'd fitted me up, the judge who'd sentenced me, the death of my brother, or the exploitation of the working class, and my mind was filled with thoughts of larcenous revenge. Likewise, it was the German bourgeoisie who'd given Hitler and his scumbag henchmen their place on the world stage. They'd suppressed the revolutionary wave in Germany after the First World War, and virtually everyone on the planet was paying a heavy price for that.

Two years is a long time to be put away, but the sentence will weigh far more heavily if, like I was, you also happen to be innocent. One night locked in a cell can seem like forever, with a million and one morbid ideas rising from the black depths of your mind as you wait for daylight and the unlocking of the door. Multiply that by seven hundred and thirty and then throw in the humiliations of pointless work, enforced cleaning and assaults from the screws. Next add the endless turmoil in my head as I went over and over the court case: the self-satisfied words of the scummy beak as he sent down an innocent man; the endless lies on the part of the prosecution who had their day in court and won because they perjured themselves; the bullying cop who'd assaulted me, whingeing about me knocking him out when I'd only acted in self-defence. During all that time inside when there was little to do but contemplate the injustice I'd suffered, the only way to stop the cynicism that constantly gnawed at my guts from turning into cancer or some other disease was by transforming it into a hatred of the bosses and their slimy capitalist system.

I didn't necessarily have to serve my full two years inside as the government wanted to reduce the prison population and free up manpower for the services. That said, the armed forces didn't want most of the cons who were released; they were interested in the screws and other support workers required to run a jail. I talked with the prison authorities about their ticket of leave scheme only to be told they weren't gonna release me while I continued to protest I was innocent of the two crimes of which I'd been convicted. So I stayed in jail and did my two years and I never got to fight the Nazis because I was perceived as having an attitude problem that made me unable to accept discipline. This was nonsense! Whoever heard of a successful boxer who lacks discipline? They don't exist, coz to fight professionally you have to train and train and train.

Anyway, as far as they could, the authorities were emptying the prisons of ordinary decent criminals and filling them up with conscientious objectors. I didn't mind the COs; at least they took a stand on what they believed in and were prepared to go to jail rather than be conscripted. In fact they seemed a little like me, since I was rotting in jail because I insisted on my innocence. Another thing that happened during the Blitz which had the effect of reducing the numbers doing porridge was that the arrest rate of juveniles shot up, and kids weren't gonna be sent to adult prisons. In parts of London juvenile crime accounted for roughly fifty percent of those being nicked. I think this was mainly coz youngsters were less adept at looting than adults—and therefore more likely to be caught emptying coins from gas meters in bomb-damaged houses or stripping clothes from dead bodies. Juvenile ineptitude took up lots of police time, and made life easier for the adult professionals of the criminal underworld.

One of the rank and file cons I came across at Chelmsford was Billy Hill. He gave me good reason to punch him out later. Hill got let out early, in late 1941, which was well before me. You had to give it to Hill that he had brains, but he was a bully and personally I can't stomach men who pick on those who are weaker than them but need a gang to take on a single person who is stronger. I came across Hill again and again over the next ten years, until I became one of the few men to get the better of him in a fight. He always preferred to take on the elite who were superior to him with their fists by stealth or from behind a mob of his own men. While he was in Chelmsford, Hill befriended Frankie Fraser, another bullyboy who failed to intimidate me. I wished I'd punched out Fraser when I had the chance, because when this idiot got around to having his autobiography ghostwritten in the 1990s it included some choice bullshit about me. But I'll return to these matters later.

When I got out of Chelmsford in 1942 the war had really changed some aspects of life in London, but in other ways everything was still the same. British society wasn't nearly as brutal as Germany under the Nazis, but it remained a racket organised to benefit rich toe-rags. One of the most striking ways in which London had been transformed from when I'd gone inside was that rationing had turned everyone into a criminal. It wasn't like that in the early months of the war. I'm told there was a similar atmosphere after the outbreak of World War I, with most people thinking that the hostilities would be over in a matter of weeks, but once the fighting had carried on for a couple of years the realisation that everyone was in it for the long haul really sank in. So even your so-called honest citizens wanted their extra bits of food and clothing, and while the rich were in a position to stockpile goods, the working class had little choice about paying over the odds for them on the black market. Both that and the Blitz, which necessitated blackouts, proved handy for me once I settled down to a life of crime.

As soon as I was released from nick, I went to see my mum and dad in Wales. When I got back to The Smoke, I headed over to Paddington to get myself trained up in the family trade of larceny. My Uncle Dinny wanted to celebrate my joining the firm with a drink, but for my whole life I abstained from touching alcohol. This was initially because of my ambition to become a champion boxer, but as I got older I just wanted to stay fit so that I could rob the wealthy and revenge myself against those who got all the benefits from a society that had treated me — and my kith and kin — so cruelly. So Dinny and my cousins Dennis, Michael and David had their whiskies and I joined my cousins" mother in having a cup of tea. My cousin Dai had grown up a lot in the two years I'd been away and was now accompanying his older brothers as they broke into homes and businesses all over west London. I may have been older than these boys, but even Dave had more experience than me as a thief.

The first job I did with my cousins was a smash and grab on Ernest Lowe, the jewellers in North Audley Street in Mayfair. We began by stealing a car; Michael drove it to the West End. It was around 10am, so the premises were open but there weren't too many people in the street. The office drones were already at work and the shopping crowds wouldn't build up until a bit nearer lunchtime. Michael brought our wheels to a screeching halt outside Ernest Lowe, mounting the pavement. Dennis and Dave leant out of the passenger windows, while I ran around the car and threw a 14lb hammer through the shop window. My cousins scooped up all they could from the display without having to get out of the motor. When I grabbed a bunch of watches, I cut my hand on the broken glass but the injury wasn't serious. I dived through the open window of our motor and landed on Dave. As my cousin and I rearranged ourselves on the back seat, Michael gunned the engine and we sped off with a good haul of swag. We weren't even chased, so I thought it was pretty much money for old rope.

Dennis told me afterwards that the number of smash and grab raids had fallen dramatically as the war progressed. Most criminals were going for other cons; burglary and looting were easy under the cover of the blackout and falling bombs. When I asked him why, if that was the case, we'd just committed an unnecessarily high-risk crime, he told me he'd wanted to test my nerve. To be honest, I wasn't particularly keen on the targets my cousins picked for me when I came out of nick in 1942 and on through the following two years, but this was my apprenticeship in the art of burglary. I needed to learn all about larceny and I'd passed my first test with flying colours.

The next day we headed to Grafton Street, just off Piccadilly, to do a run-out. This time we didn't even bother to steal a car. I walked into Catchpole and Williams smartly dressed in a new suit, put on a posh accent that was a million miles away from my natural Welsh lilt, and asked to see some jewels. When an assistant showed me a tray of sparklers, I grabbed it and ran out of the shop. As soon as I was in the street, Dennis stood in the doorway and prevented anyone from following me — he was holding the door to the shop firmly shut. I emptied the jewels from the tray into a briefcase I was carrying for this very purpose, threw the empty dish into the road and ran down the street. As I careered past Michael, who was standing at the far end of Dover Street, on the corner with Piccadilly, I dropped the bag at his feet and jumped onto the first bus I could find. Less than an hour later we all met up in Praed Street. At that time the fence we mostly dealt with was Bertie Holliday — the man I'd been with when PC Spratt stopped me for SUS back in 1937 — and he gave us a fair price for furs and jewels. But since it was wartime these weren't the only things we'd steal; we also had a roaring trade in cigarettes and clothing coupons going on with people who'd never have given us the time of day back in the 1930s.

You had to keep up with the times and be able to adapt to them. My cousins taught me to drive — in stolen cars of course! They said I might need this skill when I was out with them on jobs. My Uncle Dinny was still doing a bit of protection but the opportunities for that had been cut back. Horse racing was severely restricted, down to about a fifth of the meetings there'd been before the war; even the dog stadiums were closed on more days than they were open and weren't allowed to operate during the evenings because of the blackout. Although my family boasted many fine fighters, I was the best one it had ever produced and Dinny wanted me to work with him on protection, but bullying and intimidating people into parting with their cash simply didn't appeal to me. After many arguments it was eventually agreed that I didn't have to involve myself in family operations I didn't like. Returning to the type of crime I was up for, we'd swap around who did what during a run-out, so sometimes I was the man blocking the door and if I had to use my fists, then that's what I did. But I preferred to fight by the Queensberry Rules and favoured burglaries over run-outs, stealth to intimidation.

Which reminds me that one of the early house jobs I did was lifting the Marchioness of Queensberry's jewellery from her gaff on Charles Street. This was just the other side of Berkeley Square from where I'd done my first run-out from Catchpole and Williams. It obviously wasn't a good war for her ladyship because my cousins had also robbed her at the end of 1939. They thought enough time had elapsed to make it both safe and worthwhile going back. In 1942 it was Dennis and me who done the old sow. We took an unsecured ladder from outside a property further down the street that was under repair, and placed it against an upstairs bedroom window while the household and a number of guests were at supper. I climbed up and in through the open window, with Dennis acting as my outside man. I threw eight furs down to my accomplice, then I loaded the jewels that were spread across a dressing table into my pockets. I was in and out of the room in a couple of minutes — the blackout provided me with good cover.

The furs were of excellent quality and, since coats of this type weren't made during the war, there was a ready market for them. I put ten percent of my cash from this theft into an envelope and addressed it to the South Wales Miners" Federation. Alongside the big-denomination bills, I placed a note saying I was an ex-miner who'd had a bit of luck but still believed in working-class solidarity — hence my donation to the cause. I signed my message as "A. Friend". For the next thirty years, whenever I plucked swag from a rich parasite's home, ten percent of what I made was donated anonymously to a working-class organisation — but never to sell-out scum like the Labour Party.

With the money I was making from my robberies I'd moved into a room on D'Arblay Street in Soho, where I'd befriended a number of working girls. Most of the rooms in this property were taken by prostitutes and, since we all shared a kitchen and bathroom, I got to know them well. The mysteries were able to dispose of furs for me. After robbing the Marchioness of Queensberry, I sent two of them off for a weekend in Reading where they sat around bars and hotel lobbies getting into conversation with less fashionably dressed women. When the impossibility of acquiring fur coats came up, as it always did, they'd offer to sell the one they were wearing to their new friend, at full market rate of course! This way it looked like the fur changed hands as part of a private agreement and the purchaser didn't need to feel bad about buying stolen goods. I made more money selling coats this way than offloading them to a fence like Holliday, but if we had a big haul we wanted to get rid of quickly then we'd give some to our middlemen and the rest to my ladies.

I loved stealing coats from parties, so that their rich owners had to suffer the indignity of going home without a fur. They'd never really understand what it had been like for me as a boy when I'd had to go without a coat because my family couldn't afford these things — but it gave them a little taste of what I'd suffered. Years later when I was banged up in a cell with a college graduate who got into fraud to fund his anarchist political activities, he was most impressed when I told him about my single-minded cat burgling campaign against the rich. He replied by — as he'd describe it — rapping about one of his favourite Russian writers, a guy called Vasily Vasilievich Rozanov who virtually no one else I've ever met has heard of. My cellmate quoted the following from the works of this spectacularly unsuccessful author: "The audience gets up to leave their seats. Time to collect their coats and go home. They turn around. No more coats, no more home."

Rozanov provides a nice poetic image but that's all it is. Coming from an impoverished background, I never got much formal education and didn't have the opportunity to spend my time looking at sunsets and dreaming my life away. I got on and did things because otherwise the rich would have left me to starve to death. It is up to the working class to make the world a better place — the eggheads can't do it for us! When I said this to the anarchist who told me about Rozanov, he looked a bit sheepish but agreed with me. I never read much, but over all the years I spent inside I did go through *Capital* by Karl Marx — and some other political and historical works by him and others. I considered reading fiction or the Bible a waste of time. If I wanted to be entertained by a story I preferred to go to the cinema than read a novel.

Roland Martin, the guy who told me about Rozanov when we were banged up together in the 1960s, wasn't the first intellectual I met. I came across a load of them during the war, since they were all over Soho. I'd go to clubs not to drink, but for a game of cards. The eggheads could never understand why alcohol didn't appeal to me, even when I explained this was because I wanted to confront reality no matter how harsh it was, and had no desire to escape into fantasies fuelled by booze.

I'd got particularly friendly with Sarah Dixon, one of the mysteries in my building, and she was a bit of a bohemian as well as a working girl. She'd take me to the Gargoyle Club looking out onto Dean Street, and at this establishment the eggheads were always out in force. One of the planks I'd see there was A. J. Ayer, who someone told me was the cleverest man in Britain — but if that was the case then I always wondered why he looked so miserable. Philosophers like Ayer may have interpreted the world, but it was the working class who were changing and transforming it. My cousins couldn't abide the Gargoyle — they preferred places with a more mannish atmosphere — but Sarah loved the club. You went through a small door on Meard Street and up in a tiny lift. It had been a hangout for flappers back in the 1920s, but by the time I got there it was shabby. Still, it appealed to Sarah and all her bohemian friends, who all seemed to see her work as a prostitute as frightfully sophisticated, whereas I never viewed it as anything other than an economic necessity.

When I wasn't with Sarah I preferred to go and play cards in the innumerable illegal clubs that sprang up — and disappeared just as quickly — in the streets running off Shaftesbury Avenue. In these you could gamble for decent stakes, hundreds of quid often riding on a single game. I liked playing cards best but I wasn't averse to dice or even roulette. The places I went to gamble generally didn't have names — we'd just refer to them by their street address. Often they would harbour army deserters and those operating them acted as fences too; so you could take in tom and exchange your stolen jewels for money to gamble with. You could get booze as well if you wanted it. I was glad I didn't drink when I saw my fellow gamblers incapacitated by hooch that had been badly distilled or made up from industrial spirits with a little added flavouring. In odd instances this illicit booze killed, blinded or brain damaged those who drank it, although more often than not it just left them puking their guts up or unconscious for a few hours because it was so strong.

There were some amazing gambling dens that opened up during the war. For a while me and my cousins were going up to Kings Cross for fun and frolics at an unbelievably huge illegal spieler. This massive gambling hall was housed in a former warehouse. Along one wall people played nothing but poker, both five-card stud and the draw variety. Opposite, the punters were playing twenty-one, farobank and the dice game birdcage. At the far end of the warehouse, frenzied betting went on over rolls of the dice, and there was a huge bank accompanying it. They had coins and notes piled up in a series of glass containers to really feed the money hunger of those gambling. Outside of the vaults of the Bank of England, I can't imagine where else you could have seen so much ready cash in one place.

My cousins liked establishments in which they could booze and watch scantily clad dancers at the same time, so we sometimes went to the Kit-Kat Club on Regent Street, or The Blue Lagoon which was close by. More occasionally we went to the Panama Club in South Kensington. A few years later the Panama Club became notorious as the place Neville Heath and Margery Gardner went drinking before heading off in a taxi to the Pembridge Court Hotel. In his room, Heath got Gardner to strip, tied her hands and legs, then viciously whipped her before suffocating the poor woman. I never liked the Panama Club because it was always full of toffs on their uppers, and while many of them had turned to crime, they couldn't be trusted to observe the professional code adhered to by those of us who came from less privileged backgrounds. I didn't drink and the dancers failed to excite me because I often saw the prostitutes who had rooms in the same building as me naked. But I liked my cousins and they dug things that bored me, so I'd go along for the ride, especially when I was able to gamble.

I was still relatively young and I had no responsibilities, so it was easy to have a laugh in Soho. But this fun required money and, by 1943, it was mostly the London suburbs that supplied the readies we spent so freely. On jobs we usually headed west, sometimes north, less often south, and never east. Everywhere was under blackout but anywhere bombs were particularly likely to fall—such as the East End and its docks—you had the emergency services running around. I may have been a professional fighter but as far as larceny was concerned I did what Dennis wanted. It was Dennis I mostly worked with after Michael was called up. Dave was too young to join the military and it seemed the services didn't want Dennis coz his criminal record was even worse than mine. After a while it was just my oldest cousin and me. Dave got sent to borstal after being caught flogging clothing coupons we'd half-inched from some government offices in

Hounslow. This robbery, like so many others, had been like taking candy from a baby. We just kicked in a back door, no alarms (not many premises were alarmed in those days), no guards, no nothing. It was a Friday night and we could have been there the whole weekend if we'd wanted, but we went through the place in twenty minutes. All we were interested in were coupons, and we found them in an unlocked cupboard. We loaded them into suitcases we'd brought with us. Then it was back into the stolen car and a fast ride to town.

Dennis loved stealing coupons and we went all over west London and beyond nicking them from barely secured premises. You could sell coupons in batches with little risk, or a book at a time in pubs and cafes for more money but with a greater chance of getting caught. Dave got nicked in a Paddington cafe where he'd been offloading stacks of ration books. Dennis thought coupon theft was great because it was a victimless crime; the government could just print up more books and the ones we stole were used by ordinary people to buy things they needed. My cousin considered it a win-win situation. I didn't go for the idea of victimless crime much myself, since I wanted to use larceny as a way of hitting back at the rich and the judiciary, but Dennis taught me a lot about theft in the two and a half years we worked together, so mostly I agreed to hit the targets he found.

Life was sweet as a nut. Sarah moved into my bedsitter, but kept her own room on for work. Things were very different to approved school, my early working life or prison. No getting up early for me and Sarah; when she knocked off soliciting we'd usually go to a club so she could have a drink to wind down. I'd have something soft. We'd make love in the early hours and sleep late. Sarah was often on the street until midnight, and like many other working girls, flashed a torch on her face when a potential john went by. I was also mainly doing jobs by night. Teamed up with Dennis, our main target became government offices, but sometimes we'd do a bit of shopbreaking. We'd take money and goods like cigarettes from retail operations, but our best hits outside of coupon thefts came from lorry jacking.

For our big cigarette nabs, we'd steal a car and drive up to a warehouse somewhere and then follow a lorry when it came out of the gates. Sometimes we'd tail a vehicle for hours until the driver left it unattended for a moment: as soon as he did, we'd jump in and hot-wire it. We'd abandon our stolen car because we had no further use for it. Dennis had a lock-up in Richmond rented under a false name, so we'd take the goods there — then we'd drive the lorries into central London where we dumped them. There wasn't much to it really, and so many experienced coppers had been conscripted into the armed services that those who were left couldn't deal with the crime wave that accompanied the war. Of course, there were a load of blokes who for various reasons weren't shipped out to the front lines who became specials, but on the whole they didn't cut it as uniformed filth either and caused us no great problems.

Dennis didn't want to steal furs in Mayfair but I did. I also wanted Sarah to stop sleeping with johns, so we came to a compromise. I'd assist her with her work and she'd help me with mine. She didn't need me around when she was clipping, but when it came to cross-biting my skill as a boxer came in handy. If I wasn't available because I was off working with Dennis, then Sarah would tell punters she didn't have a room and that they'd have to give her a deposit to get one. She'd lead them to a building and instruct them to wait outside while she arranged a bed. The mark would be left standing there, sometimes for hours. Sarah, of course, would duck out a back entrance. Other times, she'd bring a john to her room and I'd give them enough time to undress before rushing in and demanding to know what the mug was doing with my wife. I'd take our mark for their money, their coupons, their watch and anything else of value. I didn't even have to pretend to be angry; I genuinely didn't want other men sleeping with my woman. I preferred it when Sarah was cross-biting to clipping, because I was there to take care of things if the john turned into a problem. I was sufficiently menacing that most punters simply handed over their valuables and left meekly, which was what I wanted coz it meant I didn't need to hurt them.

Most of the mugs I had to punch out in Sarah's room were US servicemen. They made a good target coz they had money to burn, even if a lot of them fancied themselves as hardmen. That said, they presented me with easy pickings and I wouldn't have had a problem with them even if the overwhelming majority had been sober, rather than so drunk that their reflexes were completely dulled. Most people liked the way the yanks chucked their money, their chocolate and their chewing gum around, but many blokes weren't so keen on the way they took local brides. While I was well aware that the working class has no country, the sentiment that a million and a half were "oversexed, overpaid, and over here" was something I could exploit if I needed a bit of sympathy when I had to really knock a GI around. Sarah would sometimes pick them up during the day — as well as at night — for the two of us to cross-bite, and one I knocked unconscious needed carrying down the stairs and dumping on the street at lunchtime, just as the landlord was coming in to collect rents. I told him the bloke had been causing trouble, so he helped me carry him out, all the while joking: "The yanks have brought so much chewing gum into Soho and they chuck it around so freely, that even the pigeons are laying rubber eggs."

I'd scoot around Mayfair and if we saw a party going on then Sarah would act as my outside "man". I'd go up a ladder or a drainpipe and get into a bedroom, chuck the furs down to Sarah and we'd drag them home in mailbags. Once I'd thrown down the women's coats, I'd go through the men's jackets removing any wallets I found. If I was really lucky some or even all the female guests would have left their handbags with their furs, so I'd get to half-inch those too. Mostly I didn't know who we were stealing from and I didn't care; they were rich and that was all that mattered to me. Once I'd transformed the swag into cash, I also always enjoyed deciding where to distribute the ten percent that went to working-class organisations: of course, it was the Miners" Federation and the National Union of Blastfurnacemen who got more than anyone else. The miners because I'd been one, the blastfurnacemen because steel was associated with my hometown and many members of my family worked in the industry in south Wales.

Anyway, one night Sarah and me did a job and then we went to a spieler on Dean Street. I gambled and she drank. I was losing money hand over fist and figured I might run out of wedge before my luck changed, so I sent Sarah home to get one of the furs we'd just stolen because I knew the governor of the premises would be willing to negotiate a price for the item. Unfortunately, I never was able to finish my game of cards, because Sarah came back and told me the cops were raiding our gaff and she'd seen them carrying out the coats we'd just stolen.

I quickly came up with a plan. I'd swipe the evidence of our crime from Tottenham Court Road cop shop. The governor of the spieler even agreed to take the gear off me for a reasonable price if I successfully nicked my swag back from those who'd nabbed it. There was a car park round the back of the TCR cop station, and if I was quick I'd be able to half-inch the Q van with my gear inside before the filth unloaded it. I whispered in Sarah's ear and told her to holler out that some American soldiers who'd got into a fight with an off-duty copper were getting the crap kicked out of them at Tottenham Court Road. On my instructions, Sarah then went down The Rainbow Room and a bunch of other places where there'd be shed-loads of yanks, and at the top of her voice repeated the story. I joined the mob from the spieler as they headed the short distance to the cop shop.

A large crowd of angry GIs had gathered outside the fuzz station before the pigs arrived back from the raid on my gaff. As I'd anticipated, they'd given every room in the building I lived in a good search, although the furs had been easy enough to find. The filth had taken their time in the hope of uncovering other stolen goods that had been better hidden. (I knew, although they didn't, there weren't any.) Rather than unloading my swag when they arrived at their HQ, the rozzers who'd turned me over rushed round the front of their cop shop to help their porky chums deal with the crowd of angry Americans. I nipped round the back to where they parked their vans and hot-wired the vehicle they'd used in their attack on my gaff. I drove north, then as no one followed me I turned around and headed south again, but down Gower Street rather than Tottenham Court Road. As arranged, Sarah was waiting for me in Soho Square. The furs were still in my mailbags, which I dumped on the pavement, and she stayed with them while I drove the van a few streets away to dump it. Once I was back with Sarah we lugged the swag round to the spieler and got a good price for it. However, knowing what had happened, the governor didn't want me hanging around until he'd offloaded the coats, so despite the money in my pocket I wasn't able to gamble until my luck changed.

As we walked home, I felt happy with the night's work and the dough burning a hole in my pocket. I expected to be nicked but, with the evidence gone, the case was complicated and I figured the cops would drop it. They forgot about it alright, but they knew what I'd done and they were so angry with me they decided to dump me right in it instead. They'd been banking on me making a second appearance at the Central Criminal Court as a tea leaf, but instead of taking me to the Old Bailey they dragged me before a magistrate. The charge wasn't burglary, it was living off immoral earnings, or to be more precise, Sarah's takings from prostitution. She only had one previous conviction for soliciting and although I'd never taken money from her because I earned my own, that didn't stop me being sentenced for pimping. If I'd realised this was the way things would pan out, I'd have rather gone down as a creeper. But hindsight always comes after the fact, and I hadn't seen in advance just how the cops would fit me up for a second time. Thus, just before Christmas 1944, I found myself starting an eighteen-month stretch at Horfield Prison.

The authorities were still keeping ordinary criminals like me out of the London jails. They were the preserve of prisoners of war and other scum, with Wandsworth and Wormwood Scrubs still acting as a London hub for British Intelligence, who'd be safe there unless the buildings suffered a direct bomb hit. The routine in prison was the same as when I'd got out in the spring of 1942, but in the interim the food had gone from bad to worse. Something to do with the war and shortages, or so I was told when I had the temerity to complain. The only good thing I can say about Horfield was that it was in Bristol, so when they were allowed to visit, it wasn't too difficult for my family to come over from south Wales to see me. During those meets we were strictly controlled and there was no physical contact, but that and the odd letter were as good as it got inside.

That said, one of the missives I got at Horfield was less than pleasant. It brought the news that my dad Owen had been killed in a road accident. They wouldn't even let me out for the funeral, and used the excuse that the war had overstretched HMP resources. This was a real low point in my life, and led me to swear that no matter what happened, I would attend my mother's funeral. It made me sick to the guts that the authorities wouldn't let me pay my last respects to my old man. I don't see how anyone could expect a system that treats prisoners in such a scummy way to reform anyone—what it was all about was punishment. Back then it seemed like any time I went to jail a member of my family died, and not getting to their funeral greatly added to the retribution the authorities exacted on me. Losing my dad made me feel hollow and empty. If I'd wallowed in depression I'd have become mentally ill and physically sick. Instead I did everything I could to direct my hatred against the ruling class, to focus on my release by creating mental pictures of the homes of the toffs I'd rob once I was out. Depression is anger you direct in against yourself; to stay healthy I had to mentally channel my aggression against those who were responsible for my predicament, knowing that when I was free I'd take my revenge.

Many more times than I cared to count, the cell door was slammed on me and I was caged up with dark thoughts assailing my mind until the key slid into the lock in the early morning. If you're innocent you don't expect to be convicted, and even if by the time I was in Horfield I'd committed far more crimes than I could recall, I wasn't guilty of the things for which I'd been imprisoned. This was the second time I'd found myself inside, framed by a bunch of low-life coppers who after swearing to their "almighty God to tell the truth, the whole truth, and nothing but the truth" proceeded to show the court marked card after marked card, the whole lot adding up to a pack of lies. There are only supposed to be two jokers in a pack, but every time I went before a beak I ended up with a whole hand of them, while the old bill held all the aces. The coppers, the lawyers, the judges and the property owners whose interests they upheld were the scum I was waging a war against.

THREE

ne person I didn't see while I was in Horfield was Sarah; I guess it was too far from London. Although I went down, all she got was a fine. Sarah didn't like writing letters, so while I was banged up I wasn't surprised I didn't hear from her. When I got out in 1946 I headed straight up to Soho and went looking for Sarah but she'd disappeared. No one I came across had seen her in over a year. The war was like that—it threw people together and then tore them apart. Moving on, I've said this about the hostilities but it's also true of the peace that followed it—from certain perspectives it seemed like everything had changed, and in other ways it was all still the same.

There had been a Labour Party landslide in the 1945 election while I was still "paying my debt to society"—for yet another "crime" I didn't commit. I'd always known that the reformist Labour Party only pretended to represent the working class—and was actually our enemy. Our political leaders claimed we were about to see the complete transformation of British society, and allegedly what we were going to get was a cradle to the grave welfare state. Not that we ever actually saw anything that radical; it was just that all those working men who'd been called up for service were returning home armed and with the ability to use these weapons against the bosses, so the ruling class had to promise us something to keep us off their backs. And as usual with the bourgeoisie there were far more promises than real concessions. Rationing went on and on, and a lot of those arms that floated around after World War II got used in robberies.

When I came out of nick my cousin Dennis had gone almost straight. He'd taken over a pub on Praed Street: The Great Western, on the corner of Sale Place. Although Dennis had done time for theft, with the help of some bent coppers he hadn't had too much difficulty wangling a licence. For a price, the records of his convictions conveniently disappeared. My uncle and my other cousins were up to their usual pursuits but I'd served my apprenticeship and didn't need to go thieving with them. I'd target the rich and I wouldn't use guns, I liked to keep it personal. I prided myself on being a non-violent criminal, but still I couldn't abide those thieves who tried to make out they were better than the rest of us because they only targeted businesses and not individuals. I quite consciously chose very rich people as my victims because I was carrying on a class war!

As I've said, it was a real gun culture just after the war, but I didn't want any part of it: I preferred to use my fists when force became necessary. My cousins weren't into using guns either; they viewed armed robbery as a money-making scam for mugs and the desperate. People who went out with shooters all too often ended up using them, and back then if you killed someone — especially if it was a copper — you could still get a death sentence. We all saw burglary as a better option than hold-ups, but I wanted to hit the pampered rich, while my cousins wanted to do shops and businesses.

My uncle bunged me a few quid to get me on my feet when I got out of Horfield, and I found a room not too far away from the family in London — on the Harrow Road. I went back to my old tricks of prowling around Mayfair and other swanky parts of The Smoke pulling opportunistic thefts, but while I'd been inside I'd also decided to target specific individuals who I researched by reading the papers. One man who caught my attention was Sir Hugo Cunliffe-Owen, a prominent English tobacco manufacturer. He had a reputation for being a ruthless organiser of his business enterprises but rather slack in his private life. I found his reputation as "The Human Dynamo" infuriating, since he used his organisational skills to fill his own pockets rather than benefit mankind. I decided to hit him where it hurt, by robbing his floozies. In 1946 he was dumping his second (or maybe it was his third) wife Lady Mauricia for the dancer Marjorie Daw, who a couple of years later would change her name by deed poll to Marjorie Clara Jessie Cunliffe-Owen.

I headed down to the Cunliffe-Owen estate in Berkshire and found a ladder in a shed. I placed this against the house and, while dinner was in progress, climbed in through an upstairs window. I found myself in the master bedroom where I grabbed both jewels and furs. I took the sparklers to Bertie Holliday who told me Sir Hugo's ex had some even better baubles, and by using the same entry method on her Sunningdale mansion, I made off with the biggest haul I'd had the good fortune to blag since I'd dedicated myself to robbing the rich. The papers reported the stolen tom as being worth £40,000, but as the thief I didn't get anything like that for it. I got five grand and Bertie more than doubled that when he sold the sparklers on to realise his cut. Bertie lived in the same neck of the woods as the toff whose baubles I'd plucked and, despite an ordinary upbringing in south London, he mixed with those who styled themselves "society" and I considered scum. Bertie's rich friends knew him as Barry and they had no idea he was putting me up to robbing them.

The best tip I ever got from Bertie was when that pair of Nazi-supporting royal dickheads the Duke and Duchess of Windsor were staying with Lord Dudley at Ednam Lodge in Sunningdale. On 16 October 1946, I robbed the former Mrs Simpson of a leather bag of jewels including emeralds, sapphires, diamonds and rubies. I heaved myself up a drainpipe and forced open a window to get into the bedroom Bertie had told me was being used by the royal parasites. The household was at dinner and the room I was in had been locked from the outside. I already knew there was a wall-mounted safe behind a drab landscape painting. The key for it was — as Bertie had told me it would be — in the drawer of a dressing table. The swag belonging to the woman who would never be queen was worth a bomb, but while I was at it I also half-inched some diaries and other private papers. I got out the way I'd come in: through the window, down the drainpipe and past the rhododendron bushes.

Bertie loved the royal tom I'd lifted for him but wasn't keen on my plan of taking the documents I'd obtained to the press, so that they could freely expose the former king and his concubine as the fascist-loving lice they'd always been. Holliday persuaded me to give him the disgraced monarch's documents for safe-keeping. He argued it would be stupid to put this stash of inside information into circulation right after the theft. Bertie was bang on the money about this but I never saw the papers again, and Holliday told me just before his death that he'd burnt them all. Although I desperately wanted the scandalous diaries published because they were a republican goldmine, I can still take some satisfaction from knowing that their disappearance gave the slimy House of Windsor many a sleepless night.

I often found that what at first appeared to be screwsman's bad luck would turn out for the best. That's the way it was with my purloined papers, which Bertie incinerated. I guess because Holliday fenced the Windsor jewels, even if he'd had them re-cut first, word got around that he was involved with the theft. By the end of the forties the authorities had hounded Bertie to his death. He was probably right when he said that if they'd discovered I'd planned to circulate the stolen papers, they'd have framed me up on a death charge, because knowing what I'd read they'd have wanted to stop my mouth. Not that the diaries and other documents were that interesting; mostly it was just Hitler-worshipping gibberish alongside all the usual anti-working class tirades that are stock-in-trades amongst toffs. In equally tedious detail, and at almost as much length, they also detailed the sex life of the former king. Like Hitler and Eva Braun, Edward and Wallis never had penetrative sex, because the male partner in both couplings was only capable of reaching orgasm if he was beaten and abused. Among the papers I stole were many pages of sexual fantasies in which the Duke of Windsor wrote about his love of being bound and gagged, as well as having his wife urinate all over him.

I had another bit of luck when I jumped out of a house in Duke Street and hurt my ankle right at the start of 1947. I had to abandon a bag full of furs but this led to me meeting the great love of my life. Ann Chalmers was a nurse from Hackney, but at that time she was working at Charing Cross Hospital, then located in Agar Street, running off the Strand south of Covent Garden. Like my mother, Ann was petite with blonde hair and blue eyes. But that was where the similarities ended. Ann's face was long whereas my mother's was round, and their personalities were quite different too. My wife-to-be had an easy-going manner with nothing of my mother's intensity or sense of determination, although both had a sparkle in their eyes. Don't get me wrong, Ann could stand up for herself; it was when she didn't have someone trying to walk all over her that you really saw the difference between my wife-to-be and my mother. Ann patched me up and within a year we were married and our first daughter Beryl was on the way. It was good to have a wife with her own profession; someone who didn't mix with the criminal classes. Like me, Ann mostly worked at night, so I could go out and turn over some rich scumbag's drum and then find somewhere to play cards while she was at work.

During that first idyllic year of marriage we'd sleep together in the morning, get up for lunch, then moon over each other in the afternoon. Sometimes we'd go to the pictures, sometimes we'd go shopping and sometimes we'd just stay home and enjoy the sweet hours that make up the time in which those chained to the nine-to-five routine are preparing for bed. After we got hitched we moved to Bathurst Mews between Sussex Square and Sussex Gardens in Paddington. It was the perfect location for us because we were close to Hyde Park and the mainline station. It was no trouble to get to Wales to see my mother Julia, who was getting old and ill, while whenever the weather was fine we could take a constitutional in that great green lung around the Serpentine.

What I liked most about Hyde Park was the fact it was a place where you could see the whole world go by. As Ann's pregnancy progressed, our walks around the Serpentine became slower and slower until we spent more time sitting on benches than we did moving about. It amazed me that even with rationing going on so many people managed to feed a dog, and you'd see them out exercising their pets in the park. It was people and their dogs that I liked to watch in Hyde

Park. It made me laugh when a huge dog and a tiny one attempted to have sex together, alongside the way their embarrassed owners fought to control them. When I chuckled at this sort of thing, Ann would dig me in the ribs and tell me to be quiet. Ann liked dogs but they weren't her favourite animals—she was most delighted by the horse riding that went on around us in that wondrous landscape.

When Beryl was born I felt like I was walking on air. My beautiful little girl was everything I could have hoped for—a healthy baby with a smile that would melt even the most hardened heart. Ann didn't want to give up work, so she switched to days and I carried on with my forages against the rich and late-night games of poker. After my success at Sunningdale I wanted to make the royals my special target. I looked into stealing the Crown Jewels because if I could half-inch the state regalia of the British monarch from the Tower of London, I knew it would send a chill of fear through the British ruling class. It was a big target and would take a lot of planning. Bertie Holliday was horrified by this idea, which I revealed to my fence as I was pumping him for information about other royal baubles I might pluck. Bertie wanted nothing to do with any of this. He said the cops were after him because they already suspected he was connected to the thefts from the Duke and Duchess of Windsor. At the time I wrongly put this down to paranoia; after all, I was the thief and he was only the fence.

In the late forties I had one other close call with the monarchy. At that time, if I wasn't looking after my daughter, I regularly spent my days ghosting through the rich homes of Hampstead. In 1948 I did over a queen's equerry and their family at a Hampstead grace-and-favour house. Equerries are seconded from the armed forces to help the royals during their engagements, and act as paid flunkies to the Crown. I didn't know it at the time, but the future queen—then Princess Elizabeth—and her sister Margaret were visiting the property next door when I pulled this particular piece of larceny. It caused a right security flap, but despite extensive investigations I was never caught. Bertie got word of the shock waves I'd sent through the ranks of the Metropolitan Police—and especially those charged with protecting the royals—before he fenced the jewels and furs I'd bagged. To avoid any potential difficulties, he discretely disposed of my swag abroad. He also warned me to be more careful in choosing my targets or else I'd find myself in some seriously hot water!

To keep me away from turning over the slimeballs who made up the House of Windsor, Bertie provided me with information on other wealthy gits. A lot of them were in the Sunningdale area, I guess because this was where my favourite fence both ran with the foxes and hunted with the hounds. One of the best jobs he threw my way was Lord and Lady Docker, who I would rob not once but twice, succeeding even more spectacularly ten years after my initial raid on these two degenerates in July 1949, and only in that first instance acting on a tip from Bertie Holliday. The Dockers were paradigmatic examples of the rich flaunting their wealth in front of millions who had nothing—and I mean that literally! Don't forget that when I was a boy growing up in a loving family there were times when there was no food on the table or shoes on my feet. The Docker story is so far removed from my experience it might as well have happened on Mars. It really begins with Bernard Docker's dad—Frank Dudley Docker. The son of a successful solicitor, Frank Docker attended the posh King Edward's School and then made himself a career as a businessman, being one of the biggest British employers before the First World War. He also moved into railways and banking, and became a director of BSA—originally an arms company, but it later diversified into manufacturing cars and motorcycles. Worse yet, Frank Docker was a founding member of top bosses organisation the Federation of British Industries (later merged into the CBI) and a rabid English imperialist.

Bernard Docker was Frank Docker's only son and succeeded his old man in his dad's many business enterprises.

Bernard was kept on a strict leash while his pop was alive, and parental pressure put a swift end to his 1933 marriage to "actress" and shameless floozy Jeanne Stuart—later Baroness Jeanne de Rothschild. After Frank Docker died in 1944, his prodigal son was free to fritter away the family fortune on tasteless luxury and fully indulge his penchant for fraudulent business practices. In 1949 Bernard married the gaudy Norah Royce Turner, a former showgirl who had already been widowed by two elderly millionaires—Clement Callingham (married 1938, died 1945) and Sir William Collins (married 1946, died 1948). Norah Docker claimed the working classes loved her for bringing glamour into their drab lives, but I loathed this gold digger with a passion shared by everyone else I knew.

In early July 1949 Lady Muck, a title that became synonymous with Norah Docker's name, went away for the weekend. Bertie, who'd been visiting this puffed up showgirl, kindly left some upstairs French windows at her Hays Lodge residence in Chesterfield Hill open for me. I used a ladder and lifted £40,000 worth of jewellery from the bedroom. It was one of the biggest robberies in years, perhaps only matched by my earlier forty grand raid on the Cunliffe-Owens. Given the amount of help I'd got from my fence, I made no more profit from it than I had with my less spectacular robberies. I'm not complaining; I was quite happy with the three grand I got for the job—I don't know what Bertie sold the jewels for, but I doubt it was anywhere close to the price they'd been insured against. I didn't do much with Holliday after that: by the end of the summer he struck me as really paranoid. He said he was being set up for a long sentence by the cops. Just before Christmas 1949 he booked into the Wheatsheaf Hotel in Virginia Water and used a gun to kill himself. Before Bertie died he'd told me not to worry about the cops finding out that I was the man who'd robbed the Duke and Duchess, he was the only person who knew and he'd never tell anybody…

Bertie Holliday's death is another example of how the bloated scum who run our benighted country could ruin the life of an ordinary man, and made me all the more determined to continue with my campaign to expropriate the riches of the wealthy. There were plenty of fences around but I tried to stay away from too many criminal faces. That's the way too many thieves got caught by underhand coppers like John Gosling of the so-called Ghost Squad, who were using informers to grass them up. I had a few professional friendships, but as far as possible I liked to spend my time with my wife Ann and daughter Beryl. Sure, I enjoyed a game of cards more than I should have done, and gambling brought me into contact with plenty of underworld names, but I didn't like these people knowing my business, which is why Benny Selby became the main fence I dealt with after Bertie died.

Benny Selby was discreet. He didn't put on upper-class airs and graces like Holliday, and didn't hobnob with the rich, so he wasn't able to put me up for jobs the way my old fence had done. Sax Rohmer claimed his fictional character Fu Manchu had a face that combined the features of Shakespeare and Satan. The vagueness of this sketch makes me want to apply it wholesale to Selby because he was able to blend into the wallpaper. The most important difference between Rohmer's ridiculous description of his Chinese villain and Benny is that the latter had brown rather than cat-green eyes; nonetheless Selby's peepers radiated a huge intelligence. Selby didn't like being the centre of attention, and he could easily be overlooked in a crowd because, rather than being tall like Fu Manchu, he was of average height and build — with dark hair and bland features that were pleasing rather than handsome.

Everything went smoothly for me during the first year after Bertie's demise. There were no spectacular jobs like the coup against the dirtbag House of Windsor in 1946, but a steady haul of furs and tom from the bedrooms of the rich brought me a regular income — and as I've said, I always anonymously donated ten percent of what I took to unions such as the Iron and Steel Trades Confederation. As time went by my hands were increasingly drawn towards tomfoolery, since jewels were much lighter than furs. My work as a tea leaf taught me to love all pocket-size high-value objects. Benny could get rid of anything, and had a great system with furs, so I didn't completely turn my nose up at coats. Because expensive clobber was often marked with manufacturing codes, Benny would have it re-made just as readily as other fences had easily identifiable jewels re-cut. Minor damage would be inflicted on the coats and they'd be hung with repair tickets before being made over, which meant if the old bill raided Benny's sweatshop then there was a cover story to explain away the goods.

Bertie Holliday's death, which came just a few years after that of my father, really brought home my own mortality. I wasn't gonna be able to carry on my own private class war against the rich forever, so I decided to train up some of the youths I'd observed drifting around Soho. I'd see them in dance and pool halls, and by checking their moves and engaging them in a bit of chat, it was easy to sort the wheat from the chaff. There were so many lost boys in central London, it would have been stupid wasting my time on those who'd rather hook up with a rich man or woman than pursue a career as an honest and decent working-class criminal who'd dedicate their life to the redistribution of wealth. I'd take the kids who looked like good prospects ghosting in exclusive residential areas by day, and have them break into rooms at plush hotels such as the Ritz and Savoy by night. Sometimes I'd make them scale the walls just for the practice, even when there were simpler ways to get in. And those that showed real promise, I'd introduce to country house screwing.

A boy called Michael Hackett—who I spotted in the Billiard Hall in Windmill Street—eventually became my greatest *succès de scandale*. He later changed his name to Michael Black, and shortly after the Great Train Robbery in 1963 managed to blag a load of the money from that infamous job, despite having no direct involvement with it. He disappeared, and it seems he was responsible for at least one of the actual thieves getting nicked. I don't like that sort of thing, but Hackett was one of only two of my lost boys to disappoint me. My other failure, Peter Scott, I'll deal with later. I had more fun with Hackett than Scott, because when I met Scott I needed an outside man for some big jobs. I wasn't in such a rush when I came across Hackett. I'll never forget the look that came over Hackett's face halfway through the first night I'd taken him out, when he realised how I liked to work the kids I trained up. After I'd made Hackett use a grabbling iron and rope to get in and out of the Dorchester hotel on Park Lane – via guest balconies – I took him through a gap in the fence and into Hyde Park, where I delivered the punch line to the little joke I'd been playing on him.

"Mike, now you've done it the hard way, I'm going to show you the easy way to get into the rooms at fancy hotels like The Dorchester."

"What!" Hackett exclaimed as I took a chef's hat and apron out of a suitcase I was carrying.

"Put these on, go through the staff entrance and then find an empty corridor where no one will observe you breaking into the rooms."

"Why the fuck did you make me haul myself up a rope to get in before?" Hackett spat.

"Because I wanted you to learn there is always more than one way to get into a building."

"You could have just told me about the hard way and left me to do it by walking in through the door."

"Sure, but because I made you do it the hard way first, you'll never forget to look for the easy way into a building. If I just explained it to you, it could go in one ear and out the other."

"You're a right bastard."

"I need to be if I'm to turn a boy like you into a good burglar. So many kids today are too lazy to really make it in the world of crime. If you accept my way of teaching and apply yourself to what we're doing, then you won't fail as a thief."

As a result of exploits like this, by the early fifties I had a reputation as a canny talent spotter who'd find up-and-comers, and put them to work on more remunerative — not to mention class-conscious — criminal endeavours than those they'd been pursuing as layabouts in Soho.

As I've already made clear, I learnt some hard lessons from Bertie's death, so I put my plans to rob Buck House and other high-profile royal targets on hold. I was keeping my nose clean and staying away from bad company. Then in July 1951, when my brother Patrick was up from Wales to visit me, we had a touch of bad luck. We'd gone to a spieler in Soho and Pat got into an argument with some card sharps. He was a top-notch gambler and he'd become suspicious of the way the games we got involved in went. It took him a few hours but eventually he put his finger on what was wrong. The high-denomination cards in the packs had been very slightly bent. Anyone who knew this, and the guys winning most of the games were clearly in on it, didn't know exactly what someone had in their hand but they knew if it would fall high or low, which in terms of odds gave them all the edge they needed to win time and time again. Pat knew he'd been cheated and like me he wasn't the sort of man who'd keep quiet about it. But when he made an issue of what was going down, the so-called "Godfather" of the West End, Billy Hill, pulled out a knife and stabbed Pat in the face.

Pat was never as good a boxer as me, although under normal circumstances he could look after himself. That said, Billy Hill was your typical bully who'd never take anyone on unless the odds were in his favour. One of his men had grabbed Pat from behind before the gangland boss wielded his knife, which made me see red. I didn't think twice about it: I'd take on Hill and his whole gang, since that's the only way to deal with overgrown schoolyard creeps, which is exactly what this crew were. I launched myself at Hill and it only took one well-aimed punch with my right fist to lay this tosser out on the floor. I have powerful fists and when I hit Hill he didn't know if he was a man or a mouse. The bozo was out for the count, but sticking to my three strikes street fighting rule, I got in a couple of swift kicks to his head to make sure he stayed down.

In the confusion that followed my unexpected attack on the plastic gangster, Pat had broken free from the goon who'd pinned his arms and he'd kicked the would-be hard-man with considerable force in the cobblers—so the failed heavy was bent double clutching his bollocks and wailing like a baby as tears streamed down his face. We had the upper hand but most of those in the spieler would side with Hill's gang if the fight continued for very long. So I did what I didn't do often enough when I was at the card table—quit while I was ahead.

"Let's go Pat, these punks ain't worth a light," I shouted for the benefit of both my brother and Hill's men.

Hill's henchmen knew that if they swarmed me and Pat they'd eventually get the better of us, but they also understood that I had the best punch in London and a few of them would get it before they got me. So we sauntered out of that club at just the right speed, taking advantage of their shock at discovering the fact that there was still the odd man around who had the guts to floor a yellow-bellied coward like Billy Hill, the man with the biggest gang in London, which was his only way of making up for being under-endowed in the family jewels department.

The next day and for months afterwards, Hill sent his men out to get me, but I know when to stand and fight my ground, and when it's better to retreat and fight another day. So every time a dozen or more plastic gangsters jumped out of a van armed with iron bars and knives, I would outrun them. When I came across a couple of Hill's bozos who weren't out looking for me, I'd knock their heads together and leave them seeing stars. It was funny, but you never encountered Hill's men on their own; they went about in pairs or in bigger numbers. They didn't feel secure unless they went about mob-handed. Pat, who'd returned to Wales a couple of days after the incident in the spieler, was safe enough at home. If he'd been spotted in London he might have been attacked, but it was me who'd hit Hill, so I was the one being targeted for a beating.

Hill was the kind of guy who, if he couldn't win a fight the fair way, would play dirty. He had plenty of cops in his pocket and he knew I was the top cat burglar in London, so he ordered his tame rozzers to get me locked up and to ensure the judge threw away the key. Now by this time I wasn't so stupid as to have bent gear in my home in Paddington; I had a slaughter in The Avenue, Willesden. Hill was putting pressure on all the cops in his pockets to arrest me, and if they couldn't nick me fair and square then I could be sure they'd plant stolen goods on me. I knew all this because I'd befriended George Taters Chatham after being introduced to him in a spieler. Taters had been working as a cat burglar far longer than me, but in the early 1950s he was mostly working for Billy Hill, although we also did the odd job together. However, nothing as spectacular as the Eastcastle Street mail van raid in which Taters played his part as one member of a team put together by Hill. That was one of the biggest robberies ever to take place in the UK, and Taters was paid a small fortune, which he soon lost in rigged card games run by Hill.

Taters warned me I was gonna be nicked, but there wasn't much I could do with the information. I just carried on robbing the rich. The holiday period was always a good time for someone like me who liked to do live burglaries — hitting the bedroom where the guests" coats have been stored while they're letting their hair down over dinner elsewhere in the house. During the Christmas period of 1951 I walked around swanky Hampstead and Kensington looking for parties to poop. I'd get into an upstairs room, take whatever coats and jewels I could find and be gone before anyone knew I'd been there. New Year's Eve found me in Ingram Avenue, an exclusive street situated between Hampstead Heath and Hampstead Golf Club. There were several celebrations going on, so I picked the noisiest, climbed a drainpipe and got in through a bedroom window. I threw the eleven fur coats I found on a bed down into the garden, pocketed the baubles that were lying on the dressing table, and got out of the house the way I'd come in, shinning down the conveniently placed pipe. I was using Allan Grant as my outside man that night, and by the time I was on the ground, he'd packed the coats into a mail sack and hauled the swag into a stolen car we'd parked nearby.

I got Allan to drop me off at Uncle Dinny's pad, letting him take the swag back to his place. I arranged to meet up with him in two days" time. Before that I was gonna see in the New Year playing cards with my cousins. We paused briefly at midnight to toast the start of January but otherwise gambled solidly from 11.30pm until 2am. With a young daughter it wasn't possible to celebrate New Year at home. Ann and Beryl were both asleep when I got in. We got up together in the morning and had breakfast as a family. I went round to see Allan again the day after the New Year holiday, which I'd spent at home with Beryl and Ann. He kept three furs and some jewels that he'd arranged to fence. I packed the other eight coats and the rest of the tom into a suitcase and took a bus to Willesden. Allan had decided to come with me to look at some silver I had stored there; he thought he might be able to flog it. As we approached the house in The Avenue in which I had a room, the doors at the back of a van were flung open and four men jumped out.

I didn't need to think twice about what I was going to do in a situation like that; I was fit and I could run very fast, even when I was carrying a suitcase loaded with eight furs, which I was only going to dump if that became absolutely necessary. Allan didn't have the discipline or fitness that comes with serious sports training and the men caught him, but I ran over walls and through gardens, tearing my clothes and cutting my hands — but I didn't care because what were a few cuts and bruises against my freedom? I kept hold of the coats and, once I'd evaded the cops, made my way over to Benny Selby's drum. Once I'd got some readies off him for my gear,

I told him that the cops had been chasing me and asked him to pass a message to Ann.

It looked like I wouldn't be seeing my wife for a while coz the rozzers would be keeping tabs on her in the hope of nabbing me. I needed to get away from my usual haunts but didn't want to go somewhere totally unfamiliar, so I rented a room in Feltham. All I had to do was head south into Surrey and there were plenty of rich burglary pickings to hand. I was only thirteen miles west of Trafalgar Square but it felt like another world. There was plenty of light industry in Feltham but there was a lot of greenery as well. It almost felt as if I was living in the country. Everything went well for a few months but as the weeks passed I really started to miss my wife and daughter. I was also missing my card games in central London. It wasn't that I couldn't find anywhere to gamble locally but the low stakes made Feltham games seem tame and boring.

Benny Selby was more than happy with the tom I was bringing in — a lot of top-class jewels and plenty of furs to boot. That said, by the end of March I was feeling dejected. I'd given the heat three months to cool off so I figured a trip to a card game in Notting Hill was in order. That went well, so the next thing I did was arrange via Benny to meet my wife and daughter in Hyde Park. When that and further meetings with various family members passed without a hitch I got bolder. A man can't change his passions, and throughout my adult life mine was sport. When my boxing career was snatched away from me I had to make do with cards. Having said that, in many ways being a high roller is even more satisfactory than being a world-class boxer.

When I was a boxer and I made my way through the crowd to the ring it was like going through a tunnel of light, and those who'd come to cheer either me or my opponent seemed to melt away into nothingness. There was a sense of total concentration during a fight. I wasn't in this world any more and I didn't even hear the roar of the crowd, unless I was hit very hard on the head; then the effect was like a pinging in my ear and for a split second the cheers and boos and shouting were registered by my conscious mind. You have to banish distractions like the crowd in boxing or you're a goner who's never gonna win the fight. Cards are similar – they take you right out of yourself and the world around you, albeit with the difference that you never get slapped hard enough in the face to bring you back to reality as the game goes on.

You've got to remember that because of my commitment to the art of boxing I've been teetotal all my life. I wanted to be fit even after I stopped boxing professionally, so there was never any question of allowing a drop of alcohol to pass my lips. That might be a release that a lot of men crave, but it wasn't my vice. I had no poison of choice, so it was cards or nothing – and in the early fifties I knew of nowhere to get a better game of cards than in Soho. It was stupid of me but by the middle of April 1952 I'd started gambling in London's West End again. It didn't take long for word of this to reach Billy Hill, and he was the scumbag who tipped off his bent copper friends. There might be honour among thieves, but what you've got to remember is that Hill was a gangster, a thieves" pimp. Thus it was that I got lifted in a Soho spieler and on Thursday 24 April I found myself up before the beak at Highgate. I pleaded not guilty to robbing Martin Charteris, alongside the fit-up charges of receiving stolen goods in the form of coats, jackets and a motor car. I was committed for trial at the Old Bailey and my application for bail was refused.

At the Bailey I denied having a suitcase in my possession when the cops tried to jump me and Allan Grant. I explained my problems with Billy Hill and said that when the plain-clothes cops steamed out of their van to arrest me, I assumed they were gangsters sent to beat the living daylights out of me. That was why I ran away. The prosecutor was that arsehole Christmas Humphreys. You can't win when you're up against a liar of his calibre. Humphreys was well known for his ridiculous Buddhist beliefs, which he left behind in the street every time he entered a courtroom. As a prosecutor he managed to get poor kids like Derek Bentley hanged — although the misdirection of the judge, that bastard Lord Chief Justice Goddard, played a major role too. Bentley had already been arrested when his burglary accomplice Chris Craig shot a copper. Now I'm a man who didn't ever carry a weapon because I could use my fists, but despite my dislike of those that deploy shooters, Bentley being hanged for a murder committed after he'd been nicked was bang out of order. He even got a posthumous pardon but what good was that to the lad? That trial took place six months after mine for the Charteris robbery, but from what I read about it in the papers Humphreys used the same lies and smear tactics against Bentley as got me a six-and-a-half-year sentence in June 1952.

When he prosecuted me, Humphreys should have had the death of my fellow Welshman Timothy Evans weighing heavily on his mind — the fact that he didn't proves that this cold-hearted parasite had no conscience whatsoever. Humphreys prosecuted Evans for murder in early 1950, and the judge decided he should be hanged by the neck until dead. Only a few years later it had become apparent that the murderer was actually Reginald Christie. Some say it was the storm of controversy around this case that led to the abolition of the death penalty in the United Kingdom. But before that happened, Humphreys served as the prosecutor who sent Ruth Ellis to the gallows, the last woman to be hanged in Britain. If the full circumstances of her case had been taken into account, and she hadn't suffered the Humphreys smear treatment, then she's someone else who might still be alive today. And things didn't get any better when Humphreys got made a judge. In the mid-seventies there was a House of Commons motion to have this cunt dismissed, and he only clung onto his job because the Home Secretary defended him.

Humphreys is representative of everything that's wrong with English society. He was the son of a judge and attended a top fee-paying school and then Cambridge University. He didn't make it in life on merit — he got on because of his privileged family background. He was an upper-class plank who against all the evidence absolutely refused to believe that an ordinary man with no family or educational privileges could write the greatest works of English literature. The fact that Humphreys headed a band of nutters dedicated to proving the obvious fallacy that the works of Shakespeare weren't written by a commoner but by the 17th Earl of Oxford, Edward de Vere, is proof enough that he was a bird-brained fantasist and all-round upper-class git. When in 1983 I finally heard the good news that the slithering piece of shit known as Christmas Humphreys had died, I let out several whoops of joy!

FOUR

After sentencing I found myself in D wing of Wandsworth Prison. It's one of the biggest jails in Europe. It had been built in the middle of the nineteenth century and my abiding memory of it is slopping out every morning. You'd take your bucket of piss and shit out of the cell when you were unlocked and you'd empty it. So the cell stank and so did everything all the way to the tipping-out point.

My first visitor was Uncle Dinny. He told me he'd had a meeting with Billy Hill and it had been agreed that, since we'd each had a pop at the other, we'd call it quits to avoid ongoing warfare between Hill's men and my family. I didn't see Hilly grassing me up as a particularly sportsmanlike pop but agreed to go along with what Dinny had sorted out. Billy Boy had a reputation to protect and I'd take my revenge anonymously later. I was still in Wandsworth when Hill launched his ghostwritten "autobiography" at Gennaro's Restaurant in Soho on 15 November 1955. Among the guests were Lord and Lady Docker. Word quickly spread that Norah Docker and Hilly spent more time talking to each other than anyone else. Given this, I decided I'd rob the Dockers a second time once I was free again.

Mostly prison is a case of the same thing day after day — wake at the crack of dawn, slop out, eat breakfast, prison work, lunch, more prison work, bit of exercise, evening meal, association with other prisoners (which I mainly used to get more exercise in my cell; I wanted to keep myself fit), go to sleep. Then repeat ad nauseam. But there was one event in Wandsworth while I was there that really stands out and which wasn't like anything else I've ever experienced in nick. Everyone knew the execution of Derek Bentley was a complete injustice. But nonetheless, at 9am on 28 January 1953 he was hanged in Wandsworth Prison. There were protests outside the gates and even arrests. The atmosphere in a clinker changes both before and after a man is hanged. But when that man is as obviously innocent as Bentley was, it brought down a fog of anger and depression thicker than anything I've ever experienced in my life. You could have cut the atmosphere with a knife, and our hatred of those guarding us was stronger than I'd ever felt it before. And screws are despised at the best of times – like coppers they're just lackeys of the bourgeoisie and traitors to the working class!

One thing that made a difference in Wandworth was when my friend and fellow cat burglar George Taters Chatham turned up to do porridge. Despite being tiny, like me he was a sportsman. While I was a boxer, he'd been a top London schoolboy footballer. And he could play a good game of cards too. That was one of the things I really missed in prison, being able to stay up all night gambling. It took me out of myself and into another world, a total escape – whereas inside my nose was rubbed in shit day after day. Of course there were card games, but the players were crap and the stakes were cigarettes, and I didn't smoke. Nevertheless, the fags were useful as currency although Taters was the only guy I came across in my whole time in Wandsworth who could hold his own against me in a game of poker. Playing against anyone else was an exercise in tedium.

Taters came in after me and got out earlier. As I've already mentioned, he'd taken part in the Eastcastle Street postal van robbery of May 1952. A couple of cars were used to force the target to stop and it proved to be the biggest theft for years – the whole thing had been masterminded by Billy Hill. Taters didn't normally go in for coshing people but it happened on that job, although he wasn't the guilty party – luckily for him no one was jailed for that bit of larceny. Like me, Taters enjoyed carrying out risky live burglaries of the rich, although he was also partial to doing over shops. We agreed we'd work together once again once we were both out of Wandsworth.

One of the worst things when I was banged up were the visits I had from Ann and Beryl. Or rather it wasn't the visits – I always looked forward to those – it was the comedown afterwards, the harsh reminder I was being kept away from my family. My little girl was growing up and I was missing most of that. It isn't natural to keep hundreds of men locked up away from the company of women. I wouldn't advocate the complete abolition of prisons since you need somewhere to put nonces but, that said, kiddie fiddlers and rapists make up a very small proportion of those in jail.

While I was inside Ann got a job at the Queen Elizabeth Hospital for Children in Hackney Road, so when I finally got let out just before Christmas 1956, having served two thirds of my sentence, I found myself living in east London for the first time in my life. It was where Ann came from, so there were plenty of relatives and friends around us. We had a family Christmas in my new home in Brougham Road but I was itching to get back to work. There was urgent business I wanted to attend to. It wasn't that I needed the money, since as soon as I left prison my Uncle Dinny had bunged me enough quids to ensure I didn't have to ponce off the wife over the holiday period.

After a fabulous Christmas with all the trimmings, and Beryl being overjoyed at being given a bicycle, my first robbery of 1957 was at the St John's Wood home of arch-reactionary Christmas Humphreys. I couldn't find any ladders lying about nearby so I shoved a dustbin against the house; standing on this I was able to haul myself up to a bedroom window, which with my knees resting on the sill I jemmied open and climbed through. I didn't net anything of great worth since my victim was a mystical cretin who had no taste. Nonetheless, it was a curious experience.

My toff target was having dinner with a guest when I arrived at his less-than-humble abode. So much for the Buddhist principles this rich toe-rag professed to the world at large. It goes without saying that, like all the major world religions, Buddhism is a racket designed to keep the ruling class in power with their collective boot up the arses of the ordinary working man and woman. That said, Buddhism is particularly scummy in this respect since it was used to prop up completely repressive feudal regimes in places like Tibet. Humphreys had, of course, chummed up to that notorious snot-rag the Dalai Lama.

As I rummaged about for valuables, my victim was having a tête-à-tête over the remains of a meal. I still hadn't located anything of worth when I heard Humphreys and his guest making their way towards the room. I dived under the bed, and listened as they placed various items on a table, which from their conversation I understood to be some supposedly very valuable personal effects of the Zen master Soyen Shaku. Next they undressed and both got into the sack. I was stuck right under the bed as they kissed and caressed. I guess I could have come out from my hiding place and beaten the living daylights out of the two men, but I prefer not to use violence unless it is necessary. Judged on the sounds I could hear the kissing became cocksucking, then the man who'd let Humphreys come in his mouth was jerked off by the Brit toff. Not long after this they were both snoring, so I crawled out from under their love nest.

Humphreys" chum looked to me like he was Japanese. I could have threatened the pair of them with blackmail but I don't believe in that sort of thing. Homosexuality was still illegal when I made my raid on Humphreys" home but, while I personally go for women, I've never had any problem with consenting adults doing anything they like with each other. Since Humphreys clearly valued Soyen Shaku's effects, I took them, and grabbed two wallets while I was at it. I wanted to send Humphreys the message that he wasn't safe but I didn't want him to know why. It didn't matter where Humphreys went—Mayfair, Guildford, the Old Bailey, or even home to St John's Wood—the working class would be there and ready to strike against him! I felt I'd done something to avenge Derek Bentley—as well as myself.

Once I was south of Regent's Park, I emptied the wallets of cash, or at least their British notes, then dumped them in a sewer. I also slung Soyen Shaku's personal effects into the waterlogged shit. I had no use for his papers or Zen stick, and didn't know of a single fence who'd be interested in them. Since I had a few quid in my pocket, I wandered into Soho in search of a card game. Fortuitously I found myself sitting at a table in a spieler with Taters Chatham. I'd been meaning to ask around about how to reach him — but since I'd got out of Wandsworth, the holiday season had kept me close to my family in Hackney. Taters had some jobs he'd eyed up, and needed someone to help him with them. I agreed to work with him, although to be honest doing over shops in Mayfair wasn't really my thing. Still, I needed to get back on my feet and a steady series of thefts was the way to do it.

The first place we done was a jeweller in Dover Street. Around midnight we broke into the building next door and then smashed through an internal wall with sledgehammers. We took watches, silver and gold, as well as diamonds. The next night we got into Hemmings & Co. on Conduit Street — between Bond and Regent Streets — by going over some roofs and in through an upstairs window. The night after we used the same approach on Phillips in New Bond Street; the following night it seemed as if there were cops all over the West End, so we switched our attention to Cornhill jewellers in the City of London. The night after it was back to Mayfair but this time it was a furrier in Regent Street. Stealing furs is harder work than taking jewels or precious metal. We took a supply of mail sacks with us and loaded them up. We had to drag them across a roof and then throw them down into the street where we had a getaway car parked. Taters had sorted out the jobs so he took the gear to his fence, then came back and gave me half the money. We quickly lost most of what we made in spielers and on the ponies.

There are many stories about Taters and me losing our money gambling; one turns up in *The Brutal Truth: The Inside Story of a Gangland Legend*, an autobiography of old-school heavy Eric Mason. After flashing up the name of Peter Scott, Mason gives an account of Taters and me loosing heavily in a Notting Hill spieler, and then slipping out to do a quick robbery. Upon our return we allegedly negotiated the price of a jewel with the governor of the spieler before resuming our places at the gaming table. I can recall things like that happening more than once, but I think the incident Mason is alluding to took place in the Number 51 on Westbourne Park Road, and I don't recall Taters being with me that time. That said, I guess I should add that Taters and me weren't the only creepers to pull this sort of stroke. It was run-of-the-mill behaviour among burglars who were also heavy gamblers.

Going out and doing a theft wasn't the only way I managed to return to my place at a gaming table after the money I'd taken to it ran out. When the Kray twins first went west in the mid-fifties, they were minding Jack Spot's spieler in Covent Garden. Early in 1957 when I ran out of readies at that establishment, The Twins said I could have all the dosh I'd lost back from the bank if I'd take on a bare-knuckle fighter in a warehouse around the corner — and that, win or lose, the loot was mine. Everyone knew I'd been a boxer, and you only had to look at me to see I kept myself in shape, so it didn't surprise me I received this offer. It seemed a straightforward enough proposition, although obviously I was gonna have to win the unlicensed boxing match — otherwise I'd be too dazed to gamble. One of the combatants had failed to turn up and a lot of betting money would walk out the door unless something was sorted out quick.

I didn't have time for a warm-up: it was off with most of my clothes and straight into the ring. I steamed into my opponent and he was unconscious within seconds of the match kicking off. A hard jab in the stomach and he dropped his guard, then I smashed a hook into the side of his head; when he went down I kicked him a few times to make sure he didn't get up.

After putting my shirt and jacket back on, I'd returned to the gaming table in little more time than it would have taken me to go and have a piss. I had no intention of taking up the bare-knuckle game once again as a regular fighter, I was too old for it, but running out of funds while gambling was a desperate situation, which is why I grabbed that one-off opportunity for a final triumph in the fight ring with both hands. Of course, having won the match I simply done my money all over again and walked out of the spieler with nothing. Still, it was fun losing my shirt twice in one night.

The Krays said they were impressed by me and the way I fought; I didn't let on I wasn't too taken with them. Since they were minding a club I wanted to play cards in, there was no point in getting myself barred. And let's face it, The Twins got worse as time passed by; they were run-of-the-mill figures when I first encountered them. Nonetheless, they were gangsters not fighters. The Krays may have done a bit of boxing early on but they hadn't stuck at it because they weren't that good. They were prepared to beat, maim and kill people, as long as the odds were on their side; that's what made them good as gangsters. To me The Twins were just a pair of overgrown schoolyard bullies. There was nothing impressive about them at all. It's easy to extort money from cowards — whereas it takes guts to go into a house on your own and do a live burglary, with your only support being an outside man who collects swag as you throw it to him, and sounds a warning if he sees something untoward.

Returning to the campaign of looting me and Taters had undertaken, we went on for weeks robbing central London shops and wholesalers. I told Taters it had to stop. We were taking the piss and the cops couldn't let us get away with it forever. He said not to worry. I insisted I wasn't frightened, I was merely using my noodle. In the end, we decided to switch tactics for a while and do a long firm fraud. We set ourselves up in premises under some railway arches in Brixton as V. P. Legrand & Son, wholesale suppliers of beauty products to chemists and chain stores. We then placed some small orders with a lot of different manufacturers of toiletries — and to establish a good reputation, we paid promptly. Once we'd been offered extensive credit we simply made huge orders and disappeared with the goods. Since no payment was made on them, our profit on their sale was massive.

One of the firms we swindled was Elizabeth Arden Cosmetics. We'd been invited up to their offices and our jaws nearly dropped when we saw how much money was passing through the place. We weren't frightened of being identified; investigating long firm frauds was a slow process, and those who got dunned were usually insured. After the Board of Trade took a year to check out what had gone on, it was very unusual for the victims to want to tie up their staff in pursuing "justice" instead of making profits. From the point of view of the capitalist, being defrauded was simply something you wrote off in your double-entry system. Of course, we didn't use our own names when working on cons, but beyond that we went to no great lengths to protect our identities.

Elizabeth Arden beauty products were an upmarket global brand used by the likes of royalty, the super-rich and A-list female Hollywood stars. As far as I was concerned this was a class war target, and having done a long firm fraud on the operation, I wanted to hit them again. We got Eddie Chapman, who Taters knew, to come with us when we broke into Elizabeth Arden's London HQ one dark and wet night. Chapman had been in the top pre-war jelly gangs and knew everything there was to know about blowing safes. Understanding how much explosive to use was an art I'd never mastered. Too much and you destroyed the contents as well as the door of the safe — and possibly blew yourself up in the process — while too little left the box secure, and necessitated further attempts on it. A series of explosions usually led anyone who may have heard them into either investigating the noises or reporting them. When someone hears one explosion they're unlikely to react because they think their senses may be deceiving them, so they wait to see if they can hear another.

When I opened safes it was either by finding the key or peeling the protective layers of steel open piece by piece with wedges and jemmies. Small safes I found difficult to unlock I might take to my slaughter to attack later. Combination safes were more common in the USA than the UK, but I came across them occasionally. The way movies show guys cock-ing their heads and listening to the fall of the tumblers in order to determine the combination went out in the nineteenth century safe-makers introduced technological innovations to render this impossible more than a hundred years ago. The way I dealt with combination locks was firstly to look around and see if the code had been written down somewhere to prevent the owner forgetting it. If I couldn't find a record of the combination near the safe then it was easy enough to indulge in some inspired guesswork.

Although a four-tumbler lock has one hundred million possible combinations, mostly their owners set them to easily divisible—and thus easy to remember—numbers. Cashiers and accountants loved combinations like 4-16-32 and 12-24-36. If I knew my target was a keen bridge player then I'd try 4-13-26-52, and if he was a golf fanatic 9-18-36-72 seemed likely. If all else failed and I had the opportunity, I'd knock the dial off a combination safe, turn it on its back and whack the hell out of the locking mechanism using a hammer and metal stake. If this didn't work, then I'd try wedges and crowbars.

Eddie Chapman was a war hero and had received a pardon for all his crimes. He'd served the British as a double agent after telling the Germans he wanted to work for them. Chapman had pulled all sorts of daring stunts in the war, but when it came to crime he saw himself as the crème de la crème, and expected me to perform the lowly job of breaking into the Arden offices. Taters stayed outside to keep watch as I hauled myself up a drainpipe to the roof and then let myself in through a skylight. Once inside I padded down the stairs to the ground floor and opened a window, which Chapman climbed through. He blew hell out of the copper safe in the Arden offices. We shoved the contents into a holdall and as we finished this work we heard Taters whistle, a warning that the cops were approaching. We went out through the skylight and escaped across the rooftops with thousands in cash. Taters had no need to utilise his athletic skills to get away. He was on the street and simply walked to the nearest pub where he enjoyed a couple of drinks.

Taters was reluctant to put in extra time travelling to jobs away from The Smoke, but eventually he agreed we'd done over more than enough central London businesses, and it was high time we targeted some country houses instead. This was my speciality, so I drew up a long list of potential victims. We didn't want to do another long firm fraud — they simply lacked the excitement and exhilaration we got from burglary. To be frank, we both found using a telephone to obtain goods by deception extremely dull. Unfortunately, before we could embark on a fresh campaign of plunder against the aristocracy and the nouveau riche who aspired to join their ranks, Taters was nicked doing a piddling little job in Mayfair. I knew Taters wouldn't talk, but just in case his arrest brought any heat onto me, I decided to take a trip to Wales to see my family.

There was a house on the edge of Bath I'd had my eye on doing over, and I figured I could take a crack at this piece of business on my way to visit my mother. I'd decided to drive, and as I made my way to the property I noticed a big party going on at Widcombe Manor. Jeremy Fry and his then new wife Camilla Grinling had bought the house in 1955. It was supposedly designed by my namesake Inigo Jones, but then rebuilt in the first half of the eighteenth century. There were marquees out on the lawn and guests milling about with drinks in their hands. I was wearing a good suit and figured I'd be able to mingle unobtrusively amongst these upper-class arsewipes.

Jeremy Fry's father had sold off the family chocolate business against the wishes of his relatives, and junior managed to piss off his family just as much by earning himself a reputation as a wild man of the fast set. This public image overshadowed his involvement in product design, at which he was very successful. Fry was educated at Gordonstoun, as were many members of the parasitic British royal family. The jelly bean's younger sister Princess Margaret — and Lord

Snowdon, her husband by a 1960 marriage — are typical of the rich scum who frequented the out-of-order parties Fry organised at Widcombe Manor from 1955 until he sold this pile in 1974 — to pay for his divorce from Camilla.

Having parked outside Widcombe Manor, I donned a pair of white gloves that I had with me in my car. Next I grabbed a glass of champagne from a butler who was offering them from a silver tray. Holding the booze in front of me, I made my way into the house, where I loaded my pockets with cash I found in handbags and jackets, jewellery from various bedrooms, and some silver napkin holders. I went through pretty much every room in a fairly leisurely fashion, and no one asked me what I was doing. Rather than drinking my bubbly, I threw it over an expensive dress that had been laid out in a bedroom ready for use. Considerably enriched, I made my way back to my wheels and headed on to my next target, before motoring into Wales for a week of relaxation with my family in the valleys.

The contrast between the way my folks lived and the affluent luxury of those I was plundering only served to confirm my belief that my career as a modern day Ustym Karmaliuk was morally right. Karmaliuk was a Ukrainian peasant hero whose life straddled the eighteenth and nineteenth centuries, and who — like a well-known medieval brigand popularly associated with Sherwood Forest in England — is said to have robbed from the rich and given to the poor. The idea of outlaws redistributing wealth in this way occurs in folk tales from many different parts of the world, and other examples that I know of include the Slovak Carpathian highwayman Juraj Jánošík, Lithuanian Tadas Blinda, the Estonian Rummu Jüri, the Japanese pillager of swordsman aristocrats Nezumi Kozo, the Mexican bandit Chucho el Roto, Kobus van der Schlossen in the Netherlands, and in India Kayamkulam Kochunni.

When I arrived in Nantyglo I found my mum sick in bed, and that was where she stayed for most of my visit. I would have bought her some comforts but she knew how I got my money and wouldn't accept anything from me. Nonetheless, she still loved me in all the other ways a mother should love a son. I wanted to give her books but she insisted I get her reading material from the library. One night when my mother was asleep a valve went on the family radio, and I managed to buy a replacement for that early the next day without my mum noticing I'd done so. I enjoyed going home to Wales but I had business to attend to, and so after a week it was back to London, with my first task being to take the stuff I'd nicked on the way down round to my fence Benny Selby.

Before Taters found himself facing yet another lagging, I'd already decided we should hit a country pile I'd had in my sights some years previously but had never got around to cracking. Newspaper baron James Gomer Berry was the kind of right-wing berk I instinctively despised. But what kept my hatred of the toff in question sharper than the blade of a Samurai sword was the fact that he came from Merthyr Tydfil in my native Wales. Jimmy-boy's wife, Mary Holmes, was a bejewelled and empty-headed socialite who needed taking down a few pegs. This unholy union produced offspring who became prominent Tory MPs, as well as directing such establishment newspapers as the *Daily Telegraph* and *Sunday Times*.

I wanted an outside man and I met one through my cousins. Peter Scott was a middle-class Ulsterman turned bad. A small-time thief whose takings over the previous two years came to less than what I often stole in one night... But Taters wasn't available, so I decided to try out the posh upstart. I cased the joint, Dropmore House at Burnham Beeches in Buckinghamshire, on my own. I didn't know if Scott could keep his mouth shut; he was clearly a rank amateur who needed the type of training only someone like Taters or me could give him in the craft of screwsmanship, so it was best not to let him in on where we were going until the last possible moment.

I decided I'd go in over the conservatory while the toffs were gorging themselves at their Saturday evening dinner party. On the night of the raid, I left my hire car well away from the house and, with Scott beside me, we walked through a light drizzle and the fading afternoon light to the Berry mansion. Scott was mesmerised by the silver laid out on the dining table in readiness for the evening meal. Eventually the Berrys and their house party guests started filing into the room. When a butler drew the dining room curtains, I instructed Scott to stay where he was before making my way up to the house.

I climbed a drainpipe and made my way along one edge of the conservatory roof to the main part of the house. Using a jemmy I forced open an unlit window and climbed through. I found myself in a guest bedroom with a mink coat carelessly strewn across the bed. I stuck this valuable garment in one of the mailbags I'd brought with me. There was a jewel case in the room too but it was empty. It was the same story in all the guest rooms; furs but few jewels, because the latter were being shown off over dinner. Before I moved between the rooms I'd listen at the door, and then open it a fraction to see if there was anyone in the upstairs corridor. At one point I had to wait for a maid to make her way downstairs, but beyond this I had no problems. My real prize was, of course, in the master bedroom. Mary Berry and her husband may have had a safe, but in their hurry to get down to dinner they'd forgotten to shut it. That saved me the trouble of getting it out of a window and breaking into it later. I put an assortment of pearls and jewels into a small case that had been left in the room, and slipped this into my pocket. The press baron's wife also had enough furs to fill a second mail sack.

It was raining heavily when I slid the bulkier part of my booty off the conservatory roof and down to my outside man. Moments later I'd made my way onto the lawn and had picked up one of the sacks. I told Scott to take the other. He complained that the expensive suit he was wearing had already been half-ruined by the rain. I told him if he knew what I'd got beside the coats he'd stop moaning. We jogged back towards the car, with Scott struggling to keep up with me: his love of the good life meant he was carrying a certain amount of extra weight. It was an overcast night and in his state of high excitement Scott had forgotten that on our way in we'd gone through a field of cows. The herd must have moved while I was at work and in the darkness we ran smack into them. I had many an encounter with cattle as a boy growing up in the valleys, so I just made my way through them. Upon making contact with their warm wet rumps, Scott let out a scream.

"Quieten down," I instructed in a firm but low voice.

"Get me out of here!" Scott wailed. "I'm being attacked by something hellish."

"There's nothing hellish about a herd of heifers! Pull yourself together you stupid cowson."

Scott had gone to pieces. He was petrified. In the end I had to go back amongst the cows and lead him out from among them. Once we emerged from the field he managed to regain his composure and redeemed himself somewhat by running the rest of the way back to the car. After that it was me who dubbed Scott with the ironic nickname of The Human Fly — because the cows that so terrified him had treated his intrusion as no more of an irritant than a bluebottle buzzing amongst them.

"What did you get?" Scott demanded once I'd started up the motor and we were heading back towards London.

"Aside from the furs, Mary Berry's jewels."

"What!" Scott exclaimed. "Are you telling me we've just robbed Viscount Kemsley and his wife?"

"Don't be impressed by silly titles, it is no measure of a man. Berry and his missus shit the same as me and you."

"But imagine," Scott let out, "he was born a commoner like me, then ennobled."

"It means nothing," I assured him, "or rather it means that someone has proved their worth to the ruling class. He got the titles for making money and championing the vested interests of the rich."

"You sound like a bloody red!" Scott chided.

"Don't knock it!" I replied. "It's because I'm a red that you'll get half the money we see from the fence for this job. A lot of guys without my political convictions only give an outside man a fraction of what they make. But for me the meaning of socialism is share and share alike."

"That's what it might mean to you, but to me it means people who run down the queen."

"She's an old whore, and don't say anything more on this subject unless you want twenty-five percent of the booty instead of fifty. Of course I won't keep that extra twenty-five percent for myself, I'll donate it anonymously to the NUM. Unlike me and my family, I bet yours didn't go short of food in the 1930s."

"No we didn't. And let's change the subject. I don't want half my lolly going to the militants at the National Union of Mineworkers." Scott's voice rose at least an octave as he said this.

"What do you wanna talk about?"

"Who's your fence?"

"I'm not telling you."

"I thought you were a socialist who shared everything."

"I'm a socialist but I'm not a nark. I tell people about my fence on a need-to-know basis."

We tried to talk about sport instead but Scott liked tennis and knew nothing of the art of boxing. By the time we reached London the topic of conversation had changed to the miserable weather. I dropped my outside man off in Paddington, then drove back to Highgate. I did eventually introduce him to my fence Benny Selby, but I felt that first he had to prove that he was trustworthy.

Benny couldn't believe his eyes when I presented him with what were allegedly a string of Marie Antoinette's stomacher pearls. This or a similar set had previously been owned by the late-nineteenth-century New York socialite Caroline Astor—whose perfect posture is sometimes attributed to the fact that she wore jewellery all the way down her back to her waist, making it painful for her to sit back in a chair! I'd also brought Benny a rather nice Van Cleef & Arpels diamond bracelet with matching 2.2-carat baguettes. Not to mention various other trinkets including diamond clips.

When I presented Scott with three grand the following day, I told him not to put it in his post office account unless he wanted the taxman and the cops asking questions about it. I instructed him to get a safety deposit box. And since he followed my advice, I later said I'd bring him along in the art of cat burglary by taking him out on another job, but this time he could go inside the country pile and I'd act as the outside man.

Since Scott was obviously impressed by nobs, I picked one of the grandest English country seats for our next raid: Hatfield House in Hertfordshire. This was the family home of the Cecils, a scummy bunch of Tories whose right-wing lineage stretched back to Robert Cecil and beyond. On the death of Francis Walsingham, Robert Cecil took over the role of running England as a police state on behalf of first Elizabeth I, and later James I. His rewards for pissing all over the common people included being bestowed the title 1st Earl of Salisbury. This line of scoundrels even produced a shitty Victorian prime minister also called Robert Cecil. The house was chock full of rich pickings because it had once been a royal palace, but James I didn't like it so he'd swapped it with the first Robert Cecil for a different property.

Given that I was training Scott up, and he'd proved almost adequate on our first sortie, I took him with me when I cased the joint and talked him through the various possibilities for breaking in. We returned a few days later and once again left our hire car about a mile away from our target. While a dinner party was in progress we manoeuvred a ladder from an outbuilding up against a bedroom window. Scott ascended the ladder and that was when things started to go wrong. I'd told him to jemmy the frame but he punched in the glass with a gloved fist: this was evidently his standard breaking and entering technique. Fortunately he'd covered the pane he smashed with his left hand as he did it in with his right, and so the noise was muffled. He'd got away with what he'd done but it was an unnecessary risk. Rather than bagging up furs, Scott simply threw the first one he found out of the window. I caught it but didn't like this unprofessional approach.

Instead of searching the first room thoroughly, Scott was impatient to move on to the next. Lacking my caution, he simply opened the door of the room he was in and walked into a hallway, in the process startling a maid who let out a scream. He was down the ladder in a flash, but seemed to think that a jog was enough to secure our freedom. I ordered him to sprint back to the car. At first he seemed to lack the energy for this but got a second wind when I told him he might end up spending several years breaking rocks on Dartmoor if he failed to run like a Fury. Rather than heading back to London, the direction in which the cops would doubtlessly assume we'd fled, I drove to St Albans and we made a guesthouse our flop for the night. The fur we'd stolen would cover our expenses but beyond that we had nothing to show for our efforts. I was happy enough with Scott as an outside man but, until he learnt some discipline, I decided it was best if I pulled off the actual larceny when we were working together.

While Scott was working with me, I knew he was doing smaller jobs on his own and with others too, although following my lead these were getting more ambitious. He was forever hassling me to introduce him to my fence, coz the people he knew were useless. I told him that when he'd demonstrated he was worthy I'd make him known to a man who'd pay him properly. Scott whinged once again that if I was as socialist as I claimed, then it wasn't just money I should share equally, but knowledge too. My rejoinder was always that I was no grass and wouldn't share anything I knew with the cops. Not that he was a rozzer, but in the filthy capitalist world in which we lived information could only be distributed among those you knew you could trust.

In the end it wasn't trust that led me to introduce Scott to Benny Selby, but his idiotic behaviour. He'd arranged to meet me in The Star Tavern, which was in a quiet cobbled mews at the end of Belgrave Square. I arrived slightly early. When I got there Scott was wandering around offering drinkers he wasn't even acquainted with watches he'd lifted from some jeweller the night before. If he carried on like that he was going to get himself nicked in short order, even if a publican like Paddy Kennedy had no problem with his mode of conduct.

"Drink?" Scott offered.

"A glass of water," I told him. He knew I didn't drink.

"Sure you wouldn't like something stronger like milk?"

"I'm an athlete, water is the right thing for me."

"I'm a sportsman too and it doesn't stop me drinking."

"Huh, you call tennis sport? You're not even very good at it."

"That's easy to say but I bet you don't have any tennis tips for me!"

"I've got some really good advice for you on that score."

"What?"

"Cut the bottom six inches off the handle of your racket!"

"What's the idea?" Scott asked as he leaned in towards me. "Am I supposed to practise like that to make playing harder, then when I use an ordinary racket I'll win?"

"What do you think?" I replied.

"It might just work!" Scott conceded. Then he added: "Do you really think that will improve my game?"

"No!" I shot back. "But it would make disposing of your racket in a rubbish bin easier! You're terrible, you should give up tennis."

There were eruptions of laughter all around us since many of our fellow drinkers had tuned into our conversation. Scott tried to even the score but the pub crowd quickly lost interest because it was obviously game, set, and match to me.

"You might have been good at boxing but look where it got you. Two years inside for assaulting a rozzer," Scott shot back forlornly.

"You'll get a tariff of at least two years if you carry on attempting to offload watches the way I've seen you do it tonight," I told Scott.

"In that case introduce me to your fence."

"I will if he agrees to meet you."

"When?"

"Tomorrow. Catch me in Chapel Market at noon. But I can't guarantee my fence will want to meet you, so it might be a wasted journey."

"If you put in a good word for me..."

"It'll probably be alright."

Benny gave me the okay when I phoned him, so I took Scott from Islington to Highgate to meet one of the greatest receivers in the history of London crime. To make a point, I insisted Scott buy some flowers and place them on the grave of Karl Marx before I took him round to see Selby. Not even this soured the mood of my reactionary little friend; after all he was getting what he wanted. Being introduced to Benny Selby was the making of Peter Scott—without it he'd have remained a petty thief for his entire life. He made great use of the connection over the years but it wasn't of much immediate help. Scott was nicked within a week of me taking him up to Highgate. The introduction had come too late to save him from the consequences of his previous haphazard methods of disposing of bent gear at rock-bottom prices. He did two years for a stupid larceny I wouldn't have even considered carrying out.

After Scott was nicked, I concentrated on out-of-town jobs for a while and built up a nice stash of cash. One of the funny things that happened in this period was that I managed to steal the same mink coat twice. On my way to Benny Selby's I'd go past a big house at which there were always loud parties. It was an easy target, and the first time I did it over I took seven fur coats and a load of jewels. I left it a few months and then went back again. The second time I got five furs and not that many sparklers: it appeared that the insurance money had yet to be spent on replacing what I'd half-inched on my previous raid. When I went round to Benny's he chuckled and said:

"Blimey, you've done over Florence Thompson again!"

"How do you know that?"

"Does this fur look familiar to you?" Benny asked rhetorically as he threw it at me.

"To tell the truth yes, it's unusual, very similar to one of the ones I nicked from the same house a few months ago. The owner must have searched high and low to find another that looks like this."

"It's not similar, it's the same. Mrs Thompson put word around that she'd pay over the odds to get it back, so through a third party I arranged that."

"Fuck me," I laughed, "you gonna do the same thing again?"

"Nah, too dangerous," Benny spat. "You know I think you're alright Ray but please don't rob the Thompsons again, their house is only a couple of streets away and it might bring heat on me."

"I won't Benny, you can trust me."

"You're a man of your word, proof indeed that there is honour among at least some thieves!"

As it turned out, I didn't get to do too many jobs after stealing Florence Thompson's mink for a second time. In June of 1957, Uncle Dinny had a word in my ear, warning me that I'd been put under close observation by the filth, and that if I tried pulling any jobs the cops were bound to bang me up. I had a bit of money saved and figured it would be nice to spend some quality time with my family. I went home to south Wales to see my mother Julia and the rest of the clan. My mum was in poor health but that didn't stop her questioning me closely about how I was supporting my family. I was too old for her to tell me what to do but I know she didn't approve of my lifestyle. Still, she was my mother so I took her chiding and enjoyed her company, since most of the time she didn't treat me as if I was still wearing short trousers.

I got back to London for the start of the summer holidays because I wanted to make sure this was a really special year for Beryl. Every day I took her somewhere different—funfairs, the cinema, the circus and all the big museums. What should have been the best thing we did was go to the Victoria & Albert Museum. Beryl really enjoyed me telling her all about the jewels, gold and silver. We lingered over the Bingley Cups, and I explained to my daughter how they'd been presented to Baron Bingley as a thank-you for his work as Ambassador to Spain at the beginning of the eighteenth century. I knew all about this item and many others because I'd cased the joint a number of times with Taters.

My fellow tea leaf had made a successful raid on the V&A back in 1948, when among other valuable items he'd half-inched the Duke of Wellington's swords. Taters was keen to break into the museum a second time to liberate a few more of its fabulous treasures. I'd been up for this because I found the way it displayed the fabulous wealth of aristocrats and royalty obnoxious. Beryl, being young, enjoyed the spectacle of riches without having yet developed the critical faculty to fully understand that such wealth was the result of the ordinary man and woman being ground down and exploited.

We'd enjoyed a fun afternoon at the V&A and were making our way out to catch a bus home when I was pulled over by a plainclothes copper. He told me he wanted a word. I pointed out I was with my daughter. He spat that he didn't care. I could feel anger boiling up through me because this authoritarian lickspittle couldn't let my little girl enjoy a trip with her dad without spoiling it. It took a great effort of will on my part to resist the urge to punch this crumb's lights out.

"I've been watching you," the detective informed me, "and in my opinion you're planning to rob this museum. Let me tell you that if you try it then I'm gonna come down on you like a ton of bricks."

"Look," I told the old bill, "my daughter is on her holidays and I'm just trying to make sure she has a nice time. I'm not thinking of nicking anything from here; I was telling her about the jewels and silver because that's something I know about."

"You know about it because you're a tea leaf."

"I'm not planning anything here."

"You better not be because when your mate Chatham robbed this place nine years ago and got away with it, the Mets took an awful lot of grief over the theft, and we never even recovered the gear."

"Of course you didn't, it was melted down hours after it was nicked."

"Wanton destruction of treasures that were once the personal possessions of national heroes! It makes me sick!"

"They didn't belong to heroes, they belonged to exploiters. The ruling class makes me sick!"

"You're not just a thief, you're a flamin' red!"

"I've done nothing, so can I go?"

"You can go but if you try and break in here you're for the high jump."

I took Beryl by the hand and led her out to the bus stop. I was seething. My daughter had heard every word but she said nothing. I pointed out buildings and people from the top deck of the bus as we headed back to Hackney. I didn't want to talk to my little girl about what had just happened. It had ruined my day and I didn't want it doing the same to hers.

Once the holidays were over I started getting restless. I couldn't go to work coz I had the filth on my back, and I didn't have Beryl to entertain, so I definitely needed something to take my mind off my predicament. I knew George Mizel as a fence but he also had a Hatton Garden jewellery business that he used as a front for his receiving activities, so I asked him for a job on the straight side of the operation. Punters would come in to trade jewels, and I had more than enough knowledge to be able to buy at low prices and sell at high ones.

So I saw out the autumn of 1957 commuting from Hackney to Saffron Hill. By day I worked as a shop assistant and at night I was mostly a family man – although I also did enough training to prevent my boxing and other athletic skills from going to pot. What I didn't do was go gambling, which I missed but I really didn't have the money to finance a decent game of cards, and I knew if I got back into that way of life I'd have to go out stealing. Ann was happy about this and my mother was cock-a-hoop. I knew that eventually I'd go back to robbing the rich, but while I had the police on my back I decided to play it cool.

I needn't have bothered going straight coz the filth used the blameless life I was leading to fit me up. When Mizel was out of London for the day, we got a call asking for someone from the business to go over to west London to look at some jewels. After Mizel, I was the man best qualified to do this, so I went. When I got to the house I'd obviously arrived quicker than expected and was told the man with the sparklers would be arriving shortly. I waited half an hour and then, far from being high quality, the merchandise I was eventually shown was just junk. Even a rag-and-bone man would have turned his nose up at this low-grade crap.

I'd been lured to a cul-de-sac and when I left the house I knew something was wrong. Parked virtually outside the property was a car with the number plates removed — the plates were on a nearby wall and a pair of gloves were sitting beside them. Before I had the chance to go anywhere, I was grabbed by half a dozen old bill. They accused me of having stolen the motor and changed the plates. It was a simple set-up. The gloves didn't even fit me, they were too small to go over my hands! My trial was a farce. I'd hired a top silk but when I was taken to the court I was told he was no longer representing me — and despite all the cash I'd laid out for a proper defence, the brief that had been assigned to me at the last minute did the prosecution's work for them. With a defence lawyer like the one I'd had forced on me, they might as well have done away with the court and trial and slung me straight inside.

Worse yet, the prosecution went way beyond just fitting me up. When my wife Ann came in to see me on remand I'd told her I was innocent and the situation was very different from when I'd first been convicted by a kangaroo court in 1940. Then the war was on, and while I would have made the most of any opportunity that presented itself to me to escape from jail, I wouldn't have gone out of my way to find one. This time it was different; if I escaped from nick there was a good chance the press would publicise my grievances with the so-called justice system, whereas during the war there had been no hope of them running stories about an innocent man being wrongly convicted. A screw overheard this conversation and he reported it to the prison authorities. It should have been put in my prison records but the law says it should not have been brought up at any trial. The illegality of mentioning them didn't stop my escape plans being aired by the prosecution during my December 1957 hearing. It was all part of a character assassination carried out against me, to make me look like an incorrigible rogue and lend credence to the pack of lies the filth had made up about me stealing a motor. I knew I'd be done: once you've got a criminal record you don't stand a chance in court even if you're innocent.

Things became even more peculiar when it came to sentencing because the preventative detention (PD) system was used for prisoners who looked like they weren't going to cause too much trouble inside but were likely to re-offend. Since I was innocent but had been fitted up, I could hardly re-offend, but it was also obvious PD wasn't a suitable punishment for me because the fact that I planned to make a jailbreak had been illegitimately brought to the attention of the judge. Under PD you went to places like Chelmsford and Nottingham, or if you were really unlucky Parkhurst on the Isle of Wight. If you were considered a real hard nut then they were supposed to give you a stiff sentence so you could get packed off to somewhere like Dartmoor.

With preventative detention added on because I was a so-called persistent criminal, I ended up with an eight-year stretch. When the grim gates of Pentonville swung open and I was driven inside the prison after being sentenced just before Christmas, I swore I'd escape from jail rather than serve out my term. Not that I would see it out in The Ville; I was only being held there, and it seemed most likely that the place they'd transfer me to down the line would be Parkhurst, since even if you broke out of that prison you then had the added difficulty of getting off the Isle of Wight.

While I was in The Ville I put in an appeal against my conviction, and it was dismissed almost immediately by that dried-up old jam-rag Rayner Goddard, just before this arch-reactionary retired as Lord Chief Justice of England. A typical establishment figure, educated at a costly fee-paying school and Oxford University's Trinity College, Goddard was a complete tosser known for his harsh sentencing — as well as his advocacy of the death penalty and corporal punishment. Goddard's valet told people that his "justice-in-a-jiffy" master had an orgasm every time he sentenced someone to death, and his trousers would have to be sent off to the cleaners as a result of him having a "good day in court" at the expense of some poor sod who'd probably been fitted up. I jumped with joy when in 1971 I heard that Goddard had popped his clogs; my only regret was that I'd not succeeded in robbing him before he died.

FIVE

Prison — same thing day after day! Get woken up early, slop out, eat, do prison work, eat, do prison work, eat, a bit of association, then lock-up. And so it went on. I was in London until the authorities got around to transferring me but I might just as well have been in Siberia. There are always gangs in prison and you need to be in one of the better ones if you want to avoid trouble. It doesn't matter how tough you are; if some guy sneaks up behind you and batters you about the head with something hard, or catches you in your bed when your cell is open, then you'll always get the worst of it — because they have surprise on their side. You've even less chance if it is a bunch of blokes. It is easy to offend people in the clinker and so even the hardest man is vulnerable unless he has people to back him up. The way it works is that if anyone from a prison gang gets battered, then their crew will take care of the culprits. Cons rarely attack you if you belong to a dominant gang, coz they know they'll get it ten times worse in return.

The way the gangs worked was that blokes from the same place stuck together; and if there were more than a few from one area then the faces formed gangs with other faces, while the lesser lights were left to fend for themselves. East and south Londoners tended to dominate and they didn't let just any old tom, dick or cockney into their company. You had to be tough and have a reputation. I'd lived in The Smoke since the thirties and I was a face, so I could usually get in with the east London crews. Going with the best gang is always the ideal option. I liked time on my own in my cell, but if I was moving about the prison then I'd stick with the crew I'd joined. Since I'd first gone inside for battering PC Spratt, and everyone knew he was a cop boxing champ, I was able to join the best gangs from the off. In Pentonville in fifty-eight my closest gang mates were Johnny, Barry, Brian and Phil. They were all Londoners who'd been robbing banks and hijacking lorries.

There is a lot of talk of escape in prison. Often it is the main subject of conversation between cons when the screws are out of earshot. Mostly it is hot air, and even when real plans are hatched up they are rarely carried through. I bided my time and kept my eye to the main chance, and it came easier than I could have imagined in my wildest dreams. I viewed escape as a matter of urgency because I was on home turf in London, and could reach help quickly from Pentonville if I broke out. Once I got Shanghaied to another prison I was likely to be hundreds of miles from family, friends and the support network I needed to stay on the outside if I escaped. A jailbreak was what Johnny Rider and I spoke about more than anything else. For reasons unknown to me, my transfer took far longer to come through than anyone could have reasonably expected. My guess is that it was my good luck that my file somehow got lost in the system.

The roof at The Ville was being repaired and I kept an eye on the ladders being used for the renovations. They were secured at night with padlocks but if we could get out into the yard these would be easy enough to smash with a crowbar or a hammer. I could see the ladders from my cell window and I watched them like a hawk. The Ville is an old prison and the repairs were both extensive and slow, and as the work dragged on the workmen and authorities became quite slack about security. My diligent attention to this matter was rewarded on 17 October 1958, when I was able to observe from my cell that a ladder had been left unsecured. We wouldn't even need tools to liberate it! And we'd already partially solved the problem of how to get into the yard. Phil from our crew had got friendly and then fresh with a young female teacher who came into the prison to do literacy lessons. He'd been having it off with her whenever the opportunity arose. There were classes that took place during association, a period of one hour in the evening when we were allowed to socialise.

I padded down from my cell and told the chaps what I'd seen. Fortunately Phil's sweetheart was running slightly late, so when she came to get him, he told her we were all going to go across to the classroom that night. She didn't seem that pleased, I guess because it meant she wasn't going to get her oats. Anyway, she grudgingly unlocked the gate and led us out of the association area. Once we were in a shadowy part of the yard, Phil grabbed the teacher and kissed her, telling her he wanted a quick knee-trembler while the rest of us went ahead to the classroom.

Johnny and me raced up to the unlocked ladder and grabbed it. Then we ran with it to one of the twenty-foot-high outer walls. I went up first and jumped; Johnny Rider was right behind me and we ran in opposite directions. Twenty feet isn't a difficult distance to jump as long as you remember to relax a little and bend your knees as you land. Brian was the third man over the wall but he stupidly kept his legs straight and his muscles tensed as he went down, so it isn't surprising he broke his ankle. Phil and Barry never made it out of the prison yard. Despite the sexual distraction Phil provided, the teacher had clocked what was happening and was screaming her head off.

There were screws all over the yard before Barry reached the top of the ladder and they were able to pull him down. Phil and Barry were frogmarched to solitary and Brian went to the same place but via the prison hospital. Dealing with the three failed jailbreakers tied the screws up long enough to give Johnny and me sufficient time in which to escape. No doubt the local filth had also been called in to assist but they failed to muster their forces until after we'd both fled their net. Unfortunately, Johnny was picked up within twenty-four hours, but I made a record-breaking escape in terms of its duration, and it was the first time anyone had gone over the wall from The Ville since it had been reopened in 1946. It had been shut down as a regular penal institution during the war.

Once I was the other side of the prison wall, I stole a trench coat from a nearby house and put it over my prison uniform to conceal my convict garb. It was easy: the door to the terrace was open and the garment was hanging from a peg in the hall — and I could hear the household eating in the kitchen. I knew I'd be well away before they missed the garment. Still, I made a mental note of the number, so I could push a bundle of notes in an envelope through their door at a later date.

Under cover of darkness I made my way by foot to Praed Street and my cousin's pub. I resisted the urge to run until I was well away from the prison, but once I was on the Euston Road I sprinted most of the way — pretending all the time to be chasing buses but missing them. I'd have hopped on a bus and paid for a ticket if I'd had the price of a fare in my pocket. I didn't think it was worth the risk of bunking the ride. I didn't want to draw attention to myself — and a row with a ticket inspector would have done just that. When I reached my cousin's gaff, Dennis got me a change of clothes and let me wash myself up, since I was drenched in sweat. Then I was moved on to an empty property to which he had the keys.

While I was being safe-housed by my cousin, Uncle Dinny came around and gave me some wedge to get me settled. I lay low for a few days, with my cousin and uncle bringing me food, and also the papers with their front-page coverage of my jailbreak. The press was full of the standard old bill smears about me; the media quoted the cops as saying I was violent and shouldn't be approached. Scum! Okay, so I used my fists to defend myself, but I'd never hit anybody outside a boxing or bare-knuckle ring without first being provoked. Self-defence is no offence and I've never been a violent man. However, what I read in the papers then was nothing compared to the lies told about me and my escape by various two-bit criminals in their ghostwritten and largely fictional "autobiographies". Low-life chancers like Mad Frankie Fraser have been happy to bask in my reflected glory by telling ever taller tales about me. If you believe some of the accounts of my escape you'd think I was Fantômas or something!

As I've already explained, the likes of Fraser have me climbing onto the prison roof and, while scaling down the sheer face of the outside wall, smashing one kneecap, then falling and breaking my ankle. Despite these injuries Fraser has me scaling another wall, and breaking my uninjured leg when I jump from it. After that I persist in my escape by crawling into a block of flats and making my way onto a roof, where I fall headlong through a skylight as I try to prise it open. Once I regain consciousness after this accident, I make my way out of the building, pulling myself along using the railings on the Caledonian Road, crawling across the road towards Kings Cross station, over the railway lines and into someone's garden. Eventually I decide to seek help and attract the attention of some young men, who I ask for a lift "because I had had a bad fall." The men guess who I am, but don't betray me. After they've left me at a relative's flat, my wife arrives and arranges for me to stay elsewhere, where it takes me five months to recover from my injuries.

If you believe what Frankie Fraser has to say about my escape, you'll believe anything! It honestly wasn't like that. I wasn't injured and I was able to make my way to my cousin's pub without enlisting anyone else's help. My blood also boils when I look back on my '58 escape and recall that the old bill told the public I was violent. It wasn't me but the capitalist system that was violent. What with endless wars between rival bourgeois factions, the expropriation of the vast wealth of the world by the privileged few and the resulting grinding poverty and starvation of the masses, not to mention the brutality of the police and prison system, it was a classic case of piss-taking when the paid lackeys of the ruling class labelled me as dangerous. Violence is so often a matter of definition, and those who hold the reins of power are in the position to misuse words and get away with this without being challenged. My burglaries were a form of propaganda by deed against the very existence of private ownership, so it isn't surprising the system's defenders would invert the real nature of property relations by claiming that it was people like me rather than capitalist social relations that were violent.

To return to the main thread of my life story, once things had cooled a little I headed back to Feltham and rented a room. After the filth nicked me in 1952, they never discovered where I'd been hiding out when I was on the run that time, so this west London suburb was still safe. It was back to my early-fifties routine of west London and suburbs burglaries. It really felt like my life was going round in circles in 1958: back in the jug after being fitted up by the filth just like in 1940, then lying low and robbing from a furnished room in Feltham just as I'd done in the early months of 1952.

However, this time I did one thing differently: rather than going into town to see Ann, I got my wife to head my way — but only after she'd taken several trips round the houses to check whether or not she was being followed. My cousin Dennis told her how to operate: sudden changes of buses and trains, and never following the same route. We didn't get too long together since Ann had Beryl to consider too, and to minimise the risks I saw nothing of my little girl. My wife came over when my daughter was at school or in the temporary care of friends and family.

Rather than enjoying my time with Ann, a lot of it was spent talking about how to drum up publicity in the media over how I'd been fitted up. Ann and Dennis would take letters I'd written outlining how I'd been bad-jacketed in 1940, 1944 and 1957, and post them to sympathetic relatives in Wales and Ireland, who'd send them back to the national media in London in envelopes I'd pre-addressed. This was a security measure to make it look like I'd fled the capital, since we suspected at least some journalists would pass my missives on to the cops. As it turned out, the papers didn't cover the story and I suspect that a D-notice was slapped on it. After being wrongly convicted of burglary in 1953, Alfie Hinds managed to escape from custody and used this as a way of publicising his innocence. I guess the authorities learned a lesson from him. They wanted to close me down, and I was probably less attractive to the press because I never hid my hatred of the ruling class, whereas Hinds was studiously apolitical.

I've spent years trying to set the record straight about my life, and one of the things that most frustrates me is when people respond to my story by saying something along the lines of: "Well you may have been fitted up a load of times by the cops, but then there's all the crimes you got away with, so I figure the score is about even." Now those who say this—and you'd be surprised how many do—completely miss the point that if something similar had happened to them then they'd be protesting like mad about it. Supposing every weekday they have several drinks in the pub after work, and then drive home over the limit but never get done for this. However, on Sundays they don't drink because they always take their mother out to the countryside or the beach. Now supposing one Sunday a copper stopped them and made them do a breath test, and said they were over the limit, despite the fact not a drop of alcohol had passed their lips that day. You can bet your life they wouldn't think, oh well, I break this law week in and week out Monday to Friday, so although I'm innocent today, I'll accept the cops fitting me up because it evens the score. People with nine-to-five jobs don't take being bad-jacketed by the authorities lying down—they raise a right stink about it—so why should they expect criminals to behave differently?

I see part of the problem as being that those who've never suffered a custodial sentence often view prison as completely separate from the society they live in, rather than a continuation of it. Prison is an integral part of the capitalist world, not something removed from everyday alienation and exploitation. Indeed, it's my belief that many British jails are ultimately more dehumanising to the screws than the cons. The screws have to enforce an unnatural and brutal hierarchy, and act as if this is normal and ultimately justifiable. It should go without saying that prisons brutalise cons through enforced boredom and deliberately wasted lives, as much as anything else. My experiences inside may have been cruel, but they would have been far worse if the authorities had succeeded in convincing me that I was cut off from the rest of humanity, rather than an integral part of a world that needs changing. What I'm saying is, it's necessary to live out the contradictions of prisons. You've got to make some kind of life inside because you're not dead, but you can never forget you're in the jail and that it's totally abnormal and anti-life.

Being on the run meant I couldn't spend Christmas with my family and this was a drag. But at least I was free, and December 1958 did bring some serious excitement. Archie Moore successfully defended his world light heavyweight boxing title against Yvon Durelle in Montreal. I wish I could have been at the ringside, but listening to the contest on the radio was an acceptable substitute. At forty-four, Moore was a couple of years older than me at the time, and way past the age most people consider to be a boxer's prime fighting years. Moore was knocked down three times right at the start of the match but he came back and gradually gained dominance in the fight. He was fifteen years Durelle's senior but it was the younger man who began to tire as the rounds progressed, and in the eleventh Moore knocked his opponent out. Moore's fight struck me as being every bit as epic as mine against the British authorities!

While I didn't have any success in getting the press to cover the multiple injustices I'd suffered at the hands of the British bourgeoisie, things did advance on other fronts. The complaint me and my wife Ann made about our overheard escape conversation being ventilated at my trial was picked up by some papers after it had been discussed in Parliament. Everyone admitted there was a real danger that if such breaches were repeated then briefs would be telling those on remand not to see their families, because of the potential consequences of their conversations. The Home Secretary R. A. Butler was quoted in *The Times* of 27 February 1959 as saying: "I have investigated this particular case... The statement was taken by police from the prison officer on that occasion, but the prison officer did not give evidence. But I should like the opportunity of reviewing the whole situation." While this report on page eleven of the paper gave me a lot of satisfaction, it didn't exactly rock the establishment in the way the front-page reports of my escape did, or the way my ongoing jewel and fur thefts threw them an equally nasty scare.

Ann wasn't happy catching nothing more than short snatches of me when I was on the run. Things got even more complicated when we discovered she was pregnant with our second daughter, Ann-Marie, who was conceived after I went over the wall from The Ville. In the early part of 1959 my wife offered me a stark choice: either give myself up to the authorities and settle down with a steady job once I'd done my time, or else she'd dump me. I was in two minds about what to do, but then my brother Dai, who'd been killed in the Blitz after visiting me at Chelmsford, appeared in one of my dreams. My brother told me not to give up on my campaign of burglary against the rich and that my greatest triumphs were yet to come! I know it was only a dream and it wasn't really Dai speaking to me from beyond the grave, but he was right and I couldn't ignore his advice.

I loved Ann and my daughter but I wasn't about to submit to a system that had fitted me up not just once but three times. I had too much pride to do that. If it hadn't been for that shithead Spratt I'd have been a famous boxer rather than an infamous criminal, and my brother David would still have been alive. The authorities had taken away two of the things that most mattered to me, and now my defiance of them took away my marriage, my wife and my kids. With Ann gone from my life I really focused my anger and picked myself the perfect target in my campaign of harassment against the rich, and their friends the boys in blue; not to mention Billy Hill too! I was going to hit the Dockers once again—ten years on from my previous big strike against them!

The Dockers" social life had been the focus of endless press gossip since I'd last robbed them a decade before. Lady Muck was without doubt the pre-eminent gaudy socialite of the grey 1950s in the British Isles. You could barely move without coming across her name and photo. Everyone knew the Dockers were low-life who had to look up at their shoes, and they were popularly associated with every form of luxury and indulgence from champagne to mink. Their customised cars were kitted out with everything from gold plate to crocodile coverings and zebra skins.

Rather than paying for this themselves, the couple plundered Sir Bernard's BSA expense accounts to cover the cost of such treats. By 1956, BSA shareholders had finally had enough of Lord Docker's famous freedom with their cash, and staged a boardroom coup to get rid of him when he tried to con them into covering the twenty grand cost of a gold dress for his floozy. Lady Muck claimed she was simply acting as a model and ambassador for BSA, to help sell their luxury Daimler cars. After Sir Bernard's frauds resulted in him getting his marching orders from the company his father had run before him, Norah Docker decided that from then on they'd travel in Bentleys rather than the BSA Daimler.

On 9 March 1959, Lady Docker was in Southampton with her arsehole husband to open a hairdresser's salon. I was there too since I knew she took her jewels with her to show off when she travelled, and they'd be even easier to lift when she was on the move than from her home. The bimbo was wearing her best sparklers for the opening ceremony with cocktails afterwards. Using a hire car I then followed the money-grabbing shits to the Royal Hotel. When Norah got out of the Bentley, I could see she wasn't wearing her jewels and that the couple had decided to leave their luggage where it was. I presumed they were going to send a porter to collect it.

I watched for half an hour but no one came, so I broke into the car and lifted Lady Muck's jewel case. It was easy; I simply smashed a side window using a toffee hammer I had with me. Then I undid the lock and opened the door. The jewel case wasn't even hidden—it was sitting on the back seat of the motor. I took Lord Muck's personal papers while I was at it, not that they were worth anything; I simply wanted to cause him as much hassle as possible. As soon as I'd bagged the swag, I drove my car back to Winchester where I'd hired it, and from there I caught a train to London.

I headed straight for Benny Selby's in Highgate. He'd agreed to fence the jewels a couple of weeks before I stole them.

It was my extensive knowledge of radical history that had first tipped me off to the usefulness of the small hammers used for breaking up toffee and often included as a novelty item in packs of the sweet. The suffragettes had used them to smash windows when they'd been campaigning for the vote for British women. They look completely inoffensive and are less likely to attract attention from a cop who searches you than a regular hammer. And if questioned I could always say it came with a pack of toffee I'd bought and eaten!

A rozzer would look a little silly charging you with going equipped for a burglary if all you had on you was a toffee hammer, so unless you were caught in the act or with the goods, it was a pretty safe item to carry around. Leaving aside, of course, the all-too-common practice of cops planting evidence to fit people up! Since I was on the run, I couldn't afford to risk being searched and being found in possession of burglar's tools. Should I be stopped by a copper who didn't recognise me, then there was a chance I'd get away with providing a false name and address if they emptied my pockets and found nothing more offensive than the remnants of a packet of toffee.

The day after my theft from the Dockers" car, the linens said the gems were worth £100,000 and that the theft had been committed just 150 yards from Southampton Police HQ. I loved the press reports that quoted Lady Docker as sobbing: "I've lost all my jewels – they have all gone!" To underline the fact that this was an act of class war I sent a few letters to the papers using fake names. A couple were published. Here's one of them: "Why should we feel sorry for someone who stupidly leaves £100,000 worth of gems in a car? I'm sick of the childish activities of Lady Docker, the pathetic behaviour of the Mayfair set, and the tantrums and publicity stunts of third-rate entertainers. These people ought to try working down a mine or doing something else that is useful and productive for society as a whole."

Lady Muck had once invited miners onto her yacht for a game of marbles and then told the press she brought glamour into drab lives. My theft from this dirtbag was payback time and an opportunity to let the rich know what the working class thought of them. It was a reminder that, when they were driving down the street in their Bentleys, we were always there; when they were drinking Pimm's on their yachts, we'd be there watching. I wanted them to understand that all the wealth they had was stolen from us, and that one day those whose sweat had made everything worthwhile in this world would take back what rightly belonged to them!

There were some further amusing outcomes to my robbery of Lady Muck's sparklers. This social climbing slag had got close to Billy Hill. So close that the notorious bullshit merchant Mad Frankie Fraser claimed to have seen them making the beast with two backs in a little room off the main reception area at Gennaro's Restaurant in Soho — when Bully Hill was launching his ghostwritten autobiography on 15 November 1955. For an arriviste rat like Hill, hobnobbing with rich douchebags wasn't enough — he wanted to knob them as well. Personally I wouldn't have touched Lady Muck with Billy Hill's dick, and while I suspect Frankie Fraser was fibbing about seeing them doing the business at a book launch, this pair of colostomy bags were extremely close in the mid-to-late 1950s. So immediately after my theft, the tabloids were chock full of stories about Half-Arse Hill visiting Lady Muck at her country pile and promising not to leave a stone unturned in his campaign to recover the jewels.

Since the boys in blue were unable to finger me as the thief, Hill didn't stand a snowball's chance in hell. He was made to look like an impotent fool coz Benny Selby could be trusted and wouldn't grass me up, and he'd shipped the diamonds out to a buyer in Amsterdam. Beyond me and Benny there wasn't a soul in England who knew I'd half-inched this prize. Hill's clowning about as a class traitor in front of the press reminded me I still had a score to settle with this son of a bitch. Beyond Benny and a few of my relatives, all of whom could be trusted, no one in the criminal fraternity knew where I was. I was off their radar and off their map. I hadn't been seen in London since my breakout from Pentonville, and my cousins told me the consensus of opinion was that I was hiding out with relatives either in Wales or Ireland. So early one morning I broke into the 21 Club, a bent gambling joint owned by Hill, and stole the previous night's takings from a safe, knowing no one would suspect I was behind the job.

I crawled in through a toilet window at the back of the building after forcing it open with a jemmy. I made my way up to the top floor and found the administrative office with its combination safe. I'd heard Hill didn't trust his own employees so he regularly changed the code. Frequent combination changes make the codes hard to remember, so I suspected the current numerals would be written down somewhere. I looked on top of desks, in drawers, under ashtrays — nada! Then I realised the answer was staring me in the face. A hand of cards was laid out face down on a desk. I turned them over and tried the numbers on the safe. When the door opened I smiled and imagined Hill doing his nut about my successful raid. The theft not only provided me with a small fortune in untraceable cash, it resulted in this plastic gangster losing a lot of face in his immediate circle. He certainly wasn't going to report the theft to the old bill — he didn't want word going around that he was a soft target. With these pleasant thoughts running through my mind, I went out the way I'd come in, and disappeared into the night.

On the whole I stayed away from central London, but having done one man who made heavy dough off bent gambling, I couldn't resist doing another very soon after. I robbed John and Jane Aspinall but rather than going for their club, I lifted the wife's jewellery from their home at 93 Eaton Place. I went in through an open upstairs window, which I accessed via a ladder. The sparklers were in a dresser drawer, so I just slipped them into my pockets and retraced my steps to get out. When I took the tom to Benny Selby he was incredulous. The gear was worth over ten grand but it had been hot before I lifted it. Aspinall had been buying his missus bent gear from a fence called Mister Money who did a bit of work for Billy Hill on the side. Benny decided the best thing to do was send word in a roundabout way to Aspinall that he could buy back his wife's stones at the knock-down price of two grand. Aspinall didn't want to know. He'd had the jewels valued in Burlington Arcade by a firm that didn't know the gems were dodgy. He collected ten grand off his insurance company, while Benny had to offload my hot pickings abroad.

Mostly I was doing my thefts in an arc around the west and north London suburbs: other than the 21 Club and Eaton Place, I didn't pull any burglaries in the centre of the city during my time on the run. I didn't normally steal dresses but I had need of one when my beloved mother Julia died in the autumn of 1959. I could list the diseases the doctors said my mum had — but my opinion is she was worn down by poverty and that had she been rich she'd have lived a much longer life. The cops knew I'd make it my business to attend the funeral but they were looking out for a man, not a well-dressed lady. I'd have gotten away with this without the boys in blue cottoning on if I'd still been with Ann. But we'd split up and I'd been nowhere near the hospital when our second daughter was born just three days before my mother's wake. If I'd had a woman to put the finishing touches to my outfit, then my petticoat wouldn't have been hanging down beneath the hem of my dress. As my mother's coffin was being lowered into the earth, a female copper spotted this and cried out I was the man they were after. I had to scramble over a wall to escape my pursuers and, as I'd demonstrated more than once before, I was able to outrun them.

There is a long-established tradition of revolutionary cross-dressing in Wales, and so I felt no embarrassment about the way I'd evaded the filth. Between 1839 and 1843 there was mass resistance to unfair taxation in mid and south Wales, with groups of men dressing up as women and wrecking toll gates. Those involved in these actions against the repressive British state were known as Rebecca Rioters because they would shout out this slogan from the Bible: "And they blessed Rebekah and said unto her, Thou art our sister, be thou the mother of thousands of millions, and let thy seed possess the gate of those which hate them." While there are men who get a sexual thrill out of dressing as women, the Rebecca Rioters were doing it to make a point. By attending my mother's funeral while on the run, I too was defying the state and its lackeys: it was a political action as well as a mark of my respect for my mother Julia, whom I loved deeply.

Everyone should love their mother, and losing your mum is one of the worst things that will happen to most people during the course of their lives. Mothers outliving fathers is the usual course of things, and when both your parents are dead that's a real wrench with the past. Being around my beautiful Beryl and newborn Ann-Marie to take my mind off such things would have been great, but that just couldn't be. I regret not being able to spend more time with my daughters as they grew up. Time inside, time on the run, and the break-up of my marriage were all contributing factors to me being a less-than-perfect father. I loved my kids but I wasn't always there for them when they needed me, so I never expected them to be around for me when they became adults.

Looking back on it, I think I was lucky I was on the run when my mother died. If I'd failed in my escape bid from Pentonville then I'd have been in prison brooding on my loss. That happened when my brother David died in the Blitz, and then when my father Owen was killed in a road accident. Julia's passing was the third time someone who meant the world to me had died after I'd been fitted up for a crime I hadn't committed. I was on the run and I had to focus on staying free, so I did my mourning but didn't let dark thoughts and feelings on this score envelop me.

The only way to avoid sinking into a depression over my mother's death was to go robbing morning, noon and night. So I ghosted my way through the rich ghettoes that litter the London suburbs. I couldn't even go into central London for a game of cards with sufficient stakes to let me escape my everyday reality. I was able to gamble in the west London suburbs but couldn't do so at the level I craved. This did mean that I was able to save money and give dosh to my family. I paid back Uncle Dinny and my cousins for all their help too. I didn't really need much – a room and some food – but I wanted to keep on hitting the rich because my thefts were a settling of scores in the class war.

I wasn't aspirational or interested in enriching myself. I moved every few months, and for obvious reasons I was unable to develop close friendships. I'd go out and meet people, have a chat and a game of cards in a pub or a cafe. People liked me and it was easy to make new acquaintances, but my social contacts had to be fleeting. If someone got to know me well they'd become too curious about my life and start asking difficult questions. What happened when I met people playing cards was no different to the way things developed in the places I lived: after a while other tenants would start asking more and more questions about my background and activities, so I'd leave.

I had to keep moving for my own safety. I was on my own really, a ship in the night to nearly all those I mixed with. I saw little of my uncle and cousins, which made it very different to when I'd been on the run in '38 and '39 and was seeing them every few days. My fence Benny Selby was the only person I saw more than once a week who knew who I really was. By February 1960 I was living in Staines, still close to London Airport. If I had to be in the suburbs I liked being near this aerodrome. I'd never been anywhere outside the British Isles but my proximity to those who were travelling further afield was somehow reassuring. The airport has always been a magnet for criminals, so I stayed away from it, but it was somehow heartening to know there were so many men like me close by.

While my workaday raids against the bourgeoisie continued apace, I was looking for another big score that would make the national press and television news in the way my theft of Norah Docker's jewels had hit the headlines. In the end, the spectacular I wanted came to me. Benny Selby told me that Peter Scott was out of jail and looking for an expert housebreaker with whom he might carry out a very high-profile theft. I told Benny I'd be back in a week and that he should tell Scott to visit at the same time.

I met Scott at Selby's Highgate home but we didn't have our discussion of what we were going to do there. We went up to Hampstead Heath, and during our walk Scott told me a couple of bent coppers wanted him to half-inch film star Sophia Loren's jewels while she was filming *The Millionairess* in England. Naturally they expected a cut of the profits for providing inside information. That wasn't a problem: I personally didn't like coppers but it wasn't me who was going to deal with them — that was Scott's department. This was a theft that would definitely make major headlines, and having to pay off the filth was a small burden to bear if we successfully carried out this particular act of attrition against the super-rich. Scott told me his rozzer friends wanted six grand for providing our game plan, and that was fine by me as long as we were paying them after we'd offloaded Loren's jewels.

I told Scott to go back to Selby's house and arrange for him to fence the jewels. He was to meet me at Staines railway station at 3pm the next afternoon. It was a beautiful late spring day in May when we drove to Elstree to check out the lie of the land. Loren and her bigamous film producer "husband" Carlo Ponti were renting the swanky Norwegian Barn, which we located in the 43-acre grounds of a country club close to the film studios where she was filming with Peter Sellers.

We parked well away from their luxurious accommodation and walked briskly to the building. There was some pretty thick undergrowth near the house, which turned out to be a chalet bungalow — that is, a two-storey building with the upper floor built into the roof, with the bedroom windows protruding from it. We returned to our transport — a Rolls-Royce I'd hired — and it didn't look at all out of place parked amongst the expensive motors owned by the rich cunts availing themselves of the country club facilities. I'd dressed up as a toff in a posh suit, while Scott was mortified to discover I'd hired him a chauffeur's uniform as his disguise. At first he'd refused to put it on, but he'd been persuaded to do so when I told him the job was off unless he did as I said.

We went back the next night, parking once again in the country club car park. We donned coats to cover our travelling disguises before creeping through the undergrowth to get to the house. Sophia Loren wasn't there. Scott's bent copper friends had told us to strike when she was out at the airport picking up her lover. There were a couple of domestics watching TV and they had the sound right up. I used a toffee hammer to break in through a downstairs window. I couldn't jemmy it open because it had been fitted with locks.

I climbed through the window I'd opened and into the house Loren was renting, then made my way to the upper floor. The filth who'd put us up to the job had drawn me a plan of the property, so I went straight to the star's bedroom and used the toffee hammer to force open the locked dresser drawer. I picked up her eighteen-inch-square black leather jewel case, opening it briefly to check the contents were inside and it hadn't been weighed down with some dummy materials. Everything was present and correct—four sets of necklaces, earrings, rings and brooches.

When I exited the property, I let myself out through a door rather than using the window. We'd been told by Scott's fuzz friends the jewels were worth plenty and so not to risk fucking things up by taking anything else such as furs. Aside from the fact that I was a far stealthier burglar than my outside man, who had an uncanny ability to make even the most solid of floors creak, I'd insisted I be the inside man because he was a pervert and would have wanted to lift some examples of Loren's smalls. Scott preferred dirty knickers to clean ones, so he'd have probably gone raking around the house looking for a laundry basket if he'd been given half a chance.

I made my way over to where I'd left my accomplice, told him I had what we'd come for and pushed through the undergrowth ahead of him. When we got to the Roller, Scott wanted to see the tom. I told him not to waste time. We needed to get back to London. He could examine the sparklers once we'd got them to Benny Selby's pad. We reached Highgate in north London and had left the jewels in the hands of our fence before the theft was even discovered. The domestics heard nothing and the alarm was only raised when Loren returned home with her "husband" and went upstairs to get ready for bed.

The film star was furious, and it cracked me up to see her impotent rage when she talked to the papers and appeared on TV. I hoped all my overprivileged targets felt as gutted as Loren obviously did after I'd done them, or at least their insurers, out of thousands of quid. That said, my jubilation proved to be short-lived. The bad news took a bit of time to reach me. The first thing to happen was Peter Scott leaving a message with Benny Selby saying that he needed to see me. Scott knew roughly where I was living, but I hadn't told him the actual address. When we caught up with each other I discovered our meeting wasn't, as I'd assumed, to go through the details of another big job. We'd both had an even split of the Loren jewel money from Benny Selby and now Scott was telling me I had to give him three grand of it back.

Scott's story was this: when he'd gone to the dog races at White City where he'd arranged to pay off his bent copper friends, they'd told him six grand wasn't enough for their inside information. They now wanted twelve grand because according to the linens we'd pulled off the biggest ever jewel theft in the British Isles. I told Scott there has to be honour amongst thieves and a deal is a deal. The filth had asked for six grand and we'd given it to them. At the time I thought Scott was lying and all that was going on was that he was trying to con me out of three grand. I found out later, but too much later to do me any good, that he was telling the truth — which isn't something you really expect when you pass the time of day with the Belfast Bullshitter, Scott's unaffectionate nickname in the circles I frequent.

The jewels I stole were worth £185,000 but obviously a fence needs a cut and often sells at a big discount. So what we got from Benny was £44,000 to split between us. That was £22,000 each before expenses which were to be shared equally too. The cost of carrying out the job was the hire of the Roller and our costumes, so I'm just gonna forget about that and stick to round figures. Take away six grand for info and we were left with £19,000 each. But since Scott had to pay off another six grand, only I got nineteen big ones, and he ended up with £13,000. That ain't bad for a night's work as an outside man, and if I'd known he wasn't lying he'd have had £16,000, but none of this satisfied Scott.

Before I move on to the fallout from the bent old bill wanting extra wedge, let me demolish Scott's claims to have been the inside man on the Loren job. Put simply, his descriptions of it made in the mid-1990s don't match press reports from the time of how the robbery was executed. Anyone who wants to check this out can do so at their own leisure, so I won't waste any more time on it. The Belfast Bullshitter's autobiography is filled with self-aggrandising lies. It's more than just a guilty conscience that leads him to fraudulently claim I was nicked very soon after my escape from Pentonville—he's completely unable to admit I was a far better criminal than he ever was, and it was me who trained him up.

Scott was so angry about my refusal to hand over another three grand for his bent friends in blue that he grassed me up to them. I found out years later that my supposed partner-in-crime was the dirty squealer who'd tipped off the filth to the fact that I was living in the Staines area. I guess he gave them the wink in the summer, but I was careful and it took them until 23 November to catch up with me. It was a Wednesday night and they grabbed me in digs I'd moved into only ten days earlier. At least I'd been out when they arrived and plod was forced to conceal himself uncomfortably for six hours to await my return.

And the filth didn't recover anything either! Unable to gamble, I'd anonymously donated the fortunes I'd been making to good working-class causes — rather than merely giving away my standard ten percent. My twenty-five months over-the-wall from Pentonville was a record-breaking escape from that particular institution, and my recapture made the front pages of papers like the *Express* on the Thursday morning. I was returned to Pentonville to cheers from my fellow cons, who considered me a hero for making this successful bid for freedom.

I was called up before the governor to be rapped over the knuckles for going absent without leave. This was a formality since the authorities were relieved I'd been recaptured and didn't want to push matters in case something was picked up by the press or I came to be perceived as even more of a hero by my peers. If he'd wanted to, the governor could have accused me of escape from lawful custody, but all that meant was I'd broken the prison rules and I could be tried in a prison court. I'd have happily gone to a prison court over the matter, and I told the governor that this was what I wanted, because then I'd be able to use the fact that I'd been fitted up by the filth — and therefore wasn't in legal custody — as my defence.

If I'd been guilty of prison breach then it was a criminal offence, and in theory I could have had up to seven years added to my sentence, although in practice this rarely happens. The difference was this: to break prison you had to threaten or enact violence on a screw, or make copies of keys and use them, or else undo bolts on prison doors or gates. I'd simply picked up a ladder that had been left unsecured and used it to get over the wall — and while I had broken prison rules, I hadn't committed a crime. And although five of us had gone up the ladder, we couldn't be charged with conspiracy either, if — as we'd all claimed — the action was spontaneous. And if it wasn't, that had to be proved. The governor had no proof we'd discussed escape in advance, and by the time I was recaptured he didn't want the press covering this embarrassing breach of security again. In the end I was put on two weeks" bread and water and that was that.

Once I'd had my punishment in The Ville, the prison authorities sent me on to Dartmoor. They'd had enough trouble in The Ville while I'd been on the run: the hanging of alleged cop killer Ronald Marwood there on 8 May 1959 had resulted not only in a rowdy demonstration outside the walls, but with disorder from the cons inside who smashed the place up. Marwood denied he'd made the confession that the cops used in court to get a conviction. They claimed he'd stabbed PC Raymond Summers to death. If he'd been found guilty of stabbing a civilian to death without premeditation he would have only got life, not a hanging. Everything about the trial and sentence was unfair, and it was one of the key cases that eventually led to the abolition of capital punishment in the UK. I should also mention that the prosecutor responsible for Marwood's judicial murder was that two-faced toad Christmas Humphreys.

Marwood's hanging had created a lot of headaches for the authorities at Pentonville, so they wanted to get me out of there as quickly as they could to avoid any more trouble. That's why before I'd even had a chance to get used to being back inside, I found myself in The Moor. This wasn't even a preventative detention jail, but the "prison service" didn't seem to care about flouting its own rules. The Home Secretary's annoyance about my escape conversation being brought up during my trial was no more than a seven-day wonder — and by the time I was recaptured, everything I'd done and that had happened to me was simply viewed as so much water under the bridge. The authorities didn't want to risk pushing these matters back into the public eye by subjecting me to anything that might be construed as harsh punishment for my escape.

It was in The Moor that I first heard a very funny, but utterly untrue, story about the Loren jewel theft. Scott had been around dozens of London boozers lying to people about having been the inside man on the Norwegian Barn job, so an underworld wag had made up an equally preposterous tale to deflate the pretentions of the Belfast Bullshitter. This shaggy dog story goes that, upon examination, the Loren "treasures" turned out to be paste copies, and not the valuable originals. Fortunately, Peter Scott had also lifted this Italian sex siren's smalls and he did terrific business flogging off her underwear. The Belfast Bullshitter certainly enjoyed bragging about targeting female film stars and he claimed he got a sexual thrill from riffling through their possessions and stealing their knickers; so this story about Loren's paste jewels and stolen underwear is credible, albeit untrue. According to this tall tale, Loren herself was doing an insurance scam and copped a quarter of a million pounds for not letting on that it was the paste copies and not the actual jewels that were stolen.

I hardly need to say you couldn't believe much of what you heard in prison, coz half the guys you met were drugged up on medical prescriptions to get them through another day of incarceration. You'd see the treatment queue every morning lined up to get whatever the prison doctor had given them a script for. They were a sorry sight, both in The Moor and every other prison that held — or in the case of The Ville, failed to hold — me. Before they shaved, dressed, or ate, the prescription junkies would be waiting for their medical tots to be placed before them. They'd throw back the brightly coloured fluids and after each was consumed chuck an empty container into a metal bowl. Those on this regime would walk around like zombies, all their higher intellectual faculties blocked out. I never wanted to join them. Even if it was painful I needed to keep my hatred of the bourgeoisie at boiling point, and myself in good shape, so that the moment I got out of nick I could once more take up the class war by robbing the rich of their ill-gotten gains.

SIX

Having been recaptured, it was back to the same prison routine. After months of sewing mailbags, I finally got to work in the kitchen. I played cards in the evening and ran through my exercise regime—but mostly it was a living-death "eat, work, eat, work, eat, sleep" routine. One day was pretty much the same as another. In the winter it was cold, damp and foggy; in the summer it still felt damp, but wasn't quite as cold. The miserable weather was enough to ruin a man's constitution if he didn't keep himself healthy, but as a fitness fanatic I wasn't in any danger from the shitty climate. Since I'd escaped from Pentonville I wasn't allowed to work outside the prison, and I wouldn't have wanted to either because it meant labouring on a Duchy of Cornwall estate, and I wasn't going to do anything to help the royal parasites who lorded it over the working man.

As a successful escapee I was considered a security risk and thus had patchman status. I had to dress in a regulation prison uniform but with a twelve-inch-square bright white patch on the front and back of my jacket; taking up slightly less than half the area of this at the centre was a black patch. I had similar, albeit smaller, patches on my trousers, on the front of the right knee and the back of the left one. This led to me acquiring a new nickname. From the mid-forties to the end of the fifties I'd been known as Raymond The Climber because of the frequency with which I used ladders during my thefts. Thanks to my patchman outfit and the fact I was a jewel thief, a couple of wags in awe of Billy Hill started referring to me behind my back as Magpie Jones. This didn't go down too well with the majority of chaps who regarded me as a hero, and so they called me Ray The Cat—in honour of my leap to freedom from the twenty-foot wall at Pentonville. The moniker stuck. Returning to my patchman status, aside from the magpie suit I also had to carry around a book with my photo on the front. The screws would sign it as I was passed from one to another of them.

Being bigots, the guards called me Taffy Raymond, and they'd often quote the racist "Taffy was a Welshman" nursery rhyme at me:

> Taffy was a Welshman, Taffy was a thief
> Taffy came to my house and stole a piece of beef
> I went to Taffy's house, Taffy wasn't home
> Taffy came to my house and stole a marrow-bone
> I went to Taffy's house, Taffy was not in
> Taffy came to my house and stole a silver pin
> I went to Taffy's house, Taffy was in bed
> I took up a poker and threw it at his head.

A few of the London villains associated with Billy Hill also took to insulting me as Taffy Raymond and spouting versions of "Taffy was a Welshman" at me. They tended to prefer renderings such as:

> Taffy was a Welshman, Taffy was a sham
> Taffy came to my house and stole a piece of lamb
> I went to Taffy's house, Taffy was away
> I stuffed his socks with sawdust and filled his shoes with clay
> Taffy was a Welshman, Taffy was a cheat
> Taffy came to my house and stole a piece of meat
> I went to Taffy's house, Taffy was not there
> I hung his coat and trousers to roast before a fire.

All I'll say by way of reply is, as Karl Marx pointed out in The Communist Manifesto: "The working class have no country." The racists were class traitors.

For a while in The Moor I shared a cell with a university-educated anarchist called Roland Martin, and he said I should view the racism the screws directed at me as indicative of their alienated identification with their oppressors. His take was that the bigotry they heaped on me as a Welshman provided a paradigmatic example of the way racism works, turning the victims into victimisers and laying at their feet the accusation that they were responsible for the very things their oppressors had done to them. It was the English ruling class that plundered Wales, but in "Taffy was a Welshman" and similar racist caricatures, their victims were portrayed as thieves. When I'd become a cat burglar it was to expropriate the expropriators, but even so there were still far more English thieves in the British prison system than Welsh crooks.

The racist aggravation I suffered from a few of the other cons never went beyond verbals, since there were plenty of Londoners and other Englishmen banged up in The Moor prepared to stand shoulder to shoulder with me; not everyone wanted to bow down before the reputation of a bullyboy like Billy Hill. Besides, everyone knew the issues between Billy Hill and me over him stabbing my brother in the face were officially sorted. So despite ongoing rancour on both sides, people knew it wasn't something Hill wanted going off again as a full-blown row.

Moving on, my parents were dead and my marriage had broken down, so I didn't get too many visits, but a handful of my relatives did come along to brighten up my time inside. Under preventative detention I was entitled to a thirty-minute visit every two weeks, but because I was in Dartmoor rather than a PD prison, I got twenty-minute visits once a month. My sister Catherine was incredibly supportive. Dinny and the boys came down now and then, but one of the best visits I had was in early 1962 from my cousin Julie Callan. She'd grown up in Newport and although I hadn't seen her since she was small, I'd always felt a lot of affection for Julie because she'd been named after my mother. She was taller than my mother but still petite, blonde and blue-eyed.

Julie shared my mother's sense of determination, but was delinquent with it. She'd moved from south Wales to London in the summer of 1960 and had been working as a hostess at Murray's Cabaret Club—alongside the soon-to-be-infamous Christine Keeler. Julie had only turned eighteen a few days before she came to visit me, but was already really streetwise. She didn't know that I didn't drink and smuggled a bottle of whiskey into the prison under her skirt. I was really touched by the gesture. I managed to get the booze back to my cell where I was able to swap it for a massive amount of tobacco.

I didn't smoke either, but baccy was the prison currency and so I was able to gamble with it. We had regular card games and various cons ran books so that you could bet on the racing. That bottle of whiskey gave me funds for an exciting few weeks of gambling.

Julie promised she'd come to visit me again but I didn't see her for at least eighteen months. A couple of her brothers were banged up not so long after my recapture so, among other things, she was also taking care of them. I didn't say anything because the subject was never mentioned, but the first time Julie visited me she was quite heavily pregnant. I've no idea what happened to the baby, since Julie never talked to me or anyone else in the family about her tot. The last time Julie visited me in Dartmoor she said she was making some interesting connections around Europe and told me that I was to get in touch with her once I was out, because she had some friends who could put work my way. Her brothers, who had merely dabbled in burglary rather than made a full-time career of it, went straight when they got out of nick. I suggested Julie try using our cousins in Victoria until I was released, but she told me to forget it because they didn't have my experience of robbing country houses, and that was what was needed. She also suspected they lacked the discretion the jobs required, and would plunder items of value rather than just going in and doing what they'd been told to do and leaving everything else alone. The victims of the thefts her friends were setting up were not supposed to know they'd been turned over.

Dartmoor wasn't a top-security prison, but as a famous escapee the authorities kept a close eye on me and, as I've already told you, had me done up as a patchman in a Class A kit for several years. As I keep saying, I was an innocent man who'd been fitted up not once but three times by the old bill. If I'd seen a chance of escape I'd have taken it, but none came up. So I kept my nose relatively clean and they let me out in 1965. In the end I think they just wanted to get me off their hands, and Hackney council even provided me with a home. This was Flat 9, St Andrews House, Cranwich Road, Stamford Hill, London N16 5JB. My council flat was to the north of those parts of the borough in which I'd lived before but I liked the area and having a place of my own. The year after I was released, one Dartmoor prisoner did succeed in escaping. The story of Mad Frank Mitchell is a sad one. He'd befriended Ronnie Kray in Wandsworth jail, and everyone was of the opinion that by 1966 he should have got parole.

It could have been my cousin Julie who had a rotten time because of those arseholes the Krays and their antics with Mad Frank Mitchell. She spent several years working as a hostess in Churchill's Club and only quit the job in November 1966 when she moved to Paris. One of Julie's fellow Churchill's hostesses, Lisa Prescott, had a very bad break in December 1966 after being picked up by gangsters at this club. Prescott was taken to a flat in Barking where Frank Mitchell was hiding out after being sprung from Dartmoor by associates of the Kray twins. Mitchell and Prescott engaged in a series of sexual acts over a number of days. Then on Christmas Eve, Mitchell was taken to a van outside the flat and shot because the Krays found him hard to control and figured that the easiest way to save face was to kill him.

Prescott, who'd been paid about £100 to have sex with Mitchell, was taken to a party and told to forget she'd ever met him. A terrified Prescott saw in the New Year working as a hostess; she also found herself having occasional unpaid sex with Albert Donoghue, who she believed had murdered Mitchell and suspected was planning to kill her. That said, most of those I've spoken to view Donoghue as a red herring, and believe the murder was actually committed by Freddie Foreman.

But let's forget about gangster bullies for now so that I can tell you about the curious work my cousin Julie put my way. Julie was into some pretty way-out shit and she knew all the beautiful people and every place that was swinging in London. She was a very attractive girl and had plenty of marriage offers from the rich johns who paid her to sit and drink champagne with them, but I admired Julie for always — and in the words she would use — "doing her own thing". Julie would save up money from her club work and in the summer she'd go travelling all over Europe.

On the Spanish island of Ibiza she'd got acquainted with the art forger Elmyr de Hory. I don't know if it was through de Hory or via the art and beatnik crowd she said she "hung" with in Paris, but Julie also befriended the guys who passed off this forger's pictures. Fernand Legros and his boyfriend Real Lessard were not the kind of company I usually kept, but business is business, and their scams enabled me to perform double whammies against the rich. In addition, Legros had not realised his early ambition to become a ballet dancer, but that frustrated desire created a connection between us, since — and as I've made more than clear — my boxing career had been terminated by a police fit-up. Legros had the mental strength necessary for rigorous fitness training, so we had enough in common to be friendly with each other when we met, although we were never close.

Julie first told me about Legros and Lessard when she visited me in Dartmoor in the spring of 1965, just a few months before I got out. They had a problem in that their chief forger was beginning to tire of his trade and his work was becoming sloppy and difficult to sell. The fakes needed to be in the style of the modern masters de Hory imitated but they were still original works. Legros figured that if all his forger had to do was copy existing paintings then his work might improve. The dealer had a bent English collector who was prepared to pay for works stolen to order from the country homes he frequented, but to avoid any difficulties the original paintings were to be replaced with copies in the hope that no one would notice there'd been a burglary.

That was where I came in, and although for security reasons I was never told the name of the collector, I was informed he was looking forward to showing the original owners of the works I'd be stealing their lost masterpieces. He figured they didn't appreciate what they had and planned to tell them he'd commissioned high-quality copies of their famous paintings. As far as he was concerned, if they couldn't tell the original from a copy—and vice versa—then they didn't deserve to be the custodians of old masters.

I was partnered up with an art restorer who I knew simply as Sid—I gathered from the off it wasn't his real name since it always took him a while to respond to my use of it. I tried a few common names and my outside man instantly reacted to a shout of "Bob". After being introduced we headed down to Cornwall in a caravan that was kitted out as a mobile art restoration studio. Our target was the Port Eliot family seat of Nicholas Eliot, 9th Earl of St Germans. It was one of the weirdest jobs I've ever undertaken.

Having waited until all the servants had gone to bed, I entered the ground floor of the house through an unlocked door at about 1am. I had to remove a Rembrandt and several van Eycks from the living room. I opened a window and passed them out to Sid. We then used a wheelbarrow to transport them to our caravan, which was parked up on a nearby public road. Sid had placed blankets around each painting so that they weren't damaged as I pushed them along. When we got them into the caravan, Sid removed the paintings from their frames and then placed the copies on the stretchers that had until that point protected the originals. Once this was done, which took just over an hour, we wheeled the copies back to Port Eliot. I went in through the living room window which we'd left open, Sid passed the copies—which were now in the original frames—to me, and with the help of a diagram I'd made when I'd removed the paintings, I hung the copies where the originals had been.

Once I was hanging the copies, Sid wheeled our barrow away. Having completed my work, I made sure the window was closed and went out the way I'd come in, through the unlocked door. When I got back to the caravan Sid was in a state of high excitement. He liked the van Eycks but couldn't believe he'd been party to the theft of a Rembrandt—he told me it was one of the last works by the painter to remain in private hands. I told Sid that the time to get excited was once we were safely home, so I gunned our motor and we headed for London. I couldn't see what so thrilled Sid about the Rembrandt; it was a small landscape and was plastered in so much varnish you could hardly see the picture properly at all. I said as much to the art restorer too.

"But that's the old master aesthetic. People have become used to seeing them buried beneath layers of varnish so that's what they expect," Sid snapped.

My rejoinder was: "That doesn't make them good!"

"It's good for the forger," Sid insisted. "He can hide the tell-tale signs of his fakery beneath smooth varnish. You see nothing of the way the paint has been laid on the canvas; it makes forgery so much easier!"

"So what you're telling me is this Elmyr de Hory ain't so hot?"

"The fakes weren't painted by him."

"I thought he was in on this caper."

"He's lost his touch. His work wasn't good enough, even when he was simply asked to make copies, so Legros brought in an East German called Werner Tübke. It isn't just Tübke, he's got loads of people working with him, a whole school of forgers."

"What, in East Germany?"

"Yes, in Leipzig. Tübke was in charge of recreating paintings lost during the war, and those that had been replaced with unacceptably poor-quality fakes. I assume you know what happened to thousands of valuable art works during the Allied and Axis conflict?"

"A lot of treasure was salted away down mines and other places of supposed safety, but often those who put them there, or who were guarding them, stole them or switched them with inferior goods."

"Exactly, and this was a far bigger problem in Germany than in England, because the Nazis lost the war and at the end everything was chaos. If the Axis powers had won, the situation would have been reversed."

"Why are you so sure of that?"

"The masses lose sight of what is important when they lack a leader to point them towards it."

"I don't think art is very important."

"You're a philistine."

"And proud of it. Anyway, tell me about Werner Tübke."

"He has an incredible technical facility; he can imitate anything but he has no real talent, no individual vision. But that doesn't matter, because once the Soviets had rebuilt Dresden they wanted to fill their fake city with fake art. Dresden was completely destroyed by Allied bombing but it's been flawlessly reconstructed as a doppelgänger of a baroque city. It looks almost convincing but when you're there you simultaneously know there is something wrong with it. After the reconstruction, the museums had to be filled with copies of the paintings that had gone missing, and Tübke and his school were brought in from Leipzig to do the job. He can turn out a lot of art because he has so many people working under him. Tübke does some original work too, but that's simply kitsch."

"But why would the East Germans let Tübke work for Legros?"

"Because Legros pays them and they're keen to undermine the western economy, and fake art works are as good a way of doing that as fake bank notes. If a few Tübke paintings are eventually identified as fraudulent, we'll end up in a situation where even the experts won't know what's genuine and what isn't."

"But hasn't that happened already in Dresden if Tübke has filled the city's art museums with Sexton Blakes?"

"It doesn't matter what happens there; the communist leadership dictates reality and they say the fakes are real, so no one would dare question them."

After I told Sid the so-called communist leadership in the east was fraudulent too, and it was actually a boss class, our conversation lapsed into silence. I thought Sid was a queer bird but I got paid two grand for my troubles, which isn't bad for a night's work! I agreed to do the next job for the same price, and only partly because it was a little closer to London. The target was the Spencer family seat at Althorp in Northamptonshire. I'd been intending to rob this particular clan of upper-class parasites for a long time, but hadn't yet gotten around to it.

This time there was only one painting to switch with a copy, *A Commander being armed for Battle* by Rubens. It was a much bigger picture than the stuff we'd swapped around at Port Eliot, but somehow I managed to accomplish the task. On the way back to London, Sid started to piss me off. He just seemed to be talking shit. For the money I was being paid I could put up with a lot of his nonsense conversation, but when we got to Notting Hill and I ended up going into his Kensington Park Road home for a cup of tea, things just got out of hand. It wasn't too bad to start with; Sid was simply showing me some of the paintings he'd collected. He owned a huge amount of art but even more just passed through his hands and was sold on.

"We may have just stolen a Rubens, but this is a painting by that very wonderful artist that I picked up for a song. The art world won't authenticate it but I know it is real."

"How?" I asked.

"Just look at it, you can see it's genuine."

"Actually I can't."

"What about this?" Sid pontificated as he handed me a metal cast of an eagle.

"What about it?" I echoed.

"It's by Leonardo da Vinci."

"Really?"

"Certainly. I can prove it if you like."

"Don't bother, I don't care who made it."

"Now look at these works by an outsider artist who happens to be a friend of mine. You'll see from the paintings that although Scottie Wilson is self-taught and lacks Werner Tübke's technical ability, he has a vision that the Bolshevik lacks. That is why Wilson is the better artist and potentially a leader of men."

"Artists aren't leaders of men, they're dreamers," I replied.

"Artists dream new worlds," Sid shot back. "Look at Picasso! Who saw the world the way he did before he made his paintings? And his works are now recognised as the greatest examples of modernism!"

"Picasso is famous, but that doesn't make his work good! A lot of ordinary people don't think much of what he did. Why do you think he's great?"

"Picasso is great because he had a vision, he is a man of genius, and it's that top few percent of the human race, men like him, who should rule this world! I'm working on a play about Picasso to illustrate my theories of great men, and the many ways in which their lives and actions demonstrate that democracy is a form of degeneracy presided over by the rabble, the butchered and the botched!"

"I thought Picasso joined the Communist Party. Are you sure he'd go along with your theories?"

"It doesn't matter what he thinks, it is what he did that counts. He was a man of action, like all the great figures of the twentieth century. Just like He who returns whenever He is needed, the late-born child of light…"

"And who would that be?"

"A man who set out to become an artist against his parents" wishes, and ended up animating the masses with divine sparks once he started moulding them like a sculptor."

"You must mean the fella Tony Hancock plays in that movie The Rebel!"

"Don't be silly, who do you think is the greatest figure of the twentieth century?"

"Sugar Ray Robinson."

"Bah! A negro boxer? How can you compare an ape like that to Adolf Hitler?"

"Fuck you," I screamed as I slammed my right fist into Sid's face. "If I ever hear you mention Hitler again, I'll give you such a hiding that the mere memory of it will cause you to wince for the rest of your life."

Sid didn't hear my words. I'd knocked him spark out. I left him where he fell and went home. When I spoke to Legros I told him I wouldn't work with Sid again, he had to find someone else. He agreed to this. He was less ready to make a concession when I told him that I was taking big risks going in and out of country houses with big items like paintings not once but twice in the same night. If I was to carry on with this activity I wanted more money. I never had the chance to improve my deal with Legros. He was in deep shit over his various frauds — encompassing not just fake art but dodgy cheque books too — and before we reached an agreement, he and Lessard were banged up.

I suspect we wouldn't have reached an accommodation, because Legros was really pissed off when I demanded more money. He said what I was doing was risk-free because the victims never knew they'd been robbed, but of course that depended on my not being disturbed as I was doing the old switcheroo, and the victims not realising that their valuable art works had been swapped for a bunch of Sexton Blakes. I wasn't that bothered by the turn of events that ended my involvement with Legros; I simply went back to doing what I knew best, stealing jewels and furs. I was very happy to be able to choose my own outside men, rather than having Legros teaming me up with a fruit and nut cake like Sid the Scumbag art restorer.

That said, Legros wasn't all bad and when he ended up being arrested in Brazil in 1974, before being extradited back to France, he helped out his fellow international prisoners who were jailed alongside him in a special penal institution in the national capital of Brasilia. Legros bribed the poorly paid screws so that not just he but all the prisoners could have TV, special meals, extra visits and much else.

He tried to help out his fellow cons in other ways too, with advice about how to deal with the authorities and much else besides. Although Legros was extradited, Ronnie Biggs who'd been banged up with him eventually got to stay as a free man in Brazil. I never met Biggs, but his thirty-year sentence for participation in the 1963 Great Train Robbery was completely over the top. It really demonstrates the viciousness of British courts in their defence of bourgeois property relations.

Biggs became a hero in Brazil, and it was a stroke of luck he'd got his girlfriend pregnant coz at that time those who were parents of Brazilian nationals were never deported. This was a close call for Biggs, and had the British authorities not screwed up and given him extra time to smooth things out, he'd have found himself banged up once more in Blighty. I was so glad he stayed free, and in doing so totally eclipsed my two-year escape record! He'd made his jailbreak from Wandsworth rather than Pentonville, but they were both London prisons, and his 1965 escape came just seven years after mine! That said, Biggs had outside help, friends who drew up beside the prison exercise yard in a furniture van and threw a rope ladder over the wall to facilitate his escape. My jailbreak involved no outside help, no getaway cars and no pre-arranged hideouts. Nonetheless, whatever way you look at it, Biggs still done good!

Returning to my own life in the mid-sixties, after doing over a few country houses outside London, various newspaper headlines about Richard Burton and his wife Elizabeth Taylor caught my eye. Taylor was famous for her love of jewels and the expensive sparklers she wore and collected. According to the linens I read, she was spending time in Dublin with her fifth husband Richard Burton, while he was over there filming *The Spy Who Came in from the Cold*. Taylor was going back and forth between Dublin and mainland Europe where she was making her new film—I think it was *The Comedians*, but it may have been something else. It's easy stealing from hotel rooms and I figured Taylor had so many jewels she was bound to leave some lying around in The Gresham. The best time to hit it seemed to be when both she and Burton were out. The last week of February 1966 saw me and my outside man, Chris Hawkins, boarding an early flight for Dublin.

Hawkins was a market stall trader from Hoxton who I'd got to know in gambling clubs. He wasn't an experienced thief, but from seeing him around I knew that he could be trusted. I was also aware he was in desperate need of cash because he was forever losing a fortune at cards and on the dogs. I'd have rather teamed up with my old pal George Taters Chatham, but he'd been handed a five-year stretch in 1964 for burglary and was still in the jug. Stealing Taylor's jewels was like taking candy from a baby. She'd gone back to France and Burton was out filming when I walked into The Gresham Hotel. It was the middle of the afternoon and there was only one bellboy on reception. Hawkins walked up to the desk and buttonholed the kid looking after the entry.

"There's some fellas fiddling with the handles on a car outside. It probably belongs to someone in the hotel; I think you ought to come and have a look."

When the bellboy followed my outside man into the street, I nipped behind the reception desk and helped myself to the key to Taylor and Burton's penthouse suite. I was out of the reception area and at the top of the hotel before the bellboy was back at his station. Hawkins told me later that when they went out a man was disappearing into the distance and he convinced the bellboy they should chase after him. When they caught up with their quarry, Hawkins apologised and said he'd made a misidentification. I let myself into Burton's penthouse rooms, found Taylor's jewel case in a drawer and took it. I met Hawkins back at the airport, from where we caught the first flight to London. The tom had been fenced by Benny Selby before anyone knew it was missing. Burton didn't notice a thing and it wasn't until Taylor returned to Dublin via Paris that the alarm was raised. A story about the old bill watching ports and airfields on the lookout for the thief gave me a good laugh. They were way too late to catch me. I felt even happier that the spoiled and pampered actress was quoted as saying: "I'm very sad about the theft. They were my favourite pieces."

I'll admit that Taylor was pretty and a perfectly good actress to boot, but as a rich and decadent celebrity notorious for her extravagant love of sparklers she was a target begging for my attention. Having been born in swanky Hampstead to rich American parents, she was an even more fitting victim for a class-conscious jewel thief like me than Sophia Loren. The Italian actress came from a poor family and had to work her way up to a position of privilege, whereas Taylor had been born with a silver spoon in her mouth. Anyone who flaunted their wealth deserved to have it expropriated — but nonetheless I found thieving from someone like Taylor, who had always led a pampered existence, even more satisfying than taking treasures from the likes of Loren.

That said, when I saw the film the Italian sex siren had been making when I robbed her, I was very glad I'd done the job because my theft seemed like the kind of criticism Loren couldn't ignore. I didn't understand why *The Millionairess* was a hit despite mixed reviews. I thought the film was a complete turkey, with a weak story taken from a second-rate George Bernard Shaw play and a particularly bad performance from Loren's co-star Peter Sellers.

The Spy Who Came in from the Cold was a different matter entirely. This was the movie Liz Taylor's other half was making when I robbed her. Based on a novel by John le Carré, it is without doubt Richard Burton's best film. The actor came from a Welsh mining family, and my guess is he ended up a drunk at least partially because he knew he'd betrayed his working-class roots. He may have spoken out about being a socialist but he didn't behave like one. In *The Spy Who Came in from the Cold*, Burton plays himself essentially, a burnt-out alcoholic pretending to defect to the Soviet bloc and being manipulated by his British controllers, who see him as no more than a pawn in their Cold War games. I'm not one for reading novels and I've never read le Carré's fiction, but I loved the film. Knowing I'd had it away with the jewels belonging to the lead's wife while it was being shot just made the movie even better as far as I was concerned.

The money came easy and it went easy too, at that time mostly in a spieler down Jermyn Street in the West End. Rumour had it the place had been set up with the proceeds of bank robberies committed by a group of villains the press dubbed "The Wine Gang". They'd break into banks at the weekend and empty safety deposit boxes at their leisure, having taken plenty of food and wine with them to sustain their bodies over the many hours they put into these enterprises. All the bank staff found on Monday morning when they opened up were a few crumbs, a lot of empty vino bottles and endless ransacked safety deposit boxes. The gang were never caught, but I still wouldn't have wanted to work with burglars who liked to drink on the job. If it was this gang's money that went into the spieler then they eventually lost it by overexposing themselves to successful bets, so that by the time I was going down there the operation had either been bought out or handed over to someone else.

The clientele at Jermyn Street was pretty mixed. Villains and members of the upper classes who wanted to slum it were both well represented. Thieves would come in and offer bent goods around, and as often as not it was the aristos present who bought what they were selling — anything from minks to carpets to watches and jewels. There were also businessmen and accountants — such as Michael Connaughton-Hodgkins — who lost a lot of money, and left themselves open to blackmail when it came out that as a result of this they'd had to make illicit "borrowings" from company funds. I'll return to Connaughton-Hodgkins later.

I could have snared myself a high-maintenance girlfriend in Jermyn Street had I wanted one, but I preferred to stick with lovers of my own class. If you're splashing the cash in a gambling den then you're bound to attract bedmates who want all the excitement they can get. When I got out of Dartmoor it was the height of the swinging sixties and I was able to do plenty of bed-hopping. I had loads of good sex, but I wanted more than that; I wanted a real relationship, and despite having a different girl on my arm virtually every week, I never did find anyone who could replace Ann. Too many of the women I met were gold-diggers, and even those that weren't rarely saw beyond my reputation as a tough cat burglar and spieler face.

That said, I still met some women who proved more than useful to me. One called Jackie Whitehead literally threw herself at me. She was a club hostess from Churchill's and Peter Scott had made a nuisance of himself over her. The Belfast Bullshitter had eventually been barred from that club after his infatuation with Whitehead led to a fight in which Andrew, son of the venue's owner Harry Meadows, was hit. Jackie knew Scott had a beef with me and this was all that was needed to make me an attractive proposition to her. When she approached me I didn't have a clue who she was but she knew all about me. All I saw was a fine-looking woman — legs that seemed to go up to her neck, a firm body, perfect hair and clothes that had set someone back a pretty penny.

"You're Ray The Cat right?"

"Why do ya wanna know?"

"Look, I know you're Ray The Cat and I know Peter Scott has a feud going with you."

"What's that to you?"

"I hate Peter Scott; he became absolutely obsessed with me and, as I understand it, if we both jumped into the same bed it would piss him off more than anything else in the world!"

"Is that a proposition?"

"Yes."

"I can't go yet, I'm in the middle of a card game with some really high stakes."

"I can see that. I'll wait by the bar. Come and collect me when you're ready."

A couple of hours later — by which time I'd done all my dough — I took Jackie by the arm and led her into a cab. We went back to her place in Bayswater, and Whitehead had to pay the fare coz all I had was the shirt on my back. She'd had a few drinks but she could obviously hold her liquor coz she was a very active sexual partner. I always thought there was nothing worse than a drunk woman who lay back in bed barely conscious, expecting the man to do all the work in their bout of bedroom athletics.

Jackie knew a thing or two about sex and she showed me just how sweet revenge could be. I didn't want a regular thing with her and I knew I needn't trouble myself about ensuring Scott found out about what we'd done together. Jackie would take care of that—she was one hell of a woman. All the same, I'd have rather been with Ann; I still really wish my marriage had worked out. A question of lifestyles I suppose, but I preferred regular women like my wife to club girls. Given my line of work and the class war I was carrying on against the rich, I liked a woman you could depend on. Ann was everything I'd ever wanted and it was the cops fitting me up in '58 that busted us up, providing me with yet another good reason to keep my end up in my one-man war against bourgeois society.

Another woman I met in Jermyn Street was known behind her back as Poker Patsy. This particular gold-digger had married a lord and was gambling away his fortune as fast as she could. She'd come down to the spieler dripping in diamonds. By talking to her I found out a bit about her country pile and went down there to relieve the lady of jewels and furs—which saved her the trouble of losing them at the roulette table. As the nights wore on and drink loosened tongues at the spieler, I was able to gather all the information I needed to ply my trade as a cat burglar. Being teetotal I was always wide awake and my mind was blazing. For as long as the Jermyn Street spieler stayed open I didn't even need to look at the papers to find targets to rob. They'd be laid out in front of me all night long. All I had to do was listen to the conversation to gather the intelligence I required to continue with my acts of revenge against the toffs and the system that supported them.

Leaving the likes of Poker Patsy to their rotten fates, in the late sixties I met another woman called Pat in very different circumstances. This was Patricia Halewood, wife of the industrialist Stanley Halewood. I'd robbed them of jewels, furs and a model of a galleon ship made out of silver. There was something about the Spanish galleon that made me examine it closely when I took it to my slaughter. There was a plaque on the bottom of the ship and engraved on it was a message saying: "This item has a sentimental value far beyond its monetary value. If it falls into the wrong hands phone the owner and you will be well rewarded with no questions asked." I wrote the phone number down on a piece of paper and figured I'd try calling it before I offered the piece to a fence. I'd robbed Halewood during the day and I called him that night. He invited me to dinner and said he'd pay me five grand for the return of the galleon. It was far more than I was gonna get from a fence so I decided to go for it. There was something in his voice that told me I could trust him on this one.

The following night I found myself sitting down to dinner in west London with Stanley Halewood and his wife Pat. There were two cooks in the kitchen to prepare the various courses, and the food was served up by a butler in full uniform. I'd returned the ship to its owners before we started to eat, and Halewood had given me an envelope stuffed with high-denomination notes. My hosts were a little surprised that I didn't drink, so I told them my life story, my dreams of becoming middleweight boxing champion of the world, and how my ambitions had been shattered by the bent cops who'd fitted me up. They listened sympathetically and told me that the silver galleon had been the favourite possession of their son, who'd lost his life fighting the Nazis. I'd never been so well treated by rich people in my life, and before I left I returned Halewood's reward money to him.

"I can't take this," I told Halewood as I handed him the bulging envelope containing five grand in cash. "You've invited me into your home and treated me well. On top of which you've shown more sympathy for my plight than any other wealthy person I've ever met."

"You can keep it," Halewood insisted. "I'm a very rich man. I don't need the money. My son's silver galleon is priceless as far as I'm concerned. His death taught me a lesson, and that was no matter how rich you are money can't buy you everything you want or need. It can't buy you happiness and it can't bring my son back to life."

"That's what's wrong with this world," I said. "It's ruled by money instead of love."

"I agree with you. With all my money I can't buy the things I most want. That's why I want you to keep the five thousand."

"Don't curse me with your money, please accept it back. I simply can't take it. Over dinner I've got to like you. Be generous, take your money back."

We talked in this way for perhaps ten minutes, but eventually my host accepted the return of his cash. If he hadn't taken it back I'd have thrown it away in anger, but instead I left a happy man. Of course, I was going to continue with my own very personal class war against the rich, but it was important to remember that capitalism dehumanised everyone and we all needed to regain our humanity.

Although the overwhelming majority of toffs were self-seeking toe-rags, the class system was an irrational lottery and even among the upper classes there was to be found here and there a touch of common humanity. I may have hated the bourgeoisie but that was because I loved my fellow men and wanted the best for everyone! In a sane world there would have been no reason for anyone to embark on a life of crime, because society would operate on the basis of "from each according to ability, and to each according to need".

Dinner parties with the likes of the Halewoods weren't my normal mode of entertainment. Aside from gambling, I liked to go to the movies. One film that particularly caught my attention around the time I met Halewood was *The Jokers*, directed by Michael Winner. In this flick, Michael Crawford and Oliver Reed play a couple of posh brothers who enjoy pulling pranks, and who eventually decide to steal the Crown Jewels as a jest. There are lots of cheesy tourist shots of London and swinging sixties dolly birds, since the movie was shot in 1966 and released the following year.

It's a good comedy caper that pokes fun at the establishment. At the climax the stolen jewels are hung from the so-called scales of justice above the Old Bailey. That's a good symbol of how the British criminal justice system has always served the ruling class. It's all about money and has nothing to do with justice! As I've mentioned before, back in the forties I'd wanted to steal the Crown Jewels, but I never got a crack at them. It was good to see a fictional version of this unrealised crime of mine being pulled on film, but I'd have liked it better if the heroes doing the job had been portrayed as working-class and proud of it, rather than toffs!

SEVEN

When George Chatham got out of nick in the late sixties I teamed up with him once again. Taters was way better to work with than Chris Hawkins because he was a top inside, as well as a reliable outside, man. Hawkins didn't want to be anything more than an outside man. He liked the money we made robbing the rich but was terrified of getting pulled. He was worried his common-law wife, Shirley Pitts, would find out about his criminal antics. She was a professional hoister and what she couldn't get out of a shop inside her knickers wasn't worth stealing. Shirley gave Hawkins gambling money because she figured that ensured she could depend on him to look after their kids should she end up in jail. If she'd known he'd been doing jobs with me she'd have done her nut.

The first target I hit after teaming up with Taters once again was a personal one for me. I had reasons to be grateful to R. A. Butler because — as I noted earlier — when Parliament debated the issue of the filth illegally using my private conversations with my wife in evidence at the 1958 Old Bailey fit-up, he'd been Tory Home Secretary and he didn't try to bury the matter. Butler dealt with the complaints about this aspect of my trial very well, and I've no beef with him over that.

Nonetheless, he was a Conservative toff and when he retired from politics in 1965 he became master of swanky Trinity College, Cambridge. When Prince Charles was there in the late sixties, Butler was his mentor and counsellor. It should go without saying that the entire Windsor clan are a pack of scoundrels, but despite stiff competition from the rest of his inbred family, and in particular his Auntie Margaret, Big Ears has to be the most obnoxious royal brat of modern times. So robbing Butler was also a way of hitting out against obsequious lackeys of the Crown.

I planned the raid, but as Taters hadn't been on a job since getting out of jail I let him do the inside work. He went in through a downstairs window we jemmied open. Butler was dining in his kitchen and his domestic was seated with him, listening to one of the old Tory's interminable monologues. Taters placed various valuables that were on display in the living room into a mailbag, and passed this through the window to me. He then ghosted his way through a few more rooms, and passed a second bag of swag to me, before getting out. We escaped with a lot of silver, but since most of it was identifiable, it was melted down.

Robbing Rab Butler was not a particularly remunerative job, but it paid enough to be worthwhile and, from the point of view of the class war I was carrying out against the rich, it was ideologically spot on. Taters wasn't really interested in my political views, so we rarely discussed them, but being working-class he was on my side and had no problems with my reasons for doing what we did. I noticed this with many of the London villains I knew; they acted as I wanted them to behave politically, but beyond a complete and very self-conscious contempt for bourgeois authority, they never explained their reasons for their criminal activities the way I could and did. Like me, many of them had been fitted up by the old bill, but I don't know of anyone other than myself who'd been bad-jacketed before embarking on a life of crime.

My next target with Taters was Belvoir Castle, the home of the Duke and Duchess of Rutland. The Vale of Belvoir is situated between Nottingham and Grantham, so we had a long drive up there. That said, we knew this country pile was worth attacking. This time I acted as the inside man. Taters would have gone after some of the antiques and other historical shit this notable line of dirtbags and exploiters had collected over the years, whereas I wanted to keep it personal. To tell the truth, I couldn't be doing with their military treasures, tapestries, period furniture or art works. Taters told me he wanted to lift some of the bejewelled ceremonial swords displayed in the castle, whereas what I coveted were her ladyship's sparklers and furs. These items were worth just as much as the antiques and lifting them made the raid more personal, since they were currently in use, rather than being dead makeweights in an inherited bric-a-brac collection. The tom was also lighter, smaller, easier to make off with and not nearly as difficult to fence as antiques.

Charles Manners, the tenth duke, was on his second marriage by the time we done him. So the tom I pulled belonged to the former Frances Helen Sweeny, the daughter of a rich yank. Belvoir Castle was as fake as a nine bob note, the original parts of the building having been destroyed at various times, until finally the whole complex including rebuilds was consumed by fire at the end of the eighteenth century. Belvoir is a huge nineteenth-century folly masquerading as a castle. But before I relate the full details of our attack on the Rutlands, I'll indulge in a little aside for the benefit of any rich tossers who happen to be reading this.

A burglar can get into any dwelling, but a successful thief only bothers breaking into houses that contain goods worth stealing. The greatest protection a homeowner has against a professional thief like me is ignorance. Unless I knew there was something inside begging to be nicked, then I wasn't going to bother breaking into a property. That said, British society is so class bound that you can go into any posh area where the rich try to hide themselves away from the rest of us in their private ghettoes, and know there is something in every house that will more than repay the effort of ripping it off.

But if you live in a council flat or an ordinary two-up two-down terrace, then someone like me isn't going to bother you — unless they know in advance there are big-ticket valuables in your drum. And if you have people in to work on your house, or a Christmas party or other celebrations with lots of guests, then you can guarantee that if your visitors see stuff that cost lots of money, they will talk to their friends about this, and eventually someone like me or Taters will get to hear about the goodies too. That said, even if you keep your stuff locked up, or don't have any valuables, you can't protect yourself against kids and junkies, opportunist thieves who will break in anywhere on the off chance there is something worth having away. Ninety-nine percent of thievery is by amateurs, and you can't protect yourself against them either.

And don't think security will stop a professional from stealing from you. I may have preferred live burglaries when alarms were likely to be switched off, but that doesn't mean I don't know how to disable security systems. The same logic applies to locks. No matter how expensive they are, locks — like alarms — are assembled from factory-made parts, so they can be taken apart and rendered ineffectual without too much trouble — as long as you have the right tools.

Of course, amateurs and opportunists will just smash a window and go through — not caring if an alarm is going off or not. A professional might break a pane of glass too, but they'll have a silk cushion to muffle the sound, and no copper in the world can get up in court and claim you were equipped for a burglary because you were carrying around some soft padding that meant you'd never have to park your arse on a hard surface. For me, getting into a building — any shop, office or dwelling — wasn't a problem; it was identifying the right places to hit that took puzzling out.

Returning to my crack with Taters against the Rutlands, the Vale of Belvoir is supposedly an area of great natural beauty, although if you ask me nothing you'll find in England compares to the countryside of Wales. When doing over a country pile we'd often hire a posh car, but since in this instance we were heading to the home of the Stilton cheese, we used a van belonging to a greengrocer we knew, and even brought him back a selection of local delicacies — not just in the dairy line, but also some Melton Mowbray pork pies. We picked up the food late in the afternoon and then headed to the castle, which sits on a scarp slope a hundred metres above the valley floor at the south-eastern edge of the vale. We parked some distance from Belvoir Castle and then jogged up to it. The sun had already set and an assortment of rich parasites were sitting down to their dinner.

I scooted through a side door that had been left unlocked by a servant, and stealthily made my way upstairs. I stopped every now and then to listen out for domestics, making my way unseen to the bedrooms. I'd brought mailbags with me and once these were filled with furs and secured, I opened a window and threw them down onto the lawn, from where Taters was able to retrieve them and hide the coats in the shadows at the edge of the garden. Once I'd located her lady-ship's jewel case and slipped it into my pocket, I followed the mailbags out of the window. I was wearing tennis shoes and made little noise. The jump is nothing — as I've said before, just bend your knees and relax as you land. I rejoined Taters in the shadows and, splitting the bags of furs between us, we made our way back to our van. The journey to London was a long one but we had plenty to talk about.

"I still think we should have gone for the antiques. I got a fair price for the Duke of Wellington's swords when I nicked 'em outta the Victoria & Albert in forty-eight!" Taters hissed at one point.

"You got those swords out of a museum, and you didn't get a fraction of their real value from the fence."

"I got a good whack."

"We'll get a good price for the jewels and furs we nicked tonight. With me it's personal. I want those toffs to feel some pain. They wouldn't care that much about losing some crap they'd inherited and that no one has touched for hundreds of years."

"You and your politics! All I need is money. Besides, the swords will have been touched by the servants; someone has to clean 'em!"

"You'll stick by your own when the time comes. The serv-ants may clean the swords but they're on our side."

"I stick by you coz I end up with a thick wad of notes burn-ing a hole in my pocket after we've been out on a job."

"We'll do alright from what we got tonight!"

"Do you think we'd have done better if we'd lifted some of the paintings? They've got a load of top names in their private collection — Gainsborough, Reynolds, Holbein and Poussin."

"We haven't got a fence who'd touch that type of stuff right now. We know where we are with jewels and furs."

"I guess you're right, but it seems a shame not to have lifted some of their antiques."

Another titled wanker Taters and I robbed in the late sixties was John Mackintosh, AKA 2nd Viscount Mackintosh of Halifax. The family's country pile, Thickthorn Hall, was located immediately south of Norwich in Norfolk. It had been bought in the 1950s by the father of the bumwipe we plundered. Harold Mackintosh, 1st Viscount Mackintosh of Halifax, had inherited his father's confectionery business and built it up into something far bigger than the concern his dad had passed down to him. John Mackintosh's old man had popped his clogs about five years before we robbed his son.

We'd got a bit of inside information and drove up to the property in a furniture van. The place was only four miles from Norwich but it was a different world, out in the country, just past a village called Hethersett. You reached the house from the road via a long tree-lined drive. The drum was secluded and we knew no one was inside when we arrived. It was a stuccoed early-nineteenth-century dwelling, the original part of which consisted of three widely-spaced bays at the front. These were two storeys high and there were later one-storey extensions to the south-west and east. There was also a porch with pillars to create a focal point.

Taters and I drove up to the house, parked our furniture van in front of the porch and, using copies of the house keys that had been passed to us, let ourselves in. We loaded our wheels with antiques, art, rugs and anything else we could find of value, including some fine jewels and furs from the master bedroom. I even took a miner's lamp, not that it was worth anything; it was just that having worked in the pits as a young man, I was offended that some toff would use what I once saw as my work kit as an ornament. It was lucky I took it and left it sitting in my flat. One day I decided I should give the lamp a clean, and when I took it apart I found gold coins and diamonds wrapped in white tissue paper hidden inside it. That's the closest I've ever come to releasing a genie from a bottle! I couldn't have been any more surprised if a spirit had appeared before me and offered to grant me three wishes!

We carted everything we wanted from Thickthorn Hall out through the front door. There wasn't much chance of us being seen, but if anyone had come along we'd have told them we were removal men. And in a way we were in the removals business, and actively contributing to wealth redistribution at the same time! It was an easy blag, and given the number of things we stole, one of the biggest single jobs I ever did. Benny Selby took the jewels and furs, another fence dealt with the antiques and paintings, and a third was up for handling what was left over. The paintings we half-inched weren't in the same league as those belonging to the Duke of Rutland. That was why we had a fence who was able to flog the Mackintosh pictures, whereas we didn't know anyone who was able to offload works by the likes of Gainsborough and Poussin.

I thought the Mackintosh robbery was a good move, a change of style. We wore art handler's gloves so we left no fingerprints and few other clues in terms of the execution of the crime. By the late sixties I was aware that the regional police forces were increasingly pooling information centrally. If you always performed your crimes the same way you were more likely to be caught. You needed to change the style of what you did. I'd have switched the type of target too, but I was determined to carry on with my class war against the rich. Besides, very wealthy people were a magnet for a lot of professional thieves, so I wasn't going to be the only person in the frame when it came to Viscount Mackintosh.

How many houses have I robbed? I haven't a clue! I've probably forgotten most of the jobs I've done. I guess the ones I remember are the exceptional ones. In terms of the pillage I carried out in the 1960s, rarely was anything left to chance. It was a matter of getting a good haul from someone I'd targeted and then tracked. I knew what I was doing and things seldom went wrong. There was the odd robbery where I didn't get much, but I can still remember it. When Bette Davis was making *Connecting Rooms* in west London at the end of the sixties, I happened to be passing the house they were filming inside as I made my way to a meal with one of my cousins. I was curious and pretended to be a press reporter. I managed to get into the Davis dressing room when she was on the set. I lifted her purse when no one was looking. Later, when I checked inside, I found a wad of cash and a couple of rings. The haul was worth a couple of hundred quid to me, okay for a piece of opportunist thievery but hardly the kind of take I was used to making in my role as cat burglar to the stars.

The way we got in through windows didn't change much from job to job. I had no problems with easy targets — they were still attractive. But I was known to the filth and I knew they were out to get me. At the end of the day, coppers just wanna make arrests and get convictions. They don't care if you're guilty of the crime you go down for. A rozzer who gets a lot of men banged up gets promoted, and the higher you go in a police force, the more money you can make from graft. As you get older you realise that stealing is a hard way to make a living. By the early seventies I was running through so many different outside men I lost count of them. I thought Taters was taking too many risks on central London robberies I refused to participate in, and so I didn't want to work with him. I won't detail all the robberies I can remember doing during this period — it would get boring.

Even in the sixties you could look at pigs of every rank and see they were living way beyond their means — assuming, of course, they had nothing but their official police income to spend. Cops would take money to turn a blind eye to illegal clubs, money to leave brothels unmolested, money to fail to solve a crime or convict the wrong man; in fact they'd take money for anything you could think of. Now if you had money you could pay off the coppers and have an easy life. Or in the case of the Flying Squad, for a split of the money, they had half the bank robbers in London working on their behalf. If you spent Friday night in the Eagle pub on the Farringdon

Road, you could watch the bent coppers telling armed robbers who was doing what job.

In the aftermath of the swinging sixties, the underworld had become increasingly organised and the cops controlled much of it. I figured it would almost be easier to work for a living than carry on being a burglar, since as a matter of principle I didn't want to be beholden to the filth. Besides which, furs were beginning to go out of fashion and the prices paid for them dropped. I decided to quit my life of crime right at the end of 1972, after being nicked leaving a house in Culross Street in possession of a jewel case belonging to the lady who lived there. I got in through an open window and as I came out the same way I ran into a squad of the old bill who had been called in to deal with a nearby bank robbery. Plain bad luck, but at least I wasn't done for breaking and entering. Just thieving.

My brother Dai appeared once again in my dreams and told me I'd done all I could to hit back at the rich. He said it was time to retire. I knew it wasn't really Dai; I guess a shrink would say it was my subconscious mind, but I still figured the advice was good. When I went up before the magistrate I asked him to give me a chance. I couldn't believe it when I got off with a two-year suspended sentence in early 1973. At 56 I was too old for crime, so I decided to give it a rest and get a regular job. A younger generation had taken over from me. Cat burglars—and in particular safecrackers—had become yesterday's men. We'd been replaced at the top of the criminal hierarchy by armed bandits.

Had the Flying Squad not had the bank robbery game stitched up, I may well have been tempted to get involved with it despite my dislike of guns. London's bent coppers only worked with guys who'd already proved they had the bottle to carry off armed raids, and those who'd got involved in this were the social end product of the post-war borstals. From the late forties through to the sixties, a lot of the scum attempting to grind down young offenders had been plucked straight out of the army. These screws identified with our rulers and wanted to crush the British working class in exactly the same way they'd helped smash the Nazis. They hated the welfare state and for no good reason combined this resentment with a completely false view of themselves as being better than the ordinary working man and woman.

You know the type: lower-middle-class ejits who worshipped authority but were also filled with anger that those who had less than them had failed to adopt bourgeois values. So all these borstal screws wanted to do was make life miserable for the kids who'd been placed in their so-called care. Some philosopher once said, "that which doesn't kill me makes me stronger" and that's exactly what happened to the generation of thieves who went through borstal in the 1950s. They learnt to hate authority from the very bottom of their hearts, and were resolved to defy it no matter what the consequences.

If you can't grasp this then you'll never understand the mentality of the bank robbers of the sixties and seventies. They made a lot of dough and didn't even have to go through a fence or anyone else before they were able to enjoy this money. But at the same time those armed bandits risked being buried alive. The courts were handing out thirty-year sentences for crimes against property in which no one was killed, when murderers were getting off with a fifteen-year tariff. That's proof enough of the fact that capitalism is a practical religion of money worship, and that the bourgeoisie value their own property over human life. Eventually the courts had to change their sentencing policies because they were encouraging armed robbers who used their weapons as frighteners to kill if things went wrong. It was stupid that they weren't going to get a heavier sentence if they murdered someone than if they'd used psychology to blag a load of cash without hurting a fly.

The mindset of going into a bank and doing it over for readies always struck me as having a lot of similarities with stepping into a boxing ring. The start of the set-to was all about timing and psyching your opponent out. Armed gangs would rush into a bank and the frightener among them would blast a bullet or two into the ceiling with a sawn-off shotgun. The idea was to shock those in the building into submission. The other members of the raiding party had to act fast, getting behind the tills by whatever means necessary. When glass separated the public and private sides of a bank, there was usually a gap at the top. I really admired those guys who had the athletic skills to vault onto the counter and through the gap at the top of the glass. If I'd been doing bank robberies that would have been my job; I wouldn't have wanted to be putting the frighteners on the staff and customers with a shooter. The final task of the bandit is to grab cash and get out as fast as possible. The whole thing is a psychodrama, and it is over in a few minutes.

Similar tactics were deployed by armed robbers when they went up before the beak. They'd joke and sing and generally demonstrate their contempt for the proceedings going on around them. The upper classes never understood this; they just didn't get that the whole motivation of the armed bandit was defiance of authority, not making money. Since property and money are sacred cows in capitalist societies, armed robbery was a perfect way to express disrespect for this exploitative system.

That's why burglars like me, as well as bank robbers, ran through money as fast as they could steal it. We weren't interested in improving our position in society, we wanted to live in a different world entirely, one in which every last man, woman and child was valued for themselves rather than treated as a cog in the capitalist wealth-generating machine. That said, I still considered it a mug's game to be doing robberies with shooters. If your gang has guns there's always gonna be someone who'll be tempted to let one off — and let's face it, when you're doing banks and post offices, the type of person likely to be killed is a clerk on sod-all a year, or a little old lady collecting her pension, rather than some bourgeois pig. I never robbed with a gun because I'd have been ashamed of myself if an everyday member of the working class had copped it as a result of my activities.

As I've already said, upon my retirement from crime I was 56 years old and had a record as long as your arm, even if most of it was fit-ups. And don't forget that in January 1972, just twelve months before I bowed out of the burglary game, UK unemployment topped the one million mark for the first time since the 1930s. Tory prime minister Edward Heath didn't seem that bothered about this, but Labour MPs went bonkers and their catcalls led to a ten-minute suspension of debate in the House of Commons.

I didn't exactly have employment opportunities beckoning me but I knew market stalls; as I said earlier, I'd been a fruit buyer before the war. I also had a good knowledge of jewellery, and while you don't sell top-class sparklers off a stall, there was plenty of call for cheap bracelets, rings and brooches in the early seventies. I didn't want to go and work in Hatton Garden as I had briefly for George Mizel in the fifties, since even if I could get an in with a legitimate jeweller, there was too great a risk of being left holding stolen gems and having the old bill do me for thieving or receiving them.

I set up in Ridley Road, Dalston, and became my own boss. I'd rise early and go for a jog, then get the stall up and running in the morning and work through to the afternoon. I was able to take the day off if I had something else to do, or knock off early if I'd taken plenty of money and was running low on stock. I enjoyed being my own boss. After all the years I'd been a cat burglar, I don't think I'd have taken well to somebody else ordering me about. I didn't need much and I made enough money to keep myself in house and home. Anything extra went on the horses and dogs — gambling was the only thing left in my life that generated a bit of excitement. There were games of cards with friends too but the stakes were always small. Once I stopped thieving I couldn't afford to visit the spielers that had provided me with so many thrills throughout my time as a master criminal.

The best thing about being on the stall was the socialising. You got to know the other traders, as well as your regular customers. You could always have a joke and there was plenty of music in the street, so I'd sing along when I felt like it. I didn't even mind the early starts, and I'd bob and weave behind my stock; that way I got a bit of exercise shadow boxing when I wasn't selling something. There was loads I could do in the workout line, from running on the spot to turning somersaults and doing stretches. Sometimes I even took my skipping rope down to Ridley Road and got some hardcore exercise instead of just the lighter stuff.

Skipping was a great way of attracting customers actually, since a lot of people suffer from the misapprehension that it is a pastime for girls. I'd always put them right by explaining I was an ex-boxer and that it was a great way to stay on form if you were into my sport. Not only did it massively raise your heartbeat and keep your cardio fitness up, it improved your coordination. I'd mix everything around with both single and double jumps per swing, going forward and backwards, then I'd throw in the odd trick such as adding a press-up or handstand to my rope routine.

However, I couldn't jump rope all day because I had customers to serve and I needed their money! Fortunately you don't need to skip all day to keep fit. I did it in bursts as a kind of interval training. I'd get plenty of laughs when I did jumping jacks too, since this was an exercise that people associated with girl's physical education at school. But a boxer knows that the way to win a fight is to keep their fitness level up, and although I wasn't going into the ring any more, I was determined to stay in shape and not degenerate into a shuffling old man. I found exercising behind the stall gave me a nice line in patter too. Rather than trying to cover up the fact that I'd been the world's greatest jewel thief, I played off it.

"You may be surprised to see a market stall trader working out the way I do," ran my spiel, "but actually it has served me well in all my years as a jewel thief. I've robbed the rich and famous and that's why I'm able to offer you bargain jewellery here. To climb across walls and rooftops you need to be fit, and to outrun the old bill you need lots of stamina too. I've trained long and hard but I've been well rewarded for taking a professional approach to crime. In single raids I've taken jewels worth more than a hundred and fifty grand. Because I've been so successful, you're probably asking yourself why I've got a market stall in Ridley Road. My story for the filth is that I've gone straight, but what I'll tell you is that I'm sick of fences taking none of the risks and most of the profits. So check out my stall and maybe you'll get yourself the bargain of the century. It's my prices and not my goods that look cheap."

This sort of sales talk got me plenty of laughs and brought in the punters too. Some of them might have believed my outrageous pitches but I wasn't gonna worry about that. I went for low-price items with a touch of quality about them, not junk, so I wasn't ripping anyone off. And I got some good patter back too; Brian, the bloke with the record stall across from mine, often used to help me out by trading jokes with me.

"Oi, Ray!" Mister Groove would shout. "I hope you're not planning to prowl across my rooftop and come in through my bedroom window to give me missus some extramarital passion while I'm down the pub. It's me that's supposed to be having a night on the tiles, so I don't want you coming across my slates to do your tomcat act with me trouble and strife."

"Sorry mate," I'd holler back, "I can't offer you any guarantees in that department. Don't you know I hold the world heavyweight title for bed-hopping!"

I'd also have people asking if they could join in my exercise sessions. A few even enjoyed it, but most couldn't keep up with me. More than one woman who found my boot camp-style workout too exhausting to contemplate took my fitness level as an indication that I was a world-class sexual athlete.

"Hey superman," a feisty bottle blonde called Sandra used to say to me virtually every time she passed my stall, "if I let you have a bunk up will you fly me to the moon between my first and second orgasm?"

"Don't worry darlin'," I'd reassure her, "when I slip you my salami you'll be so overwhelmed by pleasure that anyone seeing your face will think you're bobbin' for cock."

I had to explain the phrase "bobbin' for cock" to Sandra. I'd learnt it from my cousin Julie, who as I've already explained helped me out with some unusual criminal connections back in the sixties. I still saw her, but not too often as she was deep into the drug scene. The term "bobbin' for cock" invoked a junkie nodding off with their mouth open, since this looks rather like someone performing fellatio.

We'd have a right bubble bath down Ridley Road market, and it would take a whole book just to retell all the jokes I heard when I was on my stall. The social aspect of the work was something I really enjoyed, and I pulled in enough cash to see to all my material needs. As I've already made clear, any excess profits went to bookies. It goes without saying I lost more than I won but I had fun doing the money. And then there was the pools and the odd boxing match I'd take a punt on too. So I wasn't short of things to do when I was away from my stall. I settled down to life in east London and saw less of my extended family coz I wasn't travelling around the way I used to. I was no longer going over to west London to check in with Uncle Dinny and my cousins on a regular basis, because selling jewellery direct to the public kept me really busy. Still, I saw my family every now and then.

The fact that I didn't have a phone made me hard to get hold of at short notice. Just as the craze for kung fu was taking off in Europe, my cousin Dennis came and collected me from my stall one afternoon — so that I could have an encounter with a con man who claimed to have mastered the vibrating palm. Dim Mak, sometimes also known as quivering palm, was supposedly an ancient Chinese art by which you killed your enemies with gentle touches to pressure points.

According to those taken in by Dim Mak, victims could be tapped lightly on the chest by a master of the vibrating palm, and then die from this death touch three days or even three weeks later, depending upon how it had been applied.

A martial arts faker styling himself Lord Chaucer was offering his services to my Uncle Dinny, saying he would help him out in his protection rackets, although I guess ultimately he was hoping to take them over. Dennis explained everything as I packed up my stall and then as he drove me over to Paddington to collect his dad. The three of us went on to Lord Chaucer's dojo in Kensal Rise. Lord Chaucer was dressed in a black cloak and was carrying a silver-topped cane when we arrived at his headquarters. He was also more than a little tubby and spoke with a squeaky London accent. He had mouse brown hair and washed-out blue eyes.

Dinny explained that I was a relative who used to box professionally, and that if Chaucer could get the better of me in a fight then he would have proved the power of his Dim Mak techniques. I knew from the off the guy was gonna be a walkover. For a start, Dim Mak had its origins in Chinese swordplay novels and didn't work outside of books and movies. Chaucer made a truly miserable attempt at psyching me out by saying that he could cripple me without even touching my body, by interfering with its electrical elements from a distance. He demonstrated this "secret fighting art" on some of his students, who were obviously feigning being disabled before they could get within five feet of their master, and were then theatrically revived by the instructor.

"Do you realise that by taking me on you are putting yourself in grave danger?" Lord Chaucer asked me. "I know how to revive you, but if you were left unaided after I'd used one of my deadly knockout techniques on you then you would die!"

"Sure," I said. "But the thing is, it ain't gonna be you who KO's me, it's me who's gonna flatten you. And I don't have any secret techniques to revive you, but I guess one of your students can just go call an ambulance."

"I won't need an ambulance," the con man insisted.

I took my shirt off. The Dim Mak master had removed his cloak before demonstrating his fraudulent fighting style on his students. As he had with his disciples, Chaucer made some funny passes with his hands but they had no effect on me coz I knew what he was doing was a sham. I just charged right in on the twerp while he was wasting his time with his counterfeit moves designed to intimidate opponents mentally, but that were utterly useless on anyone who saw through his phony claims about them. Before he knew what had hit him, I'd hooked the bogus spiritual boxer from the right. He crumpled up like a sack of potatoes dropped from a great height, and I proceeded to stomp on his face.

Clowns like Chaucer left me feeling sick. They wanted to pretend they were hardmen but weren't prepared to do the rigorous training that would make them what they claimed to be. The twit deserved the beating I'd given him because he was stupid enough to challenge me before he'd mastered any effective art of self-defence. I spat in his bloodied face, put my shirt back on, then motioned to Dinny and Dennis we should leave. My uncle could see that working on protection with a Dim Mak master would be a waste of time. We had a good laugh about it afterwards over a meal.

I don't want to be misunderstood here. I've got nothing against kung fu and karate as sports, or in the movies. Indeed, I still think Bruce Lee is one of the greatest film stars of all time — as well as a top-class martial artist. He trained hard and he knew how to fight, and in fact on camera he had to slow down his moves because otherwise cinemagoers would have missed them. What I don't like are Sexton Blakes like Lord Chaucer who aren't prepared to put in the sweat and toil necessary to become a real warrior, but nonetheless feel at liberty to go around claiming to have mastered the world's deadliest fighting secrets. And I might as well add that while high kicks can look great in a dojo or on a movie screen, only a mug would attempt to use them in a street fight.

EIGHT

It ain't easy going straight and it didn't surprise me when, the very year I set up my market stall, bent old bill started giving me grief. A couple of Met muppets claimed robberies were being pulled all over London that looked like my work. I think they must have got home drunk one night and seen the old Alfred Hitchcock movie *To Catch a Thief* on TV. I'd seen it too. The film stars Grace Kelly as a rich American. Male lead Cary Grant plays a retired cat burglar who has to catch the person lifting sparklers in his own inimitable style, coz if he don't come up with a body then the filth say they're gonna nick him for the creeping. The premise is stupid since no self-respecting crook would do the old bill's work for them. I'm not the only ex-crim who can't stand a snout, a slag, a nark, a canary, a grass, a squealer—call him or her what you will, a budgie is always beneath contempt.

As I hope these memoirs have made clear, cat burglary is largely a matter of getting in through unsecured doors or jemmying a window open. The mode of attack is determined by the target. On the whole, there isn't a trademark style of housebreaking. That said, a professional will go in when people are eating their evening meal, an amateur — and more often than not that's a junkie or a drunk — will rob folk while they're asleep. There are differences of approach but no unmistakable signatures.

I had to play along with my tormentors and their celluloid fantasies. But I immediately had them down as a couple of crooked cops, and called them The Flowerpot Men, coz they shared their first names with the characters from the children's TV series of that name. They'd first come and hassled me on a day when I was closing my market stall up early, and made me sit with them after I'd packed up over cups of tea in one of Dalston's many cafes. They knew I had a suspended sentence hanging over me, and if I was convicted for anything at all then I'd be banged up.

"Look Ray," Bill told me, "we'll give you a break."

"Never give a sucker an even break." Ben played the tough cop and simultaneously confirmed my belief that he spent most of his free time pissed and watching old movies.

"Ray's not a sucker," Bill chirped, "he knows that we could plant some diamonds on him, and nick him right now. So if he ain't behind these thefts he'd better come up with a thief for us to take to court."

"And how would I do that?" I demanded.

"We reckon whoever is doing the climbing has a snout at the Premium Insurance Company. We have a list of the owners of the sparklers on their books, and the robberies have been committed in a clear sequence — starting with the jewels that were worth the most money and working on downwards."

"So," I laughed, "I suppose you're gonna give me a copy of the list so that I can watch the properties and catch the culprit red-handed."

"What's so funny about that?" Bill replied.

"Oh nothing, absolutely nothing," I assured him.

I wasn't going to let on but to me the whole thing stank to high heaven. This didn't stop me accepting the insurance company's papers when they were proffered. I knew there was something very wrong with what I was being told to do, I just needed to figure it all out.

"The thief has done the first four places on the list, so you need to keep an eye on the Hampstead home of the Berg-Watsons, who are next in line."

"Okay chief," I told Detective Plod. "And, just for the record, is your mate a Grace Kelly fan?"

"What's it to you if I am?" Ben snapped.

"If you want my tuppence-worth she looks like a dragged-up bit of plastic with no screen presence and I wouldn't give her a poke with someone else's dick. The marriage to Prince Rainier was ridiculous. Monaco isn't a country — it's a tax haven. I can't dig her as a film star, and it should go without saying that the very existence of royalty and princesses angers me."

"I don't want your smart-arse opinions, so shut it and do what we say or you'll be in deep shit."

"Okay, okay."

I let the old bill leave before me. I didn't want to be seen in the street with them. After that I went to see John James who'd hung around in Jermyn Street back in the day, and who I knew had been blackmailing Michael Connaughton-Hodgkins of the Premium Insurance Company. I was lucky, because James was leaving his Islington flat as I arrived. He wasn't happy to see me, but a hard punch to the gut not only had him doubled over, it also persuaded him he'd like to invite me into his home.

"Okay scumbag, unless you want me to beat the crap out of you then give me what you've got on Connaughton-Hodgkins, and it better be everything or I'll be back, and when I return I won't be so friendly."

"It's in a safe deposit box," James told me.

"Well we'd better go and get it."

We arrived at a West End bank just before closing time and retrieved various photographs and documents. Connaughton-Hodgkins had been a bit of a naughty boy. There were photographs of him having sex with more than a dozen different prostitutes, and various compromising documents that provided proof he'd been embezzling funds from the company he ran. I was alone in the vault with James, so I tapped him playfully on the head before addressing him.

"I want the photographic negatives and the second set of copies you must have made of these papers."

James opened another safety deposit box and handed over the things I'd asked for.

"How am I supposed to make a living if you take all this stuff?"

"This is just one fella you're blackmailing. Let's have a look at what else you got in those boxes."

James had compromising snaps of all sorts of public and not-so-public figures, not to mention numerous confidential documents. He wasn't gonna be short of a bob or two just coz

I'd taken the dirt he had on Connaughton-Hodgkins. I left James to stew in his own juices, and went on a tour of various London pubs. Obviously I wasn't drinking, I was looking out for information on any creepers who were thought to have had a good tickle or two in recent weeks. One name from my past kept cropping up. Those using it tended to be apologetic, but I told them I was retired and prepared to let bygones be bygones. I even said I wanted it to be widely known I was now extending the hand of friendship to all my old enemies.

I went to bed a reasonably contented man, woke early, and had to wait until 9am before I could use a call box to phone the Premium Insurance Company to make an urgent appointment to see Michael Connaughton-Hodgkins. At first his secretary told me he was out. When I informed her to tell him I'd been passed a bunch of documents by John James he was on the blower double quick. Connaughton-Hodgkins wanted to see me right away, and no doubt had me down as another blackmailer. I didn't put him straight about that on the dog and bone; it was better to resolve this matter in his office.

On my way to the insurance company's City headquarters, I clocked a billboard emblazoned with the slogan: "Plant A Tree In '73". Underneath, some wag had added: "Buy a saw in '74!" Would you believe that the UK Government had declared 1973 "National Tree Planting Year"? They'd sponsored a campaign to encourage people to plant trees that year under the "Plant A Tree In '73" catchphrase. This was at a time when a virulent strain of Dutch elm disease was sweeping the country, killing millions of trees. When people talk about the early and mid-seventies in London these days, they all too often forget about the crazy government propaganda that confronted the population wherever they turned. There was even an official 9p "Plant A Tree" commemorative stamp issued by the Royal Mail. But the cynicism of the graffiti under the poster bearing that official slogan sums up the whole era for me.

"Look," I told Connaughton-Hodgkins after being shown into his office, "I'm a retired criminal and I'm not here to blackmail you. In fact, I'm here to put an end to that."

I threw several items I'd confiscated from John James onto Connaughton-Hodgkins's desk. He looked at them incredulously for a few moments, then swept the lot into his briefcase.

"What do you want?" Connaughton-Hodgkins's voice was trembling and his whole body was shaking as he said it.

"I'm being hassled by some bent cops, and I reckon you've been tipping them off about clients of yours to be robbed in return for a small cut of the proceeds. Like you being blackmailed, it has to stop. The old bill are threatening to charge me with the crimes and they've handed me a list of your top clients. I understand the four with the most valuable gems have been burgled..."

"Not the first four," Connaughton-Hodgkins corrected. "Our five top clients. But the police have asked us to keep quiet about the last burglary because the family concerned are abroad and we don't want to alarm them. So not even they know about it."

I didn't have to tell Connaughton-Hodgkins what was going down; I could see from the way he looked at me that the penny had dropped. The Flowerpot Men had told me to stake out the address to nab the thief—but if I'd gone anywhere near it, either they or some of their pig mates would have nicked me and tipped the stolen jewels in my pocket. The insurance company wouldn't argue the toss about the date of the theft in court, they'd simply be happy that they didn't have to pay out for a loss. I'd never had the slightest intention of going anywhere near the Berg-Watson home, despite what I'd told Bill and Ben.

"As you can see," I explained to the suit, "the thief is just working their way down the list. I want you to get all your big clients who haven't been done over to replace the jewels they keep at home with paste copies. They'll need to secure the genuine items in safety deposit boxes somewhere."

"If you'd suggested we keep them in the company safe," Connaughton-Hodgkins smiled as he said it, "I'd have concluded you were the thief trying to get me to place all the items together so you could grab them in a single raid!"

"You're a sly one!" I laughed. "But will you advise your clients to do what I'm suggesting?"

"You've saved my bacon, so of course I'll do it!"

"And you don't know who the thief is coz you're just working with the cops who are putting him onto the jobs?"

"That's right."

"So I really do need you to bait my trap with paste copies."

"Yes."

"Does the name Peter Scott ring any bells with you?"

"No."

"And you do realise that I haven't given you everything I took from John James?"

"Taken onboard."

"And that if you don't stick up for me if I have any problems over any of this, then the photographs I still have will find their way to your wife, and the documents to your shareholders?"

"Yes."

After a bit more banter with Connaughton-Hodgkins, I left a happy man and spent much of the day betting on the dogs at the Hackney Wick Stadium in Waterden Road. My market stall trading had kept me away from racing at the Wick. The best time to go was on a Saturday morning, but a weekday afternoon still provided top-flight sporting entertainment. The greyhounds straining in the slips and then running out was a sight to make any betting man's heart pound. I lost more than I won, but I had fun. I fortified myself against the losses with strong cuppas from the tea bar after laying my money down.

Bill and Ben visited me the next day. They wanted to know why I'd not been staking out the house they'd told me to look after. I told them I'd had a bit of a row with some former associates and couldn't do anything until that was sorted out. The Flowerpot Men understood what I was saying but weren't happy with it. They said if it took more than a week to conclude my business I'd be in real trouble, and I was to let them know the minute I was free to do the bit of work they'd been bending my arm about. I assured them that the battles I was involved in wouldn't take long to resolve and they left me in temporary peace.

A few days later Peter Scott turned up at my stall to tell me how glad he was to hear from mutual friends I wanted to let bygones be bygones. Of course that wasn't really why he'd come to see me; the reason for his surprise visit was to complain about Benny Selby refusing to take some jewels that he'd stolen, and telling him they were paste. Now Scott was your typical middle-class dilettante — he didn't know a ruby from a sapphire (it's a question of the colour), and couldn't have told a genuine stone from a fake if his life depended on it. He pulled some paste jewels he'd half-inched the night before out of his coat pocket and I just laughed when he held them out to me in his right palm.

"Sexton Blakes!" I assured him. "What's wrong with your eyes?"

"You know I can't see the difference between a real stone and a copy!"

"In that case you really ought to take up some other line of work."

"I have, I've pretty much gone straight. I'm running a tipper truck, moving muck out of Brent Cross, but I'm doing a few jobs on the side that a couple of bent coppers are tipping me off about. They want three grand a pop for each job I pull, but I can't afford to pay them if all I'm getting are paste copies."

I told Scott to hang around coz I thought I might be able to help him out. I left him minding my stall and used a pay phone to call the cop shop Bill and Ben operated from, telling the switchboard that the two detectives ought to get over to Ridley Road sharpish as I had something they wanted. Scott no doubt thought I was lining up a dumb fence — not that

I told him I was doing this, it was simply what he wanted to believe. Eventually The Flowerpot Men turned up with the intention of giving me the third degree. Obviously if I'd been free to do them the favour they required, then I'd have already been nicked. The bent detectives were expecting delaying tactics and a further excuse, so they were all psyched up to intimidate me. I'd been a naughty boy and failed to stake out the house they'd told me was the next one to be hit by the creeper they were after. Ben tore into me with threats and insults, while Bill kept mum.

"What the fuck 'ave you bin playin' at?" Ben demanded as he approached my stall. "You weren't where you were supposed to be, you no good lump of shit. We told you what drum to stake out and now it's bin robbed."

"It was robbed before you told me about it but I've got the thief here for you, as I promised!" I said, jerking a thumb at Scott.

"Good god almighty!" Ben spluttered as he took in the familiar form of the Belfast Bullshitter. "Wot the fuck are you doin' 'ere?"

"Just passin' the time of day," Scott assured him.

"So you 'aven't told him you're the thief?" Ben snapped.

"You'd have just given the game away if it wasn't already so obvious," I laughed. "You said you wanted me to catch the thief and here he is, and, I might add, acting under your instructions."

"I'll break your balls for this!" Ben thundered.

"I don't think that would be a very good idea," was my rejoinder, "because I went to see Michael Connaughton-Hodgkins the other day. I showed him the copy of the list of his clients you gave me and he recognised it as a document he'd had drawn up especially for you. I didn't tell him how I got it, but if you try and fit me up I'll get him into the court as part of my defence. There really aren't many places I could have got it, so he may have worked out the source already. That's why he got all his top clients to put their jewels in safety deposit boxes, and told them to keep cheap imitations in their homes. So from your point of view it is best to let sleeping dogs lie, and go looking for other targets."

"Fuck," Ben screamed. "Fuck, fuck, fuck! You got your hands on the blackmail material John James has been using on him, haven't you!"

"Look," I said, "let's all be gentlemen and forget everything."

"That sounds like a good idea," Scott chipped in, "coz all I got on my last raid is copies of the jewels we were after, a bunch of fakes."

"I'm gonna get you the gems from the raid you did before that one, so that you can fence them," Ben hissed. "But you'll have to give us six grand of the money for your balls-up in taking the fakes."

"You never told me why you needed that other lot of jewels after the raid," Scott whinged, obviously hurt that the money he'd be pulling in had been mightily reduced to cover tip-offs on two thefts.

"I give out information on a need-to-know basis," Ben thundered, "and you really don't need to know anything except when and where to creep! If you weren't so half-witted you'd be able to work it out for yourself."

"Raymond," Bill put in, "we asked you to find us the thief and you've been as good as your word. Our business is concluded, so there is no need for Ben and I to remain in touch with you."

"And if you know what's good for you, then you'll forget you ever met us!" Ben spat. "Or else!"

The bent cops disappeared into the crowd and that was the last I ever saw of them. Scott left too but I was fated to see him again; I'll get to that later. Once they'd gone I shook my head in disbelief. The Belfast Bullshitter should have learnt his lesson after having to pay off double to the cozzers who'd given him the tip about the Sophia Loren jewels.

Just before The Flowerpot Men attempted to disrupt my life, the UK had joined the European Economic Community. This didn't make much difference to me, and I didn't have any strong views on the matter since I'd always believed the working class had no country. Still, I came across plenty of Little Englanders who thought membership of the EEC was a nightmare threat to the so-called British way of life. I've never paid people with such views much attention coz they were deluded fools. I got a lot more excited when an IRA car bomb blew up outside the Old Bailey in March 1973. Given that it was the cop fit-up against me at this venue in 1940 that set me off on my life of crime, I saw it as a very legitimate target. And while I didn't believe in national boundaries, if we had them then Ireland was clearly to be treated as one unit — don't forget my maternal family roots were in Cork, even if I was a Welshman. That said, when it comes down to it I don't believe terrorism is progressive either; we need to struggle as a whole class against the bourgeoisie, not indulge in elitist paramilitary actions.

Despite my rational objections to terrorism, I couldn't stop my heart from leaping with joy when I heard the Central Criminal Court had been bombed. That doesn't mean I didn't hate it when this IRA mainland campaign resulted in ordinary men and women being maimed and murdered. For very different reasons, my heart sank just two weeks after the Old Bailey explosion when I heard about the Lofthouse Colliery disaster, where sudden and unexpected flooding led to seven Yorkshire miners losing their lives. Moving on, aside from the rising tide of industrial unrest, for me the real highlights of 1973 were the Joe Frazier fights. He lost his world heavyweight boxing title to George Foreman at the beginning of the year, and that July had an incredible match in London, which he won against Joe Bugner. But all of this is really leading me towards 1974, coz at the beginning of the year Frazier and Muhammad Ali slugged it out in a non-title fight in New York. Ali, who'd lost against Frazier in 1971, won that one and their third and last match — 1975's "Thrilla in Manila". These bouts kept me on the edge of my seat when I watched them with friends on the telly.

But let's wind back to the very start of 1974, when the Tories introduced the Three-Day Week to conserve electricity in the face of industrial action by the miners. Businesses only had a power supply for three days because the miners were working to rule in protest against wage caps imposed by the government. When the lights went out during power cuts it made me especially proud of those working men still doing what I'd done upon leaving borstal. A popular slogan of the day ran: "turn something on for the miners!" I always left the lights on in my flat when I went out, to show my support for my mining comrades. The Three-Day Week lasted until the beginning of March, and in the first of two general elections that year, Tory leader Ted Heath asked the rhetorical question: "who governs the country, me or the miners?" Heath was ousted as prime minister, so he had his answer and it wasn't the one this worthless fart expected.

For me personally, life went on pretty much as usual at the market stall. The early rise necessitated by my self-employment did nothing for my love life. I had the odd one-night stand but found no one who could replace my ex-wife Ann. I wasn't lonely, there were plenty of people about the market with whom I socialised, but there was never anyone special. That said, in the late summer of 1975 there was one lady who showed a lot of interest in me. She told me her name was Marion Smith and, to be honest, from the moment she first approached my stall I found it difficult to understand why a middle-class woman in her twenties would want to hang onto the every word of a working-class geezer who was pushing sixty. Still, I was curious to discover just what the attraction was; although had Marion not been such a good-looking girl, I may not have bothered. Normally I couldn't be arsed dealing with posh women because they'd fault everything I did, but with Marion it just seemed like I couldn't put a foot wrong. She kept coming down the stall and buying bits and pieces, and would hang around after making a purchase to chat.

"Tell me Ray," Marion said on the third day in a row on which she'd appeared in Ridley Road, "just what is it that a girl has to do to get a date with you?"

"Try asking me out to have a fun time at York Hall watching boxing or down Hackney Wick for the dog racing!"

"I don't like sport."

"What, not even bedroom athletics?" I joshed.

"What time do you pack up?"

"I can knock off any time I like, it's my stall and I'm my own boss."

"Do you like love in the afternoon?"

"I like it morning, noon and night."

"So can we go back to your place now?"

"Why my place? I'm sure yours is nicer."

"I wanna see how you live," Smith told me.

"My flat is spartan and it's in Stamford Hill."

"I don't mind," Marion insisted. Then added: "Shall I go and buy a bottle of something while you pack up?"

"If you wanna drink get something for yourself, I'm teetotal," I replied.

"Have you done AA?"

"Never. I've not touched a drop my entire life. As you know, when I was younger I was a professional boxer; booze is bad for your form."

It was 3pm and I'd flogged enough cheap jewellery to keep a roof over my head and food on my table, so I tidied everything up. I sold more during the lunch hour than at any other time of day, and trade tended to slacken off later in the afternoon as the stalls gradually disappeared from the street. So ending my day just then didn't adversely affect my takings.

Marion came back to find me standing in the empty spot where my stall had been. She had a bottle of red wine in a plastic carrier. We took a bus to my flat. I didn't have that much in my drum. Beyond the items I needed to clean my teeth, plus soap, a towel and a mat, there wasn't anything else in the bathroom. The toilet had nothing in it beyond a bog brush and loo roll. The kitchen was pretty empty too, a few cans of food and some tea in a cupboard, a kettle, two mugs, a couple of plates, two knives, two forks, two spoons, two pans, a can opener. I didn't even have a fridge, so I used milk powder when I made a cuppa. I sat Marion down in the lounge, one sofa and one chair, a radio, no TV. When I wanted to watch sport I went round to the betting shop or to a friend's pad.

"Sorry," I said handing her a mug, "I don't have any glasses so this will have to do."

"You're an old lag, aren't you!" Smith was obviously thrilled by this observation.

"Yeah, how did you know?"

"I just have to look at your place to know that. There's nothing in here, so I figure you must have spent a lot of time in institutions. Since you're obviously not mad and you're too rebellious to have cut it in the army, it must have been prisons."

"Very astute."

"Have you got a bottle opener?"

"No."

"In that case I'll get the cork out with my nail scissors. Once I've had a drink let's go through to the bedroom."

When we got onto my single bed ten minutes later, what happened wasn't subtle, but then it didn't need to be. We were both extremely familiar with the fundamental differences between a man and a woman, and knew how to give each other a good time. I was glad I'd kept myself in shape. Marion screamed out in pleasure as I gave her orgasm after orgasm, and even after I'd spent my load she couldn't keep her hands off my well-defined physique.

"How do you keep your body like this?"

"I work out and I eat plenty of protein, not too much fat or carbohydrate and very little sugar."

"Are you a health nut?"

"I wouldn't say that, I just like to stay in shape, but I'm not a laziness nut. You can only grow jowls by sitting on a fat arse."

"You're funny!"

"You are too. What is it you actually want from me?"

"Tell me about your cousin Julie, the one living in the Tottenham Court Road squat right now."

"Julie's back in London?"

"Yes."

"Last I heard she'd returned to Wales."

"Well she's back in London, and she's living with Bruno but seeing other guys. Her old flame Grainger amongst others, but there are a few of them."

"You know a lot about my cousin."

"I'm sure you know more."

"I don't know if I do."

"Before you retired from housebreaking did she put you in touch with guys to work with?"

"Julie's not into housebreaking. She does some fraud and dipping but mostly she's around drugs and johns."

"And figures like Michael X."

"She told me she knew Michael X."

"She didn't introduce you to him?"

"What is this? Are you a cop?"

"No, I'm not a cop."

"In that case what are you?"

"If I tell you, will you play straight with me?"

"Depends."

"On what?"

"On what you tell me."

"What do you wanna hear?"

"The truth."

"You sure?"

"If you tell me you're an undercover cop I think I'll throw up! The thought of having sex with the filth makes me feel sick. But I wanna know the truth regardless. So shoot!"

"I work for the *Evening Chronicle*. I'm an investigative journalist."

"In that case what are you doing here?"

"I got a tip-off that Michael X organised the 1971 robbery of Lloyds Bank in Baker Street, and that through your cousin Julie he got you in on the team."

"Whoever told you that must have been on LSD or some other psychedelic drug! I did burglaries not bank robberies!"

"Come on, it wasn't an armed robbery, they tunnelled into the bank!"

"Yes, and I usually went up ladders to get into the bedrooms of the rich! There's a world of difference between that and the theft from the Lloyds Bank deposit boxes!"

"Well people are saying you were involved and Michael X organised the team."

"You hear all sorts of stuff about Michael X at the moment because it's only a few months since he was hanged for murder in Trinidad."

"And your cousin's on-off boyfriend Grainger was staying at the Michael X commune in Trinidad when Gale Benson was killed."

"Julie told me about that. It's got nothing to do with me, or her! We weren't there!"

"But you have a family connection to Michael X."

"My cousin knew him, I never met the man."

"Are you sure?"

"Of course I'm sure. He was all over the papers in the sixties and early seventies as the pre-eminent black power leader in England. I know who he was. I know what he looked like from seeing his picture in the linens. If Julie had introduced me to him then I'd remember it. I like my cousin but I don't really go for her bohemian crowd. I don't even drink, so I'd hardly be interested in their drug scene. And anyway, why would Michael X want to rob a bank?"

"Before he rose to prominence as a black power leader, he was involved in small-time crime. That carried on after he became famous, mainly drugs. And don't forget he returned to Trinidad to avoid an assault charge in London. Then there are the murders. Why wouldn't he be involved in a bank robbery?"

"Because thefts like the Baker Street bank robbery are carried out by professionals who know how to do that type of crime. Michael X wouldn't have had a clue."

"He could have recruited the necessary professionals…"

"Come on, get a grip, this is ridiculous."

"We've been told he wasn't just after money. One of the safety deposit boxes contained pictures of Princess Margaret having sex and he wanted to use them to blackmail the establishment."

"Yeah, sure, and another of the safety deposit boxes possibly contained pictures of the Pope doing drugs, and Michael X may have planned to use them to blackmail the Vatican!"

"You've really never met Michael X and weren't in on the Lloyds Bank safety deposit box robbery?"

"No, nothing to do with me."

"You're sure."

"Of course I'm sure."

"Cross your heart and hope to die?"

"This is ridiculous. That robbery took place six months after Michael X fled from Britain and he couldn't have organised it from Trinidad. That would be too complicated!"

"Are you sure you're right about the chronology you've just given me?"

"Haven't you checked it yourself?"

"No."

"Well that was a bit bloody stupid of you. Do it. Someone's been telling you porky pies."

"I parted with a few quid of the paper's cash for that information, and the stuff about you and your cousin."

"You've been had."

"I suspect you're right."

"So I guess I won't be seeing you again!"

"Don't be silly, you're great in bed."

We had a bit of a giggle about how we'd ended up in the sack. It was funny and ridiculous. I saw Marion a few more times, and since she'd checked out my flat and discovered I was a non-story on the Baker Street bank robbery front, we always ended up at her far more comfortable pad in Islington. But to be honest my heart wasn't really in relationship mode, and I didn't want to be going out with a woman young enough to be my daughter, so as the year turned and we entered 1976 I found myself resolutely single once again.

For me, by the late seventies one year felt pretty much like the next. I loved the waves of strikes and workers" militancy that threatened to topple successive governments, but in retrospect we can see that after the oil crisis, from 1974 onwards, the British proletariat suffered a series of defeats. And when Thatcher was elected as Tory prime minister in May 1979 the intensity of bourgeois attacks on our class was further intensified. To my mind the eighties started in the summer of 1979 immediately after Thatcher's election. Another reason that year didn't feel like the rest of the late seventies was my cousin Julie being found dead in her Cambridge Gardens bedsit in west London in December.

Some of Julie's friends thought she'd been murdered, and I was quickly convinced that the old bill had indeed performed one of their cover-ups. I spent a bit of time looking into Julie's death and my conclusions were that she'd probably suffered an accidental heroin overdose. The authorities claimed she'd died from natural causes, which was stuff and nonsense. The coroner system in England and Wales is completely corrupt and there are no checks or balances on it. Often the coroner will take a lead as to what happened from the fuzz, regardless of the actual evidence.

If the authorities had found that my cousin died from an overdose, then there would have been a public inquest and who knows what might have come up. Julie had been harassed and abused by a number of cops, so it may be that low-level police corruption is all the old bill wanted to hide. To avoid an inquest they said Julie was living alone when she was actually back cohabiting with her smack-dealing boyfriend Grainger, and they ignored the fact that she was found dead in her flat by a friend who got in because the door was open and the lights were on. There are loads of other irregularities in what the cops reported, but the details aren't that important. What matters is that they lied to avoid an inquest since all the evidence points to Julie having overdosed.

If you went through Julie's life you'd definitely find things in it that the establishment would have wanted to conceal, since she knew a lot of very rich and famous people and didn't exactly live a life that they'd view as "respectable". That said, my impression is that there was no high-level cover-up over her death. It was most probably low-ranking cops acting without direction from the political establishment — or even their immediate seniors — who decided they didn't want a public inquest into Julie's death (because of what might have been aired during the course of it).

I can't go into all the stories I heard about Julie from her friends after she died, but I'll provide one here to give you a taster of the kind of things I was told. Julie was part of the Christine Keeler set in the early sixties and this group of "good time girls" attracted the amorous attentions of President John F. Kennedy at that time. I know that is true and also that Julie gave birth to a son called Llewellyn nine months after Kennedy's summer 1961 visit to the UK. While the entry for father was left blank on Llewellyn's birth certificate, I was told by some of Julie's friends that he was the illegitimate son of JFK. This is just one of many fantastic stories, which may or may not be true, that I heard about my cousin. She was without doubt an incredible woman but I wasn't convinced by everything her friends told me about her, and to be specific, I don't believe — as they did — that she was murdered.

NINE

The 1980s saw a big change in my life, because at the age of 65, in August 1981, I decided to retire from running my market stall. Since I hadn't paid enough National Insurance, I didn't have a regular pension, and had to claim social security instead. This meant scraping by on a really low income. Nonetheless I didn't see why I shouldn't enjoy a work-free old age like everyone else. There'd been riots all over Britain in the month leading up to my retirement, and rather than finding myself stuck on my stall in Ridley Road, I wanted to witness this upsurge of youthful militancy first-hand.

The most impressive rioting in London that year took place a few months before the nationwide disorder. It occurred in Brixton during April. The anger of the youth was very effectively directed against the cops, although there was also plenty of looting. I really appreciated what the young were doing; offence is the only defence against capitalist oppressors. The Brixton kids were angry about swamp policing in the area and the use of SUS laws—the very thing that had led to me being fitted up for assaulting PC Spratt back in 1937.

I went to loads of political meetings about the riots and at them I picked up innumerable leaflets that explained the politics of the situation far better than I can. Here's a paragraph that I really like from one of those broadsides: "Looting is a natural response to the unnatural and inhuman society of commodity abundance. It instantly undermines the commodity as such, and it also exposes what the commodity ultimately implies: the army, the police and the other specialised detachments of the state's monopoly of armed violence. What is a policeman? He is the active servant of the commodity, the man in complete submission to the commodity, whose job it is to ensure that a given product of human labour remains a commodity, with the magical property of having to be paid for, instead of becoming a mere refrigerator or rifle—a passive, inanimate object, subject to anyone who comes along to make use of it. In rejecting the humiliation of being subject to police, you are at the same time rejecting the humiliation of being subject to commodities."

In 1982 I found myself up before a beak once again, charged on the basis of evidence given to the cops by supergrass Billy Young. I'd known Young at the end of my criminal career and now, in an attempt to get off scot-free for his own crimes, it seemed he was acting as a squealer against anyone he'd ever met who had a criminal conviction. Young was even prepared to talk about corrupt cops, but the authorities weren't very interested in subjects like that. Young put me in the frame as part of a gang who'd been robbing security vans in areas to the north of London during the late seventies and early eighties.

This was ridiculous but presumably Young was covering up for someone else that he — or the authorities — wanted kept well out of the picture. Fortunately I was able to establish good alibis for some of the robberies and the case against me collapsed. Others weren't so lucky and went down. Personally I can't stand a grass and I hope if it hasn't already happened, then someday soon someone with a grudge gets their hands on Young and gives him the beating he so richly deserves. I assume that after giving evidence for the Crown he was provided with a new identity and shipped out to somewhere like Australia to start a new life. If there is any justice in this world, this snout will hate wherever he ended up living and is rotting away there.

The fact that I'd retired from crime never stopped people approaching me and asking if I'd do jobs with or for them. By the beginning of the eighties the stream of offers I received had slowed to a trickle because a lot of people realised I was genuinely out of the burglary game. Nonetheless, despite being found not guilty when dragged before the beak on supergrass "evidence" in 1982, that court appearance resulted in a flood of new criminal work offers. I guess this is because many in the underworld believe there is no smoke without fire. Their view was that if I'd ended up in court once more I must have been doing something, even if it wasn't the crimes I'd been charged with.

I was in my mid-sixties but few people realised this because I didn't look my age. I was fit and several fences thought I might like to do some lucrative creeping for them. I was also asked if I'd like to join a number of armed gangs, and even if I wanted to participate in a raid on the Royal Mint. The strangest offer I got was the opportunity to rob a sperm bank. This came from a man with a limp who buttonholed me as I was placing a bet on a dog at Hackney Wick Stadium.

"You're Ray The Cat ain't-cha!" a bloke in his thirties said as he held out his hand.

"How do you know that?"

"You're a face, people point you out."

"And who would you be?"

"Silent George."

"And what will people tell me about you if I ask around about your form?"

"That I can be trusted and I never talk."

"Sounds good to me."

"So what about stepping to one side now you've placed your bet, somewhere no one will overhear us?"

"What if I'm not interested in knowing about anything that shouldn't be overheard?"

"Do me the favour of listening to me."

"I retired from crime a decade ago."

"You won't get to watch the dog race in peace unless you listen to me."

"Okay, but make it quick. We'll walk to the stands and talk as we go there."

"Have you heard of the Bourn Hall Clinic?"

"Yeah, it's the place in Cambridgeshire set up by Patrick Steptoe and Robert Edwards, the boffins who pioneered IVF treatment for infertile couples."

"Right. In 1978 they were responsible for the birth of Louise Brown, the first ever test tube baby."

"So?"

"They collect eggs from infertile women and sperm from their husbands. I have inside information about a number of rich women who were doing treatment there but haven't gone all the way through with it yet."

"I don't see the angle."

"You have to understand that the husbands of these rich bitches died after producing their sperm samples, but the wives can still have their babies because their spunk is in cold storage at Bourn Hall."

"So what are you planning to do? Steal this sperm and then hold it to ransom?" I was chuckling as I said this.

"Don't laugh!" Silent George hissed. "I'm straight up serious about nicking this spunk and making those rich bitches pay an arm and a leg to get it back."

"And where are you gonna keep it when it's stolen?"

"I've got access to a cold store in Smithfield."

"What about getting it there?"

"Packed amongst ice in a miniature cold storage container."

"Why not just nick it and throw it away, but claim you've preserved it to extort the money?"

"Because there are several of these women and they ain't all gonna cough up at the same time. We have to return the sperm in good nick to all of 'em, except possibly the last to pay."

"I'm not interested."

"Why not?"

"I told you, I've retired from crime."

"But this is foolproof. The women are rich and desperate to have babies by their dead husbands. They'll pay and we'll have no trouble getting the readies from them. They won't dare involve the police; it would endanger the lives of their unborn children."

"I'm still not interested."

"Once I've pulled this job, people will be queuing up to work with me. I'm an experienced blackmailer. All I need is someone to break into the sperm bank and nick the spunk."

"Sorry, I don't do that type of work."

"Well if you change your mind look for me in The Bird-cage in Stoke Newington."

"I don't drink."

"That needn't stop you walking through a pub door."

"Riddle me this: where did the vampire open his savings account?"

"I dunno."

"At a blood bank!"

"Look me up in The Birdcage alright?"

With that Silent George melted into the crowd. I never saw him again, and I heard no more of his scheme to rob the Bourn Hall sperm bank. My guess would be that it was a crime that never got beyond the planning stage. I certainly never clocked a mention of it in the papers, or heard word of it from any of the old lags I spoke to at the dogs or in betting shops. Some of them knew Silent George and told me his criminal speciality was picking up rich married men in gay clubs and public toilets, starting an affair and then threatening to go and spill the beans to his lovers" wives unless they handed him a big wedge of cash.

George's problem was that he was getting older, so he was having less luck getting into the knickers of wealthy married men. As far as blackmail schemes went, the way Silent George operated struck me as not much different to another scam I first heard about in the eighties, a bit of naughtiness that was run as a profitable sideline to a domestic cleaning agency. The agency boss would employ hookers alongside the regular domestics and get them to do the shag nasty with the male head of a household when they were out on their "cleaning" job. Next came the threat that everything would be revealed to the wife unless the victim coughed up a load of dough.

Moving on, I followed political issues closely in the eighties, and of course I put my money where my mouth is and demonstrated in solidarity with various strikes. The one I was most passionate about was the miners" strike, seeing as I'd been a miner when I first got out of borstal. The strike started in March 1984 and I marched in solidarity when there were demos in London. I wasn't at the Battle of Orgreave in June, but the way the old bill brutally attacked strikers there — and at other places too — left me feeling sick to the guts. That said, given my experiences at the hands of the rozzers, nothing these class traitors did surprised me. The strike went on until March 1985 with the miners being defeated by the combined power of the filth and scabs. This rout was a sad day indeed for the working class not just in the UK but the whole world. It was a defeat that left whole communities shattered.

Nonetheless, it was important to keep struggling against the ruling class, and so when the Wapping dispute kicked off in January 1986, I'd be down on the demos against Rupert Murdoch's plans to destroy the print unions in Britain. The protests mostly took place outside the new plant Murdoch's News International group had built well away from the traditional newspaper industry area around London's Fleet Street. For a whole year, I went down to Wapping in east London at least once a week to show my class solidarity and anger; then in February 1987 that strike also collapsed. Which was another bitter blow for the workers of the world.

I had plenty of free time, so my life wasn't all politics in the eighties. I couldn't afford to gamble in the spielers but as I've made clear I still had the odd bet on the dogs and ponies. I also had more time to spend on my exercise regime, so I actually got myself fitter than when I'd been running the market stall. I was doing everything from weights to skipping, and plenty of roadwork too. I probably averaged four hours of training a day, and never did less than three hours" exercise six days a week.

I didn't work out on Saturdays because I liked to go to the dog racing or, if I didn't have the readies for that, to watch the sport on TV with friends. There was the odd woman too, but they were all ships in the night. Try as I might I could never find anyone who could match my ex-wife Ann. She really was the great love of my life. Still, I didn't dwell on the break-up of my marriage; the past couldn't be changed and

I had to live in the present and work towards making a better future for both myself and everyone else on our planet. Nonetheless, when Ann died right at the end of the eighties it broke my heart all over again. From that point on I just lost all interest in women, because I realised there was no longer any possibility of being with the only one who meant the world to me.

It is probably just as well I'd forsaken skirt, because shortly after Ann died Benny Selby got in touch and asked me to go to the south coast with him. My former fence had emphysema and his doctor had told him to take a seaside holiday for the air. I agreed to go to Brighton with Benny on a Saturday, and then spend the week down there with him.

Selby wasn't short of cash and booked us both into the Old Ship Hotel right by the town pier. He was paying and I wasn't complaining! We arrived in Brighton in the afternoon, and that evening in a pub Benny got talking to a couple of hookers who told him they were called Janet and Babs. I'd gone to the toilet and came back to find them at our table; Benny had ordered a fresh round of drinks. Because he didn't want us to look like a pair of old squares, rather than getting me another orange juice Benny had bought me a pint. I could see the logic behind this action, and realised he wanted me to make it look like I was a drinker.

I shook hands with the hookers, before asking Benny for some change to make a phone call. While I was pretending to have an animated conversation with a bookie, I poured three quarters of my drink into an empty glass that was standing nearby. When I returned to our table with my beer pretty much drained, Benny told me we were going back to the Old Ship with the girls. We all went up to the second floor in the lift. Selby took Janet, the younger and better-looking woman, into his room after slipping her companion a score and telling Babs to give me a good time. She followed me into my suite. Seconds later, she'd taken off her shoes and thrown herself across the bed. She looked at me quizzically when I sat down in an easy chair.

"Aren't you gonna take your clothes off and join me?" Babs mewed.

"No, let's just talk."

"You're a queer one!"

"Nothing wrong with that, but the real reason I'm not interested in you is because the only woman I've ever loved is my wife Ann."

"Where's she?"

"Sadly, she's in her grave."

"Ever heard that one-liner about necrophilia?" Babs cackled.

"Which gag?"

"I used to like fucking corpses until some rotten cunt split on me!"

"Charming!"

"I know some more if you wanna hear them."

"Go on then."

"My grandfather was a dirty bastard. One time he went to a brothel and they sent him upstairs. A couple of minutes later he was back down at the front desk telling the madam that he didn't want the girl she'd given him coz this particular chick was foaming at the mouth. The brothel keeper picked up the phone and called the undertakers, telling them to bring another corpse coz the one they'd left earlier in the day was full up!"

And so it went on, with Babs telling me sick joke after sick joke. She became increasingly hysterical as she did so. I watched her without reacting and eventually she lapsed into silence. I knew something was wrong and I'd guessed what it was before there was a knocking from the hallway. I leapt up and flung the door open, and had hauled Janet into the room before you could say "scarlet harlots". I threw Janet on top of Babs and both women squealed in pain. I don't like hitting women and fortunately there was little need to do so, because they were obviously intimidated by me. I locked the door to the room and slipped the key into my pocket.

"Okay," I said, "I know your game. Slipping johns Mickey Finns to knock them out and then robbing them. You picked on the wrong people. I don't care if you rip off posh cunts, but me and Benny ain't that kind of mug. You'll have to learn not to pick on people like me. Both of you, take off all your clothes."

"What are you gonna do, rape us?" Babs asked.

"No," I told her. "Just strip. I'm gonna give one of you my pyjamas and the other my bathrobe, and you can get home in those."

"We can't do that! Our boyfriends will beat us if we go home without any money for them!" Janet wailed.

"That's your problem. If I was you I wouldn't go back to scum like that. Find yourself better men."

"How come you're still conscious? We slipped enough chemicals into your beer to put an elephant to sleep!" I don't think Babs actually expected an answer to what I took to be a rhetorical question. And I wasn't going to disillusion her if she had me down as some kind of superman.

"Shut up and just do what you're told!"

I slapped Janet across the face with my open palm, and after that she got up and stripped. As I said, I don't like hitting women but I'll do it when it is necessary. Moments later Babs was shedding her clothes too. Without shoes and dressed only for bed, I escorted the two women down to the street. What happened to them wasn't my problem. I just hoped that by leaving them without a penny it discouraged them from going back to their pimps.

I understood why women like Janet and Babs became prostitutes — economic necessity rather than choice — but I couldn't stand men who ponced off women like them. Even when I'd been living with Sarah Dixon back in the 1940s, I'd hustled my own money, not taken hers. Returning to my room I emptied the hookers" pockets, and their handbags. These contained not just Benny's watch and wallet, but items that belonged to other men. I put Benny's items to one side, then bundled up the other valuables and cash and hid this under a sink in one of the hotel's communal toilets. The women's glad rags I threw in the trash.

Next, I broke into Benny's room. I used his bank card to slip the catch, and found him crashed out. I shook him for a good five minutes, but couldn't rouse him. The Mickey Finn he'd imbibed had left him spark out. I put his watch on his bedside table and his wallet in his jacket. I thought there was an outside chance the hookers would tell the old bill I'd robbed them, which is why I didn't want any of their booty in my room. As it happened, they didn't, but there was no point in taking pointless risks. If they'd gone back to their pimps and told them what had happened, then the chances were their so-called protectors wouldn't have the bottle to come after me for what I'd taken from their girls, although they knew where I was for another seven days.

Benny was very sheepish the next day at breakfast, his only consolation for having been left looking like a complete sap being a fantastic night's kip! I gave him the watches, rings and other non-cash items I'd taken from Janet and Babs. Benny wanted to pay me for them but I refused. Knowing I was broke, he'd said he'd cover the cost of my holiday, but fencing the swag I'd given him would more than offset the bill for it — and I still had a big roll of notes burning a hole in my pocket.

Returning to the bigger political canvas, another obnoxious Thatcherite attack on the working class was the change from funding local government by rates charged on property to a poll tax on every member of the population. This came into force in Scotland in 1989, and for England and Wales in 1990. I joined the local Anti-Poll Tax Union in Hackney and this was where I met Michael Morgan, someone who was going to change my life yet again. Michael was of average height, a little overweight and balding. He was an intense bloke in his forties when I met him, and had a righteous sense of injustice, which he'd acquired as a boy growing up Catholic in Northern Ireland.

Mirroring my Welsh lilt, despite living in London for years, Michael's speech still carried strong traces of his native accent. We'd both picked up plenty of cockney patter, but these were words and phrases rather than London pronunciations. If you saw our speech written down on a page then you might wrongly imagine we'd been born within the sound of Bow Bells, but that could never happen if you'd heard us speak. I'll get back to Michael in a moment, after sketching out the backdrop to the activist scene in which we met.

There was a big push to persuade people not to pay the poll tax, and so many of us refused to do so that it became really expensive to collect. Almost as significantly, there were huge demonstrations against it. The biggest protest of the lot was held in Trafalgar Square on 31 March 1990. This was only a bus ride away from Hackney but I was too ill to get there on the day. That was a real shame because after the march from Kennington Park there was rioting and looting in the West End of London, and this went on from late afternoon until 3am the following morning. It all kicked off with a lot of pushing and shoving, then a load of unemployed miners climbed some scaffolding and started hurling missiles at the cops. This was the sign for everyone else to get stuck in. Banks, posh restaurants and upper-class drinking clubs were attacked, and some set alight. Flash motors were also targeted, with models like Porsches and Jaguars being destroyed by fire. But this wasn't random violence: everything was carefully targeted with ordinary pubs, small shops and cheap cars left untouched.

Ultimately, there was so much opposition to the poll tax that, by the end of 1990, Tory prime minister Margaret Thatcher was forced to resign from office, and eventually the so-called "community charge" was abolished. Something else I was pleased to see collapse at this time was the Soviet Union. For much of my life, when reactionaries heard my political views they'd tell me I should go and live in Russia. Why they said this I have no idea because anyone who looked at the agricultural question within the Russian revolution could see that the USSR was a capitalist and not a communist state. What the Bolsheviks did there was collectivise the small farms, freeing up workers from the land and creating an urban proletariat. In other words, they liquidated the last remnants of feudal society and replaced this with capitalist social relations. Yes, there was a revolution in Russia, but it was a capitalist revolution and not a communist one. As I'd had to reiterate again and again during the political meetings I'd been attending since I retired, there was no such thing as a communist state. One of the aims of communism is to abolish all nations because the working class has no country.

I wasn't sorry to have lived my entire life well away from Stalinist terror in the USSR, but I wasn't smug about it because I'd experienced first-hand how brutally the bourgeoisie—and don't forget the Bolsheviks were the first fully fledged bourgeois class in Russia—treats the working class in the British Isles! And while I was very disappointed to have missed the Trafalgar Square poll tax demonstration, I was still cock-a-hoop about the fact that it had turned into a riot. The bourgeois press, of course, blamed the trouble on anarchists in the hope that those who weren't there would fail to grasp that it was an act of working-class resistance.

Anarchism covers a wide variety of political positions from left to right, which is why those of us seeking to emancipate humanity from class society steer well clear of it as a label. Don't get me wrong, some anarchists are okay beyond their desire to describe themselves in this way, while others are right-wing scum. Likewise, in the UK by the 1980s anarchism had more to do with lifestyle choices and youth culture than politics. It certainly wasn't a label I wanted pinned on me or my class!

Returning to more personal matters, unfortunately by the time of the 1990 Trafalgar Square riot I was going up and down to Homerton Hospital and the doctors there eventually told me I had lung cancer. I couldn't understand this since I'd done so much to keep fit. The medics said my condition may have been caused by inhaling coal dust as a youth, or from passively inhaling the smoke from other people's fags throughout my life. Michael Morgan, who I'd met through my involvement in the Anti-Poll Tax movement, stepped in to help me out and make sure I got to hospital for my appointments. I told Michael my life story and he said I should make it public. At first I wasn't sure about this idea but on reflection, and after a lot of pushing from Michael, I thought, why not?

"Ray, my friend," Michael announced one day, "you need to write an autobiography, a book from which some lucky film producer can make both a movie and a fortune!"

"Do you think someone would make a picture about my life?"

"I'm sure of it."

"Why?"

"I can read your aura."

"What?"

"I'm a sensitive and I can see colour fields around everyone, and that tells me about their psychic life and their ultimate destiny. Your aura says that one day soon you are destined to be very famous."

"Are you sure about that?"

"Certain. You need to write a book about your life, and then as sure as night follows day someone will turn it into a blockbuster movie."

"How do you know?"

"Finish your tea and give me your mug."

"Okay," I replied before gulping down what remained of the brew.

"Look!" Michael announced triumphantly after giving the inside of my mug the once-over. As he turned it towards me he added, "You can read it in the leaves, they say you're going to be world-famous and a film will be made about your life."

"I don't know how to read tea leaves! The muck at the bottom of my mug doesn't mean anything to me."

"Fair enough, but I know how to divine the future, and your glittering ascent into the hall of fame is written out here in block capitals."

"Are you sure?"

"Absolutely positive! Now give me your hand, we'll look and see what it says there."

"I don't know how to read palms either."

"Well look at that!" Michael barked as he traced a line on my hand. "It says the same thing here—you're going to be a celebrity!"

"Okay."

"I can do a Tarot reading for you if you like; would that really clinch it for you?"

"It's okay Michael, I believe you!"

"You know I've prayed to the Blessed Virgin to guide me over this too. The very Mother of God has shown me your rise to fame. Mary is even more reliable as a guide than tea leaves or the Tarot. You're going to be a celebrity once your life story reaches the wider public."

"Well as long as that happens before I die, I'll be happy!"

"You can be sure of it Ray! I've seen it in visions."

Morgan was a bluff bloke and friendly with it. I wasn't convinced he was actually seeing my aura or my future, but I knew he was seeing something, even if it was just a product of his own imagination. I'm absolutely sure Michael believed everything he said, but just because he was honest and wouldn't knowingly lie that didn't make his every utterance true. Still, there was some sense to the conclusions he drew from what he thought he was seeing, so I went along with it all despite being sceptical about Michael's spiritual beliefs. I wondered if my brother Dai would appear once again in my dreams and tell me what I should do; sadly he didn't.

Before long, Morgan appointed himself my press agent and towards the end of 1992 contacted the *Western Morning Mail*, who in November of that year broke the story that I was the man who'd robbed Sophia Loren of her jewels in 1960. I was ill and expected to die of cancer very soon, so I had little to fear from the old bill. Even if they put me in jail it meant nothing; I was 76 and already facing a death sentence.

It was Michael's idea that after talking to the *Western Morning Mail* I should hand myself in at my local nick. The stringer who covered the story had come to see me at my pad in Stamford Hill, so when the journalist left, Michael and I went down to Stoke Newington cop shop. However, it just went against the grain to turn myself in. I simply couldn't do it, so after a bit of a row with my press agent, I turned around and went home without talking to the desk sergeant—who eyed us suspiciously but left us to sort out our differences on our own. Michael came around the next day to make up with me, and apologised for pushing me too hard in a direction I was not yet willing to travel. Nonetheless, he still insisted that confessing to the cops that I'd robbed Sophia Loren was the best way to get my story to break in a really big way.

I had no difficulty in being interviewed by journalists; I felt able to handle them from the off. The way they worked seemed to me a bit like cops. Some were confrontational and deliberately asked difficult questions. Others just let you talk in the hope that you'd hang yourself. Most were two-faced. Michael figured the best way to get my autobiography published was to drum up as much publicity as possible. I now think this was a mistake. I hadn't even started working on the book and I should have got it written before we approached the press with my story. That said, the *Western Mail* piece was picked up by other papers and my story—or at least that part of it concerning Sophia Loren—was rerun in national newspapers such as the *Daily Mail*. And for some reason there was a lot of interest in my life of crime from places such as Germany. Some of the German TV interviews I did as a result of this were surreal.

"Herr Jones," one host began, "you were a British master criminal who stole from the rich and famous. Can you tell me the names of some of your victims?"

"Perhaps the most famous of my robberies was when I nicked Sophia Loren's jewels in 1960. I was on the run from prison after going over the wall eighteen months earlier. The Italian star was making a film in England, and she had her sparklers with her, so it was easy to lift them from the house she'd rented."

"And you also stole from Hollywood legends such as Elizabeth Taylor and Bette Davis?"

"That's right."

"So can you tell me why the British intelligence agencies recruited other accomplished thieves such as Eddie Chapman to do secret work against the Nazis during the war, but not you?"

"Although I'd been to borstal as a boy, I was only banged up as an adult prisoner for the first time during the war. All my big crimes were committed after the fighting came to an end. Besides, Eddie Chapman was first recruited as an agent by the Germans; it was after this happened that he contacted the British authorities and let them know he wanted to double-cross the Nazis. Chapman ended up in the Nazi jail system because he'd been incarcerated in the Channel Islands, which Hitler successfully invaded. The Nazis thought Eddie would work for them against the Allies because he'd been punished as a criminal and resented his own country for how it had treated him. He proved them wrong coz, after training him, they parachuted him into England to do sabotage but he immediately alerted the British authorities, who made good use of him to feed the Germans disinformation. But on the whole the army didn't want criminals. Rather than fighting, they were mostly left at home during the war."

"But were not many of the British leaders criminals? For example Winston Churchill was already notorious as the Butcher of Gallipoli, and Bomber Harris deliberately had hundreds of thousands of German civilians murdered."

"You won't like this, but such figures aren't seen as criminals in England. And remember, the Nazis systematically murdered people on the basis of their ethnicity, political beliefs and sexuality. The British didn't do that during the war."

"But surely the British leadership during the Second World War were still no better than a bunch of degenerate psychopaths? And your Churchill, he simply didn't have the charisma or leadership qualities of the Führer!"

"I wouldn't say that."

"Well I would! Hitler had a vision of completely rebuilding Berlin and making the German people great once again. Churchill was more interested in long shadows on cricket grounds, warm beer, invincible green suburbs, dog lovers and football fans. Now that's not going to inspire anybody is it!"

"You're mixing up Winston Churchill and the current Tory prime minister John Major. It was Major who included that rhetoric about warm beer in a speech he made last April to the Conservative Group for Europe."

"What does it matter? Britain's so-called leaders are characterless, they are all more or less the same!"

And so it went on. This exchange must have taken place in 1994 because it also turned into a barney about the end of apartheid in South Africa. The German TV host was mourning the demise of white rule, whereas naturally enough I saw the dismantling of a fascist regime that had enforced vicious race laws as something to be applauded. For kids coming into politics in the 1980s, South Africa was the closest they came to the discussions and activism my generation experienced around Spain in the 1930s. Fortunately by the time a broadly based working-class movement smashed white rule in South Africa, Spain had long shed its fascist past, a process that started with the 1975 death of that windbag dictator General Franco.

The interview I mention above was never broadcast, I guess in part because I wouldn't agree with the host's extreme right-wing views. They'd have needed to edit out the explicitly fascist garbage he spouted too. We spent a fair amount of time in a green room waiting for a television studio to become free, and while I sipped water, the interviewer was boozing and he was drunk by the time the piece was shot.

The crew and producer appeared rather embarrassed by the whole affair. Fortunately the TV interviews that did go out in Germany were rather more balanced than this one. However, after a while media interest in me dropped off and Michael said we needed to do stunts to drum up more press coverage. That was when I really did hand myself in to the cops. Michael was simultaneously trying to organise film and book deals but nothing ever came of them.

In 1995 we travelled up to Borehamwood by train and I went to the cop shop there in order to confess to robbing Sophia Loren. It was close to Elstree where the crime had been committed, and in the same county of Hertfordshire.

"Hello," I said as I walked up to the desk sergeant.

"Hello," he replied.

"Hello," Michael echoed.

"What can I do for you gentlemen?" the cop demanded, obviously pissed off by the three "hellos" — so I refrained from adding "what's going on 'ere then?"

"He'd like to confess to a burglary," Michael said as he pointed at me, obviously worried that I'd change my mind again at the last moment, and fail to hand myself in to the filth.

"Well," the pig spat, "if he wants to confess to a burglary, he'd better tell me about it himself. However, it doesn't look like he'd be able to do much in the way of housebreaking, he looks ill."

"It was a burglary I committed 35 years ago," I chipped in.

"I suppose you were in better health then?"

"I was very fit," I boomed.

"To me you look like a shuffling old man."

"Even hobbling old men started young," was my retort, "and I'm not that old or shuffling. My punch still has a lot of power in it."

"I thought you'd come here to own up to a crime, not to threaten me."

"I'm not threatening you, I just want to make a confession."

"In that case you better tell me your name."

So I went through all the details. Eventually I was charged with robbing Sophia Loren of her jewels and released on bail. I went home feeling decidedly queasy; making a confession to the authorities just didn't feel right, but Michael was happy. Then—nothing!

Meanwhile I kept up my visits to Homerton Hospital and the chemotherapy treatments really knocked the stuffing out of me. All the while the charge against me was nagging at the back of my mind. Would I live long enough to go to court? I wasn't sure that I wanted to find myself facing a beak at my age. On the other hand, I needed my achievements as a career criminal recognised so that I might inspire the younger generation to take up burglary as a way of getting back at the rich and redistributing wealth.

At the beginning of 1996, I was informed the case and the charges against me over the Sophia Loren theft had been dropped. Michael convinced me this was a conspiracy to protect the cops who'd provided the inside information enabling me to carry out the crime. The way things went certainly surprised me; I'd been fitted up and done years of time for crimes of which I was entirely innocent, but here I was ready to confess in court to something I had done and the filth wouldn't even take me before a judge.

"It's a right liberty!" was Michael's verdict. "There's only one thing to do Ray, and that's for you to stage a one-man protest against the suppression of your story."

We kicked ideas around and Michael's opinion was that doing something in Wales would work best. There was too much going on in London for whatever I did to be picked up by the national papers, but by pulling a stunt in Cardiff and playing up my Welsh roots, I was likely to get coverage in the likes of the *South Wales Argus* and *Wales on Sunday*. So in April 1996, and at the age of seventy-nine, while sick and ill from cancer, I found myself standing outside Cardiff railway station with a placard and leaflets explaining how I'd robbed

Sophia Loren and why the cops refused to let me have my day in court for this crime.

"How is your son?" a guy who'd taken a leaflet from me said after glancing through it. "Have they let him out of the funny farm again?"

"I don't have a son," I told him. "I've got two daughters."

"Don't tell me there's been a cover-up!"

"What do you mean?"

"I reckon you're David Icke's dad!"

"David Icke?"

"Yes, David Icke. You know, the former TV sports presenter who is now even more famous for being a conspiracy nut. The bloke who told Terry Wogan on the telly he was the Son of God. The guy who claims the Royal Family and all the leading politicians in the world are really reptiles posing as humans, and that they eat babies and control the human race for evil ends."

"Icke totally lost the plot years ago."

"Like you mate, which is why I reckon you must be David Icke's dad. You stand there claiming the cops won't prosecute criminals and expect me to take you seriously. Next you'll be claiming British MPs fiddle their expenses! You make me laugh."

It was Michael's idea to play up the conspiracy angle and the issue of the filth protecting their own. But I was more than a grown man, and I went along with a plan that in retrospect I think was a mistake. I should have stayed at home and written my life story. I'm doing that now, albeit from my hospital bed, and I've nearly reached the end—but I'm unlikely to live long enough to see it published, and it's knowing that the tale gets out to a new generation that is important to me; simply writing it down isn't enough. At book length it's possible to explain how cop corruption works and the effect it had on my life; on a leaflet and placards you don't have enough space to deal with the issues in the depth they require.

Shortly after the Cardiff protest, Michael Morgan informed me he'd found a ghostwriter to work on my autobiography, a guy called Bill Hooper. I think Michael dug Bill up because I'd told him I needed to crack on with my book, and there wasn't any point pulling stunts to publicise my case until an autobiography was more or less in the bag. I didn't know anything about the book world, and when Michael told me Hooper was a talented writer, I accepted what he said at face value. I hunkered down with Bill for weeks on end and not only recited my life story for him, I even acted parts of it out. I demonstrated the moves I'd made in my many boxing and bare-knuckle fights, and demonstrated many of my breaking and entering techniques too. Hooper was amazed by my stories, since it was a slice of life he knew nothing about. He'd arrive at my flat around six o'clock in the evening most days and he'd sit taping my recollections on a reel-to-reel recorder for anything up to five hours at a time. When he told me he was going away to write it up, I had high expectations of the results.

I didn't see Bill Hooper for a month after that and when he called around I thought he'd had time to write the whole book—after all, he only had to transcribe what I'd told him and put it in order. Instead of a thick manuscript, what he gave me was a couple of pages of highlights he'd typed up. He told me this was a synopsis and that he was sending it around to all the major publishers. We waited months to hear back from them. Most ignored Hooper's letters, and those that did reply said they weren't interested. The excuses were usually along the lines of the market in crime books was saturated, or the editor had never heard of either of us. I found this odd, so six months after the synopsis had been sent out I asked Hooper about his track record as an author.

"So how many books have you had published?" was the way I framed the question.

"Well Ray, you see it's like this…," and then Hooper clammed up.

"Like what?" I demanded.

"Like this…"

"Look, just tell me how many books you've had published!"

"I'm always writing," Hooper told me, "putting stuff down on paper. It's just I haven't had anything published yet."

"No books out at all! No wonder the publishers haven't heard of you!"

"I'm just trying to make a name for myself. We'll do it with this book of yours."

"None!" I said.

"What do you mean?" Hooper replied.

"Zero! Zilch!" I shouted. "You haven't had any books published!"

"It's not my fault, I'm working hard at becoming a professional writer, I just haven't cracked it yet."

"So how many books have you written?"

"Mostly I'm just working up ideas. I haven't actually completed a manuscript yet either."

I couldn't believe what I was hearing. I'd been labouring under the misapprehension that Hooper was a professional writer, but it turned out that he had no more experience in the literary game than me. I hadn't gone around giving people the impression I was a professional tea leaf before I pulled off my first robbery. It was unbelievable; when it came to bending the truth the straight-goers were worse than those of us who worked the other side of the law. I found out later that to get books published you needed literary agents and connections; a track record helped too. Hooper had no better chance of getting my autobiography taken on by a publisher than I did on my own. He was just hoping for a ride on my coattails.

To placate me, Hooper and my press spokesman Michael Morgan came up with the idea of doing a film treatment instead. Their thinking was that although they'd had no luck flogging a book about my life, if they could sell film rights then getting my autobiography published would be a piece of piss. Hooper's synopsis was reworked and sent to movie production companies. To take my mind off the fact we were getting nowhere and being blanked by the film industry, Michael and Bill asked me to think about which actor was best qualified to play me in a major feature film. To be honest, there weren't many who could walk in my shoes. They had to be quick on their feet and able to box. Step dancer Michael Flatley was about the only person who fitted the bill. He'd been an amateur boxer, moved with speed and grace, and apparently wanted to swap small-time TV appearances for major acting roles.

Around the time I was being distracted by the film treatment nonsense, I moved flat from Stamford Hill to Colvestone Crescent in Dalston. I required a change of address because my health was still deteriorating and I needed to be closer to the shops. It was hard to reach them from my old pad. Now I was living close to Ridley Road market where I'd run my stall after retiring from my life of crime. Michael saw this as another opportunity for publicity stunts, and so from the summer of 1996 onwards you could find me in Ridley Road sticking up my own "wanted" posters, and handing out leaflets to shoppers. This got me running coverage in the *Hackney Gazette* for a couple of years, but it never went any further than there and a few of the Welsh papers.

Then Michael came up with his next big idea: making an appearance at Peter Scott's May 1998 trial for his part in the theft of a Picasso painting. Despite the fact that Scott had grassed me up to the cops in 1960, there was no way I was going to say anything in court about him until after he'd been sentenced. I didn't want to be the cause of extra years being added to his tariff. Scott had admitted to his part in the theft of the Loren jewels in his 1995 autobiography, but he'd written me out of the story and made himself the inside rather than the outside man. This left me at liberty to mention his supporting role in this crime, and my rather more leading one. Once the Belfast Bullshitter had been handed a three-and-a-half-year stretch at Snaresbrook Crown Court, I got up to tear a strip off him and the judge let me speak for fifteen minutes. By this means I was able to get my feelings about Scott off my chest, but unfortunately it was the wrong way in which to do it.

Scott was fourteen years my junior but at sixty-seven he was still too old to be facing such a long sentence. He was an idiot, but his pensioner status and stiff sentence aroused sympathy, even among those who knew just how much I'd been wronged by him. Reflecting on it over a period of several months, I knew my underworld friends were right when they said I shouldn't have slagged Scott off to a judge. My Uncle Dinny, who'd died more than a decade before, would be spinning in his grave. Michael kept urging me to do more stunts but I was not only ill with cancer, I was also sick to the guts that I'd stood up in a court and denounced Scott as a liar. What I'd said was true but the right place for saying it was in the papers and the pages of my own autobiography.

Before I fully admitted to myself that I'd done wrong by standing up and speaking at Snaresbrook, Morgan had read in the *Evening Standard* that Michael Flatley was throwing a housewarming party in a five-million-pound property he'd just bought in London's Little Venice. He decided we should try to gatecrash it so we could sweet-talk this dance celebrity into coming on board our film project, which would make Hooper's movie treatment about my life much easier to sell. Thus it was in the summer of 1998 that we headed out on our mission of recruiting Flatley. Morgan had suggested I impress Flatley by going in to his joint over the rooftops. I knocked this on the head by pointing out I was sick with cancer and just wasn't up to it. Instead Michael and I found ourselves at the front gate talking to security.

"Names?"

"Raymond Jones and Michael Morgan," I said.

"You're not on the list."

"We don't need to be on the list," Morgan put in, "this is Michael Flatley's date with destiny. He's going to play my friend here, Ray Jones, in a film about cat burglary. It will be the making of Flatley as a star."

"The making of your friend no doubt. Flatley is already a celebrity."

"Yes but this will take your boss to the next level."

"How do you know that?"

"I'm psychic."

"Okay, if you're psychic, tell me what I'm thinking."

"You're thinking you'd like to let us in and that a demonstration of my powers would convince you to do this."

"Wrong. I'm thinking you should piss off. So you'd better do just that before I lose my temper!"

That was that, we'd blown our chance. Michael should have let me front it out by talking to the security about my life as a fighter and creeper. I'm sure that would have impressed them more and maybe got us in the gate. But it was too late for that; they had us down as a pair of idiots and nothing I said after the "psychic" debacle was gonna be taken seriously enough to change their minds.

I was annoyed with myself, and despite the endless support he'd given me through my illness, I also felt angry with Michael. I knew he'd only wanted to help me but in the end that desire had led both of us astray. After the Snaresbrook Crown Court nonsense, and the Michael Flatley episode that followed on from it, I cut myself off from Michael, and I haven't seen him for nearly two years now.

I wanted to begin work on my book and somehow I knew that when Michael was around this was never going to happen. It took me a year to get over all the false starts I've had in trying to tell my story. What finally pushed me into writing everything down was being told that on top of lung cancer I'd also developed pancreatic cancer. Now I've got to the end of my tale, but I'm also realistic enough to understand that I'm never going to live long enough to become a criminal celebrity.

Death is never clean or pleasant. Nonetheless I try to put a brave face on things for my visitors. As an example I'll mention in passing my niece Tricia, who was in to see me a bit earlier today. She'd come all the way from south Wales to visit me and do a bit of shopping in Oxford Street.

"Uncle Ray," Tricia said, "I can't stand the thought of all the pain you're in. I read up about pancreatic cancer before I came here and it's almost too horrible to contemplate."

"Don't worry about me," I assured my niece. "With the amount of opium being pumped into my body by the nurses here, I feel like I'm on cloud nine."

"Really? Are you sure you're not in pain?"

"With all the painkillers I'm getting I don't feel a thing."

"Is it the same for everyone in the ward?"

"You can bet your life it is. Take a look around you. Half the people in here are nodding out. And when they wake up the first thing they think about – before food or going to the toilet – is getting more drugs."

Tricia looked a lot happier leaving than when she arrived. I was glad about that. What I said about getting the opiates was true, but for her sake I over-egged the part about them killing all my pain. I haven't even had as many drugs as I might have done because I wanted to finish these memoirs, and keeping my mind sharp meant accepting a certain amount of discomfort.

Pancreatic cancer is a quick killer – once you've got it you know you don't have much time on this earth. So let me return briefly to where I came into this world, with the Battle of Romani. That was an episode of World War I concluded on the day I was born. The Battle of the Somme was still raging on that fateful day of 5 August 1916; it ran from 1 July until 18 November and by the time it was over there were more than one million casualties. The working class paid a heavy price for the bourgeoisie's inter-imperialist rivalries, with the Battle of the Somme having a major and lasting impact on the British and Commonwealth proletariat. The British army had never seen that level of loss of life before – 60,000 deaths on the first day alone, a new and shameful record! Again this particular battle fits into the bigger picture of the First World War.

In just the same way, individual tales like mine feed into the far greater story of working-class struggle. From this perspective we can see the younger generation are not to blame for the situation they are in, and also that they must emancipate themselves from it. The only way to make this world a better place is to soak the rich. Some say revenge is a dish best served cold, whereas I think it is something that should be delivered piping hot! So let's hit the toffs where it hurts them, in the wallet! Overpaid businessmen, bankers taking home huge bonuses, millionaires and their families are all legitimate targets for our class anger. Such people have no right to the wealth they enjoy, since the working class created it and it's high time we took it back! It's not a question of demanding such ill-gotten gains be returned to us, it's a matter of deeds. My activities as a creeper demonstrate one viable form of direct action against the rich, but there are many others... Get to it kids!

Raymond Jones
Hackney, London
January 2001

EPILOGUE

Raymond Jones died of pancreatic cancer at Homerton Hospital in Hackney, London, on 4 February 2001. He was 84 years old. Jones was buried in London beside his beloved wife Ann. His dying wish was that a publisher be found for his life story, and that if at all possible this book would ultimately be turned into a movie.

I became involved in various ongoing attempts to realise The Cat's unrealised desires by accident. Until I came along, those most active in keeping the legend of Ray alive were his former press spokesman Michael Morgan and various journalists in south Wales. It hadn't occurred to me to start researching The Cat's life and crimes until the day I asked my long-term writer friend Paul Buck if he'd included my distant relative Ray Jones in his book *The E... List: Notorious Prison Escapes*. Paul said he'd covered The Cat's breakout from London's Pentonville jail but he doubted the veracity of the story.

After speaking to Buck about Jones, I posted various blogs about Ray on my website as I began to probe into his life. One of the things I was surprised to discover was that in the mid-eighties I'd lived just a few hundred yards away from where Ray had his flat at that time; and that when he'd moved to Dalston towards the end of his life, he was once again located within an easy walking distance of my own home. All of which makes it a greater shame that I never got to know Ray, and hadn't asked around about him until very shortly after his death. We come from an extremely large family and, to clarify, Ray was my first cousin once removed — or, to put it more simply, the cousin of my mother Julia Callan-Thompson. I was aware of Ray as a figure who cropped up in books about crime in London during the fifties and sixties — but up to the point I talked to Paul Buck about Ray, I'd read nothing that indicated he'd spent much of his life in east London, or that his criminal activities were politically motivated...

Paul's doubts about the veracity of the story of Ray's escape from Pentonville — which he'd got via Frankie Fraser — eventually prompted me to go to the British Library so that I could check old newspapers for accounts of this jailbreak and his various crimes. Ray's 1940 conviction for assaulting PC Spratt had generated a lot of press interest, as had his 1952 sentence for robbing Colonel Martin Charteris. Ray genuinely did create front-page headlines when he escaped from Pentonville in 1958, and upon his recapture in 1960. However, this coverage is completely at odds with the way Frankie Fraser recounts the story in his ghosted autobiography.

Why Frankie Fraser decided to spin such a ridiculous yarn about Ray severely injuring himself during his escape and yet still getting away is unknown to me, but it is obvious Ray's reputation suffered as a result of such nonsense being written about him. That's sad, because Ray was clearly not to blame for the lies Fraser spread about him. Peter Scott, in his autobiography *Gentleman Thief*, also fluffs the details of Ray's escape, but rather than over-egging the story he chooses to tone it right down by greatly compressing the time The Cat was on the run. Scott's schtick is to run Ray down, and it's evident from his text that he resorts to outright lies in order to do this.

I wanted to know more about Ray than I could find in the newspapers, and used my blog to appeal for information about him. For a couple of years I received dribs and drabs of additional material via comments and emails. Then unexpectedly in June 2013, I was anonymously mailed a package with no return address containing a manuscript copy of the autobiography of Raymond Jones. Inside there was an unsigned note: "This is yours to do whatever you like with." I settled down and read through the book in a single sitting. For me it had a ring of authenticity — either, as I believe, it was actually written by Ray Jones, or else it was ghosted by someone who knew a lot about him. The narrative matches the facts of Ray The Cat's crimes as far as they are recorded in court cases and newspapers. I've been able to find precious little about Ray's boxing career but I'm prepared to take what he — or his ghostwriter — has to say about it on trust.

Despite lacking any provenance for this text, I believe it to be at least as reliable as the ghostwritten autobiographies of those underworld figures who claim to know a thing or two about Ray. After reading books credited to the likes of Mad Frankie Fraser, I am left with the impression that the real author had produced a collective portrait of various criminals but hung their stories on a single name. Such accounts are essentially works of fiction loosely based on fact. That they are being marketed by genre as "true crime" is on the whole rather misleading. They have their origins in — and indeed are not far removed from — the earliest forms of English prose fiction: short and fanciful pieces about the lives of rogues and criminals, that from the seventeenth century onwards were generally presented as being factual despite their dubious status as historical records.

If the conventions of the true crime genre in the English language were first mapped out in Robert Greene's Elizabethan coney-catching pamphlets, they found an early crystallisation in Richard Head's 1665 novel *The English Rogue*. Although Head's text is often described as picaresque, it consists of many examples of "nugget fiction" — short accounts of criminal escapades — that have been strung together. One of the many things that differentiates Ray's writing from both Head and the ghostwritten and largely fictional "autobiographies" of other 1950s and 1960s underworld figures is that his political views are progressive. That said, it stretches credulity to claim that a career criminal can be relied upon to tell the truth about themselves and their activities — although we shouldn't forget that politicians and celebrities also tend towards the fictional in their autobiographies.

The broad outline of Ray's criminal career as given in this book is corroborated by other historical material and records. Whether all the details are correct is something we'll probably never know. In my opinion the safest approach to this type of text, by which I mean all autobiographies and not just this account of the life of Ray The Cat Jones, is to treat them as fiction. That said, Ray's views and speech are more carefully nuanced than those of most underworld characters active around London at the same time as him. For this and many other reasons, I'm very pleased that in *The 9 Lives of Ray The Cat Jones* my first cousin once removed is at last able to speak "in his own voice".

Stewart Home
Bethnal Green, London
October 2014

APPENDIX

London *Evening Chronicle*

Press File on Raymond Jones

SAVAGE THIEF BEAT POLICEMEN UNCONSCIOUS

A persistent housebreaker who had remained at liberty for two years after beating the police officers who tried to arrest him into unconsciousness was jailed at the Old Bailey today.

The thief, 23-year-old Raymond Jones of King Edward Walk, Lambeth, London, claimed to be a labourer and to have earned the money for the 21 suits and £50 in his pockets when he was finally brought to justice. He was sentenced to two years" imprisonment for causing grievous bodily harm to PC Spratt, who tried to arrest him at Marble Arch in December 1937, as well as for attempted theft from a car.

He was arrested at his home in February 1940.

Detective Hope told the court Jones had verbally confessed to assaulting numerous police officers to escape arrest over a two-year period, and that throughout this time he had been living on the proceeds of his burglaries. When asked to sign a written statement to this effect Jones had refused. His not guilty plea at the Old Bailey failed to save him from jail.

Judge Beazley told Jones he had been guilty of a savage attack.

Evening Chronicle
7 March 1940

BURGLAR STOLE FURS FROM NEW YEAR PARTY GUESTS

Raymond Jones, 35, a fruit buyer of Bathurst Mews, Paddington, was jailed for six and a half years at the Old Bailey today. He was guilty of stealing 11 fur coats and jackets worth £4000 from the Ingram Avenue house of Lieutenant Colonel Martin Charteris during the course of a Hampstead New Year's Eve party. He was also convicted of receiving a motor car knowing it to be stolen. The vehicle belonged to Mr Thomas William Wilkinson of Silverston Way, Middlesex, and was valued at £500.

Prosecutor Mr Christmas Humphreys said that 2 days after the theft of the coats from Ingram Avenue, police officers watching a house in The Avenue, Willesden, observed Jones in possession of a suitcase that contained 8 of the stolen furs. When they moved to arrest him, he ran off. A second man, Allan Grant, who was with Jones at the time, was caught. In February Grant received a seven-year jail term for his part in the theft.

Jones, who was defended by Petre Crowder, told the court that his younger brother was stabbed during an argument in a Soho gambling club, and this had led him to have a fight with gang leader Billy Hill. He was subsequently threatened with severe retribution by Hill and his men. He claimed that on one occasion prior to his arrest, gang members had jumped from a van and attacked him. When he saw the unmarked police van, he thought it was the gang and ran away.

In giving his evidence, Jones denied he'd ever been in possession of the suitcase containing the stolen coats. He said that when the theft took place he had been engaged in a 5-hour-long game of cards in a flat belonging to a friend.

Evening Chronicle
23 June 1952

PENTONVILLE GAOLBREAK — DANGEROUS FUGITIVE STILL AT LARGE

5 convicts attempted to escape from Pentonville gaol in north London last night. 3 failed to get away from the prison, but two evaded the authorities and police roadblocks. A police sweep of the area failed to unearth the missing convicts in the vicinity of the gaol. Last night Caledonian Road was filled with police cars, plainclothes and uniformed police armed with torches, tracker dogs, and wardens in an attempt to apprehend them.

One of the escaped men, John Rider, aged 34, was recaptured today at an address in Antlers Hill, Chingford. He was discovered asleep on a sofa. The search for the other prisoner, Raymond Jones, aged 42, continues. Jones, who was serving an eight-year preventative detention sentence, was described by detectives as dangerous and potentially violent. They warned members of the public not to approach him, saying he had in the past beaten police officers unconscious in order to escape arrest.

The gaolbreak took place during evening classes using ladders set in place for repairs to the prison roof. Without these the convicts would have been unable to scale the 20-foot-high walls of the gaol. From the prison wall they leapt down into an alley that runs alongside the gaol. The two men ran off in opposite directions.

Evening Chronicle
19 October 1958

PRISONBREAK MAN CAUGHT

Last night, dangerous criminal Raymond Jones—who made a record-breaking two-year escape from Pentonville Prison—was re-captured in Staines, Middlesex.

Jones more than doubled the length of time a fugitive has stayed on the run from this gaol.

Information from an underworld source sent the police to Staines. They had to wait six hours at a property in which he was renting a room before they were able to seize him.

44-year-old Jones, who grew up in south Wales and has many convictions, was sentenced to eight years" preventative detention in 1957.

Evening Chronicle
25 November 1960

CAT BURGLAR DEMANDS HIS DAY IN COURT

At lunchtime today a retired thief called Ray "The Cat" Jones staged a one-man protest in Ridley Road Market demanding that he be tried in court for his part in the theft of gems from film goddess Sophia Loren more than 35 years ago.

Positioned by a placard detailing his part in the 1960 theft, Jones handed out 500 leaflets to passers-by in the Hackney street market.

Jones, from Stamford Hill in north London, alleges that he and an accomplice gave two corrupt police officers twelve thousand pounds in exchange for the information that enabled them to steal the Italian actress's jewels when she was filming in England.

"The authorities are afraid of police corruption being exposed," Ray told the Chronicle. He first confessed to the crime in a newspaper interview four years ago, but has not yet been charged over it. He alleges there is a top-level conspiracy by the authorities to suppress his part in the crime.

Evening Chronicle
7 May 1996

This is simply the coverage of Ray The Cat Jones to be found in one London newspaper over a period of more than 50 years. The court and jailbreak stories were covered by many national newspapers too, while The Cat's admission he stole Sophia Loren's jewels was featured in both the national press and various local east London, south Wales and Hertfordshire papers. The clippings from this wide assortment of publications are remarkably similar because the journalists who wrote the pieces were working from the same sources — court proceedings, police briefings or interviews with Ray The Cat and his press agent Michael Morgan.

The London *Evening Chronicle* coverage reproduced here is indicative of the way the media as a whole dealt with these stories, and so there is little need to present them from a variety of sources. To do so would be too repetitive to be of interest to the general reader. Ray, of course, also turns up in various books about crime in London in the 1950s and 1960s by the likes of Frankie Fraser, Eric Mason, Bruce Reynolds, Peter Scott and Donald Thomas. He does so as Raymond The Climber and Taffy Raymond, as well as Raymond Jones.

GLOSSARY

ARSEWIPE worthless person. Literally toilet roll.

BAD-JACKETED fitted up, wrongly convicted, someone made to look responsible for something that has nothing to do with them.

BANGED UP imprisoned.

BEAK a judge.

BEAST WITH TWO BACKS sexual intercourse.

BENT unlawful, corrupt.

BERK a stupid person, an idiot. The meaning has changed over time, a shortened version of rhyming that originally stood as Berkshire hunt = cunt.

BIRD prison sentence. Doing bird is time served locked up. Also an attractive young woman, as in a dolly bird.

BOBBING FOR COCK heroin addict who is nodding out or falling asleep after taking the drug.

BORN WITHIN THE SOUND OF BOW BELLS a cockney, now generally taken to mean someone who grew up in east London. However, Bow Bells refers to St Mary-le-Bow church on Cheapside, which is actually in the City of London rather than the East End of London, although the bells can be heard in parts of the East End.

BRACELETS handcuffs.

BRIEF lawyer.

BUBBLE BATH rhyming slang for having a laugh, or having a joke.

BUDGIE informer.

BULLSHIT./.BULLSHITTER rubbish, nonsense. Person whose talk is filled with ridiculous and untrue assertions.

BUNK UP sexual intercourse.

CLIMBER cat burglar.

CLIMBING cat burglary.

CLINK/CLINKER jail. From the Clink Prison at Bankside, on the opposite side of the River Thames from the original walled City of London.

CLIP/CLIPPING taking money from a man looking for commercial sex and running off with his cash prior to providing the service he believed he would be receiving.

COBBLERS rubbish. Literally male testicles or balls.

CON convicted criminal. Also a confidence trick.

COP SHOP police station.

COWSON irritating and usually worthless person.

CREEPER cat burglar.

CROSS-BITING shaking down a john for their money and valuables once they are in a compromising position with a woman they believe to be a prostitute. A man who claims to be the woman's husband appears and threatens the man lured into this trap with the promise of commercial sex.

DICKHEAD a stupid person. The literal meaning of dick in this instance being cock or penis.

DIM MAK mythical branch of Chinese martial arts concerned with the "death touch", or killing by attacking pressure points.

DIRTBAG a worthless person.

DOG AND BONE phone. Rhyming slang.

DONE convicted for a crime, or losing money most usually through gambling.

DOUCHEBAG worthless person.

DOUGH money.

DRINK pay-off to either bent coppers or criminal associates in return for a favour.

DRUM home, someone's house or flat.

DUN/DUNNED con, do out of.

EJIT idiot, fool, worthless person.

FAKE AS A NINE BOB NOTE prior to the decimalisation of UK currency in 1971 the smallest note in circulation was worth ten shillings or ten bob (fifty pence after 1971). There was no such thing as a nine bob (nine shilling) note. Hence this phrase and the similar one "as bent as a nine bob note".

FAMILY JEWELS genitals.

FLOOZY loose woman.

FLOP a place to stay or sleep. A contraction of flophouse; a cheap hotel or boarding house.

FUZZ police.

GIT a stupid or unpleasant person.

GRAFT corruption, profit from corruption, hard work.

GRASS informer.

HALF-INCH steal. Rhyming slang half-inch = pinch.

JAM-RAG worthless person. Literally a sanitary towel.

JELLY BEAN the queen of England. Rhyming slang.

JEMMY lever open.

KIDDIE FIDDLER paedophile.

KO knockout term used in boxing but carried over from that sport to more general use.

LINENS newspapers. Other usages include bedding and underwear.

LOLLY money.

MUG a stupid person, an idiot, but generally also a victim of criminal activity and in particular a confidence trick.

MYSTERY woman, most usually one working in the sex industry.

NARK informer.

NICK/NICKED arrest/arrested or to steal/stolen. Nick singular also means a prison or police station (with cells).

NICKER a pound or pounds (sterling).

NONCE sex offender. Sometimes explained as a contraction of nonsense crime, it is an extremely derogatory term.

NOODLE head or intelligence.

OLD BILL police.

PEEPERS eyes.

PISS OFF go away.

PISS-TAKE/PISS-TAKING contempt, ridicule, mockery or teasing.

PLASTIC GANGSTER a would-be hardman, a wannabe criminal.

PLOD police officer or police.

POKE sexual intercourse.

PONCE a pimp. Also a blag, asking to be given something—as in "can I ponce a fag off you" or in polite speech "would you let me have a cigarette please". Also means someone with upper-class or effeminate speech and mannerisms.

POPPED THEIR CLOGS died.

PORKY PIE lie. Rhyming slang.

PORRIDGE time spent in prison. Taken from the name of the food associated with prison breakfasts.

PULLED arrested.

RATBAG worthless person.

READIES cash.

ROZZER policeman.

SALAMI cock, penis.

SCREW prison officer or burglary. Also sexual intercourse.

SCREWING burglary. Also sexual intercourse.

SCREWSMAN burglar.

SEXTON BLAKE fake. Rhyming slang, name taken from popular fictional detective.

SHANGHAIED transferred between prisons.

SHITHEAD a worthless, useless or stupid person.

SHOOTER gun.

SILK lawyer.

SLAG an informer. Also used to describe a sexually promiscuous woman.

SMALLS underwear.

SMOKE (THE) London.

SNOT-RAG an obnoxious individual. Literally a handkerchief.

SNOUT an informer.

SPARKLERS jewels.

SPARK OUT unconscious.

STRAIGHT-GOERS regular citizens without criminal involvements.

STUFF AND NONSENSE rubbish, foolishness.

SUIT white-collar worker or businessman.

SUS LAW informal name for a stop and search law that permitted English and Welsh police officers to stop, search and potentially arrest people on suspicion of them being in breach of section 4 of the Vagrancy Act of 1824. Contraction of suspected person. SUS law was finally repealed in August 1981.

SUSS/SUSSED intelligence, to work something out.

SWAG a thief's booty.

SWANKY posh, upper-class.

TAKING THE PISS showing contempt. Sometimes deliberate ridicule or mockery, sometimes exhibiting contempt in terms of behaviour that it is hoped will pass unnoticed or unchallenged.

TANNER sixpence or the lowest-value silver coin in British currency prior to decimalisation in 1971.

TEA LEAF thief. Rhyming slang.

TICKLE haul or profit from a crime.

TOE-RAG an obnoxious individual.

TOFF an aristocrat or upper-class person.

TOM/TOMFOOLERY jewels. Rhyming slang tomfoolery = jewellery.

TOT small child. Alternatively a measure of spirits (alcohol).

TOSSER stupid or unpleasant person. Literally someone who masturbates.

TROUBLE AND STRIFE wife. Rhyming slang.

TWERP idiot, fool, worthless person.

TWIT idiot, fool, worthless person.

VIBRATING PALM mythical branch of martial arts concerned with killing by a special means of touch.

WANGLE acquiring something by illicit or undeserved means.

WANKER stupid or unpleasant individual. Wank also means both masturbation and rubbish or foolishness.

WEDGE money.

WHEELS transportation, most usually a car.

WHISTLE suit. Rhyming slang, contraction of whistle and flute.

DENIZEN OF THE DEAD

THE HORRORS OF CLARENDON COURT
EDITED BY STEWART HOME

— WARNING! —

You are about to enter the City of London,
the most evil and corrupt place on the planet!

On the border between the City's Cripplegate ward and south
Islington's Bone Hill district stands Clarendon Court AKA The
Denizen - an elite and newly built luxury apartment block of
99 flats marketed to property investors.

Exclusive? Yes.
Reassuringly expensive? Yes.
Safe? Undoubtedly not!

There were stories, just rumours, about what went on there. Rumours
about perversion, orgies, ghosts, bad feng shui and shockingly
unpleasant deaths.

When a gorgeous young nymphomaniac bursts into a Clarendon Court
apartment, the whole story of depravity and corruption is revealed.

In this collection of short fiction by today's top writers the Clarendon
Court investment flats really are haunted by the ghosts of Cripplegate's
wild past, when the hood was notorious for its brothels and the ultra-
violent criminals who frequented them.

On top of this there's a problem with the spirits of hundreds of
thousands of unhappy souls whose corpses were dumped in both local
plague pits and the more recent Golden Lane mega-morgue, a huge
Victorian Palace of the Dead.

This anthology is a protest against property speculation and a new
take on the genre of haunted house horror fiction. The book itself is a
talisman that defends our communities against developers and inside
it also features Spell Series by the w.o.n.d.e.r. coven. The symbols of
this living spell are a lock and key designed to dismantle the neoliberal
project and overdevelopment as represented by The Denizen.

Featuring work from
Paul Ewen, Tariq Goddard, Iphgenia Baal, Chris Petit, Steve Finbow,
John King, Chloe Aridjis, Tom McCarthy, Liz Rever, Katrina Palmer,
Michael Hampton, Bridget Penney, Stewart Home and many more!

Lightning Source UK Ltd.
Milton Keynes UK
UKHW011830260521
384427UK00003B/26